Amazon Dreaming

Bill Keats

MINERVA PRESS
MONTREUX LONDON WASHINGTON

AMAZON DREAMING

ISBN 1 85863 261 7

First Published 1995 by
MINERVA PRESS
10 Cromwell Place
London SW7 2JN

Printed in Great Britain by
Martins the Printers Ltd., Berwick upon Tweed

Amazon Dreaming

This book is dedicated to all those I love and I love them very much - SWAShG^{2}.

ABOUT THE AUTHOR

It is with a sense of great pride, and deep and fulfilling humility that I accept the honour of penning this biography of the author for his first novel. Where should I begin? They said it should be short and pithy...

Bill Keats was born a Yorkshireman in 1949. He ate lots of Yorkshire pud washed down with innumerable pints of Best Yorkshire Bitter. He deserted Yorkshire, however, at the tender age of twenty-one as he was too short to make the cricket team and had become a geologist instead, exploring for gold. There may be brass in Yorkshire, but there's not a lot of gold to find there. But I digress...

The quest has so far taken him to the Caribbean, Indonesia, Cornwall, Australia, Canada and Venezuela; one day, he says, when he's a famous author, he might like to return and vegetate among those dark satanic hills - or was that mills?

ABOUT THE MAIN CHARACTER

Tom Askew was born in England, also in 1949. He too is a professional exploration geologist; he graduated from Cambridge and has a PhD from the Camborne School of Mines. Since 1971, he has worked and lived abroad, including Guyana, Sumatra, Western Australia, Canada and Venezuela.

He presently lives in Vancouver, British Columbia, with his wife and two children.

CONTENTS

Page

PART THREE

PART FOUR

EPILOGUE

PREFACE

They Don't Make Diamonds as Big as Stones

Diamond n., Colourless or tinted brilliant precious stone of pure carbon crystal, hardest naturally occurring substance; from the Greek, adamas, meaning adamant or invincible, of Adam the first man.

Diamond:

- is the naturally occurring crystalline form of carbon in the cubic system;
- occurs most commonly as octahedral crystals (double tetrahedron), often flattened with curved faces, only rarely as cubes;
- contains a perfect cleavage and has an adamantine or greasy lustre; is brittle and easily fractured;
- has a specific gravity of 3.5 gm cm^{-1} and a Mohs' hardness of 10 (on a scale of 1 to 10);
- is generally colourless and transparent, but may be black or shades of brown, yellow, green or red;
- gems are clear, industrials or bort are clouded, dusted with myriads of tiny inclusions or impurities;
- is formed deep in the earth's crust under immense pressures and carried to the surface of the earth within kimberlite and lamproite volcanic pipes;
- is mined from kimberlite and lamprophyre pipes, also from alluvial deposits derived from pipes which have long since been eroded away;
- is not made as big as stones:

Most of the diamond in the world has been mined over the last century and a half from southern Africa; one consequence of this is that certain major multinational/transglobal companies whose historical base is in South Africa now control, absolutely, the world gem diamond supply. They do this by means of a powerful cartel; Antwerp, Amsterdam and Johannesburg are in firm control.

In December 1985, however, mining commenced at the Argyle AK1 diamondiferous lamproite in the Kimberley Region of Western

Australia. This was the first major diamond mine development which was able to operate somewhat removed from the direct control of the cartel. Argyle would produce more than 30 million carats of diamond per year, effectively increasing world production by more than 40% overnight. With the Law of Supply and Demand, therefore, as the linchpin of world capitalism, Argyle's position in and influence on the world supply market was absolutely critical to the cartel. Fortunately, most of this huge production was industrial and cheap gem quality stones, with only 5% being gem quality and most of those coloured. Thus the cartel did not feel particularly threatened and investment and production went ahead; the Argyle Mine became the largest diamond mine in the world.

But the AK1 pipe held another secret. Among its coloured gems were very rare pink fancies, ranging in intensity from the palest pink to almost blood red. There followed some rather remarkable marketing initiatives by the Australians, and the Argyle pinks became amongst the most highly prized and highly priced of all gems. AK1 was the sole source of these stones.

Bill Keats

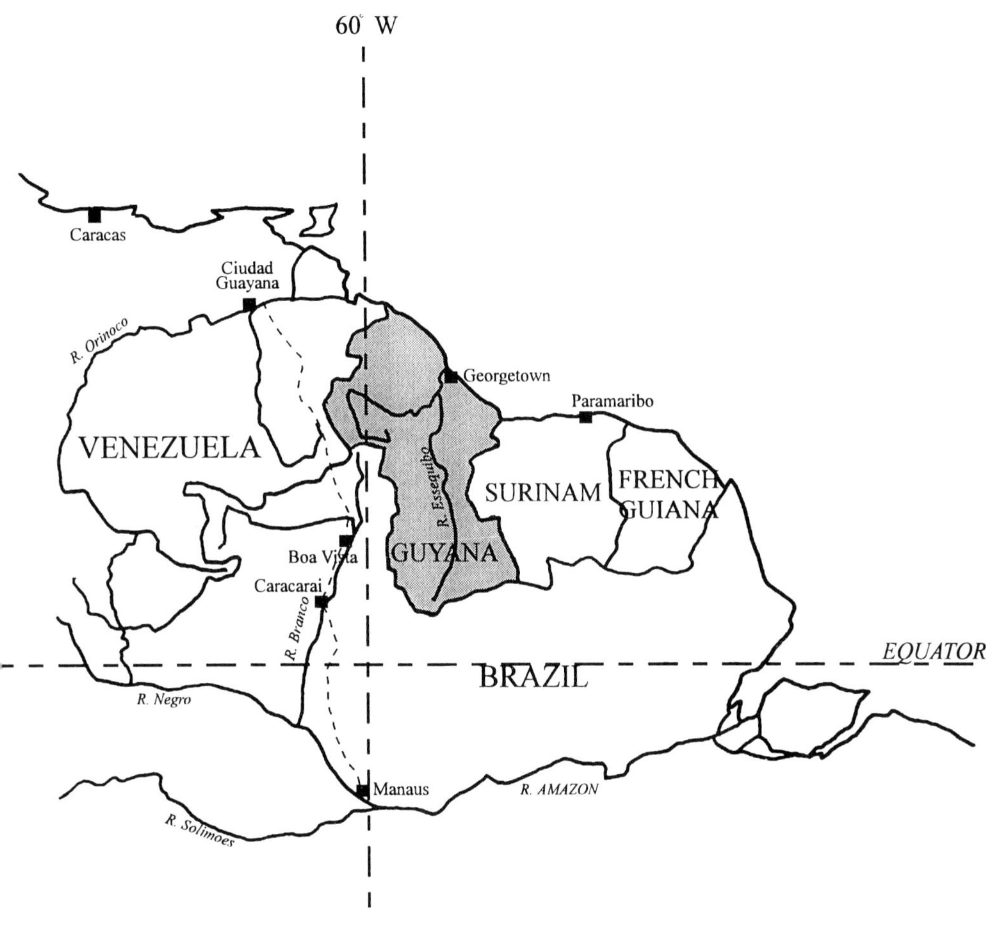

60° W
Caracas
Ciudad Guayana
R. Orinoco
Georgetown
Paramaribo
VENEZUELA
SURINAM
FRENCH GUIANA
R. Essequibo
Boa Vista
GUYANA
Caracarai
R. Branco
EQUATOR
BRAZIL
R. Negro
Manaus
R. AMAZON
R. Solimoes

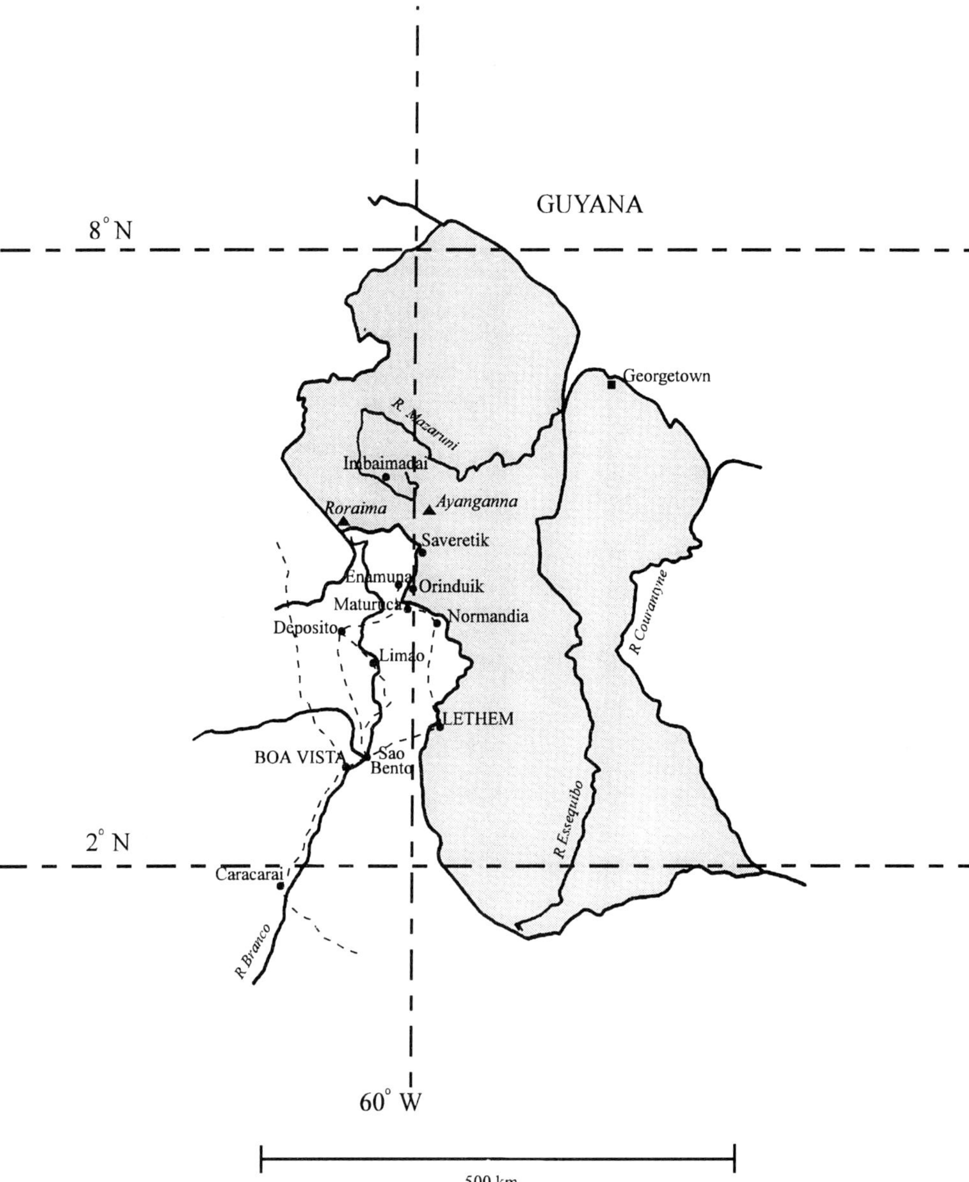
GUYANA
8° N
2° N
60° W
Georgetown
R. Mazaruni
Imbaimadai
Ayanganna
Roraima
Saveretik
Enamuna
Orinduik
Maturuca
Normandia
Deposito
Limao
LETHEM
Sao
Bento
BOA VISTA
Caracarai
R Branco
R Esequibo
R Courantyne
500 km

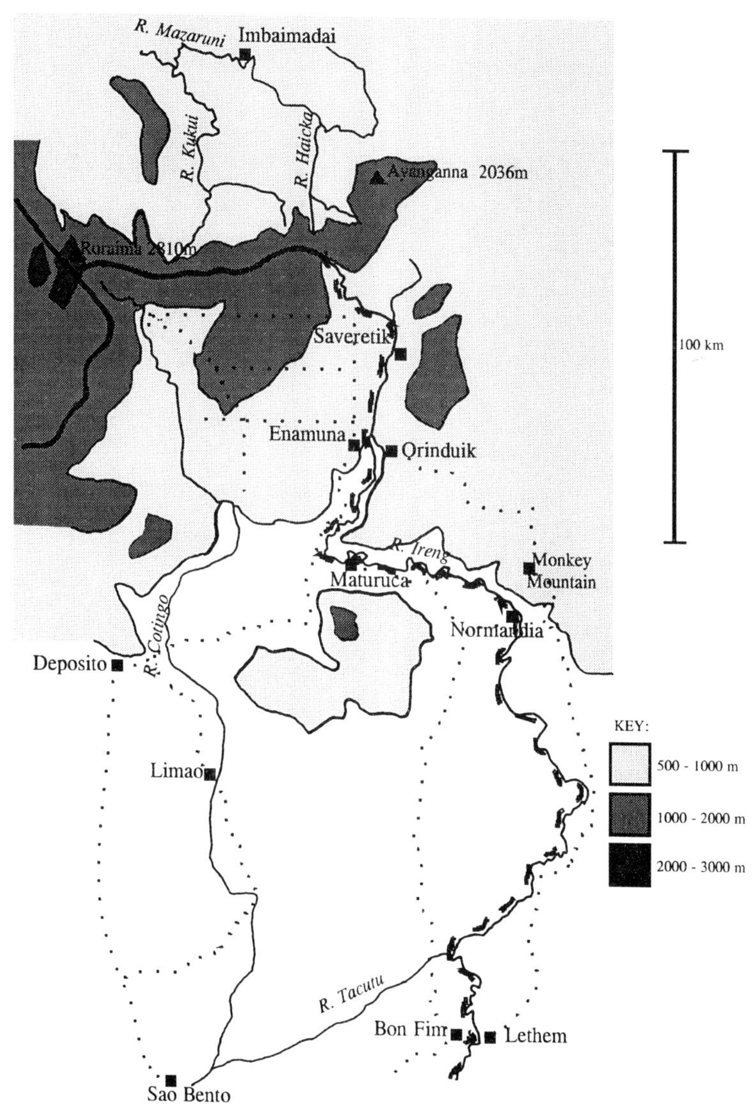
R. Mazaruni
Imbaimadai
R. Kukui
R. Haicka
Ayanganna 2036m
Roraima 2810m
Saveretik
Enamuna
Orinduik
R. Ireng
Maturuca
Monkey Mountain
Normandia
R. Cotingo
Deposito
Limao
R. Tacutu
Bon Fim
Lethem
Sao Bento
100 km
KEY:
500 - 1000 m
1000 - 2000 m
2000 - 3000 m

PROLOGUE

CHAPTER ONE

WHISKEY DREAMS

They say there is at least one book in every man. I have often meant to write mine, a novel, a travelogue, an epic even, perhaps a detective story, sci-fi; a deep and meaningful dissertation? An essay - would have to be prose, for I never was any good at poetry. A letter to the editor?

I did write a letter to the BBC once, and had it read out over the air - those famous words *This is the BBC World Service* - though I couldn't hear too clearly through the short wave static. The BEEB wrote in reply, apologising for having 'affronted my sensibilities', or was it 'confronted my sensitivities'? I had complained about some commentator's insensitivity to Man - 'hanging was too good for him' or some such phrase. I guess I was just a dreamer then.

My excuse has always been time, a common enough one. My reasons? Well, they're something different but common too, sensitivity to criticism, a wish to remain private. Once a dreamer, always a dreamer.

My excuse was gone.
My sensitivity faded,
Was perhaps a little jaded.
My excuse evaporated.

But do I have the time? My thoughts are jumbled and tumbling as though in Aboriginal dreamtime. Bright pebbles tumbling and polishing in a lapidarist's kitchen. Excuse and reason intermingle like spice in a mortar producing in chemical combination yet another taste sensation. I wish I had a dream recorder to make all this easier. I wish my wish list.

And sure there is time, plenty of it, no end to it in fact.

So here goes. I have lived experiences that no others have. You, dear reader, will share them. You can wear them and add your own fantasies. I will allow you to live vicariously in me. Am I just fantasising? Mr Dreamer of dreams.

Light weight (efficient body lipo-something-functions), short furry legs, heart, lungs and general viscera in superbly good working order, not even the beginnings of a beer gut; stealthy, wary, suspicious? Even a little smart (boasting again), just right for this place, for to dream here can be dangerous;

Hah! that was twenty years ago; start over:

Forty something, balding, close to the onset of presbyopia, have to be careful, have to be practical, no sloppy sentimentality allowed; no elephants live here, no dinosaurs, no king of the jungle, four-hundred pound lion; the kings and queens of this jungle are of a different aspect, serpentine, or small and scuffling, sucking, stinging, sessile, never ending variety, and smart.

The bush drips its load of reinforced raindrops; pale new shafts of sunlight filter through the canopy; some miles away a troop of howler monkeys cacophonies, though no doubt to them the sound is sweet; there is a muted background roar; it is a thousand miles away, thousands of miles away, Charing Cross Station, Piccadilly Circus, years away, porters smiling, civilisations away, buses honking, taxis hooting, a siren wailing...

Slowly the sounds melted with the melting sunset and I woke from my dreaming to the tumultuous roar of the waterfall and the distant machinations of the Howler troop.

My dreams had been self-indulgent and self-induced; I was sharing my hammock with the dregs of a Diamond Club whiskey bottle, local whiskey, all you could buy on the landing. A party was in full tilt in the next hut. I swung my legs out, tangling in the mosquito net. How the hell did that get there? Must have been my Guardian Angel! Boots? Shake them out first, the centipede, the scorpion, the sting in the tail.

Outside, the cool of the evening air was instantly sobering. The last rays of sunlight silhouetted the forest giants, those great buttressed plant-beasts that are a whole marvellous world to themselves. On them, in them, under and over them, a synergistic microcosmic universe of symbiosis pulsated, sweated, defecated, married, had kids, divorced, got buried, you know, the usual stuff.

The Charing Cross dreams were in reality nightmares. Who in their right mind would want to exchange this reality? Who would cross the miles? Who needs the Westminster System, taxicabs, when you could have this, the untainted and untamed beauty of the Amazon, a bottle of Diamond Club whiskey over a game of dominoes, friends, honest badinage?

Sounds of kitchen clatter came from the side of the hut as I turned back in. Harald was firing up the camp oven; a piece of pale red meat in a chipped enamel plate readied itself for its roasting. Two young Indian lads squatted in the corner, smiling widely. I started to feel sick from the whiskey hangover; I needed to talk, to reminisce. Harald and the two smiling Indians would make my captive audience, though most of what I told them I told in dreamer's silence.

"Heh, you remember when I first arrived, Harald? I was twenty-one, can hardly believe it, my first trip in aeroplane."

My dreams and memories merged.

I am leaving London behind in its pre-80s, pre-Thatcher wintry grip, wet melting slush in the streets, litter-blocked gutters, steamy, smoky station snack bars, piss swilling on the penny toilet floor, pork pies, soggy sausage rolls, white bread and butter something dead sandwich, tea bag with milk and sugar, Double Diamond; if only I had been born something a little more exotic, say Swiss, or even French perhaps, breakfast might at least be a little more exciting - coffee, croissants, black cherry conserve!

First stop is Barbados, but just a stopover; think in Centigrade, 31°, steamy 90% humidity, ice-cold rum and coke, and another ice-cold coke; how could anyone exchange this paradise, this Westminster System, for the mother of Westminster Systems? Ice-cold rum and coke with a twist of fresh lime for lukewarm beer; but many had done just that, lured by hope, money, education, betterment, the good life, motor cars, slick suits with London Transport on their epaulets, lies, tales.

"I was headed out man, but they made it so easy for me, they did everything for me."

All I carry is my education and a need to be different, a need to not be a banker, nor an accountant, nor a gas fitter, nor a bus conductor; I have the choice; I have my degree after all.

"Yeh, I remember Tom, I'd never forget such a momentous occasion now would I?" Harald was all ears, never the cynic.

"Back in the dark ages, back in the age of the British Overseas Airways Corporation if you need the historical perspective." I stood up on my soapbox. "When names were big, man, long for long's sake, grandiose and imperial. Before the Age of Acronyms, of pithy, hip, Saatchi & Saatchi. The aristocracy ruled in those days, democracy's puppeteers."

"It still does my friend. The strings are of a different colour, and you colonialists like to think you still hold some sway, but them faceless city gents they still in charge. They use they yuppie tools but they have not yet ceded that authority... " Harald could be quite the philosopher.

I've lived with Mum & Dad for twenty-one years, cosseted, fed and watered; I've been educated and welfare-stated, and still the people's government is nurturing me, providing me with more succour in the name of AID to our less fortunate cousins in our dismantled Empire; I have no ulterior motive, no guilt-by-association to assuage; the Empire is not of my making; it is my first job; it comes complete with a salary, more than I have need for, though now that I have it, I am determined to enjoy it to the full; I am going to be... an explorer... an adventurer, fine if incidentally I can be of some minor use to my less fortunate cousins; I have been pampered across the Atlantic, coca-colaed in Barbados, and am now about to be contracted south to the South American Caribbean ex-colony of Guyana.

Circling over those white sands and aqua pools, swaying coconut trees, I am not at all sure I want to go any further; imagine it, December thirty-first, short-sleeved, black-skinned sunshine faces, smiling; coming down off the plane I am hit by a wall of steam, my specs instantaneously fog and I almost go head over heels; I make for the air-conditioning of the transit area; I am being jostled by a Bermuda-shorted, middle-aged, uncouth colonial of a northern neighbour, horribly sunburnt and sweating; I am thinking that that must be where the term 'redneck' originates! He is scratching himself, chain smoking Camels, and pontificating loudly on the honesty of the barman's rum measure; maybe not such an unspoilt paradise after all?

I was just twenty-one, still had my idealism more or less intact, black was black and white white, ingenuous. But then, that is what youth is all about. I have no regrets for that.

The piece of pale red meat sizzled in the roasting pan and combined its fishy juices with shallot and peppers. Alligator tale. Alligator tail. Harald was peeling eddo and sweet potato. The two Indian lads propped themselves up in the corner, now smiling wildly, smoking sweet leaves. The camp oven belched dragon smoke. I felt really sick and went out for fresh air. Better get back on the BOAC bird and find my dreams in Amazon backwaters.

CHAPTER TWO

DEAR MR. ASKEW

'Dear Mr. Askew,

It is with great pleasure that I confirm your appointment as Geologist, Level 1... Your travel arrangements will be confirmed as soon as possible, on the first available flight after Christmas... Terms of your appointment are 24 months, with extensions by mutual agreement...Housing will be provided at subsidised rental...Tax free allowances...Enclosed information on availability of consumer items (Tate & Lyle refined sugar!)... '

Thomas Askew, that's me; the Thomas is pronounced with a Tee, not a Thee, and the Askew part I like to think of in terms of its statistical bent; newly graduated from a rather superior university, so they said, and, in these days, just old enough to vote; I am being sent, all expenses paid, generously salaried and fully briefed on the availability of refined sugar in neat and clean paper bags from Liverpool, to the experience of a lifetime; I am jumping feet first into the cane fields of adulthood.

I'm not sure whether I've surfaced yet, but now is time enough to start to share those images conjured in the early years of my independence. It is difficult to describe my feelings of twenty years ago; my memories now are corrupted with the overprint of my second twenty years. So many of the images are still hazy, but with the writing, veils are slowly lifting. Heh, I'm more hopeful now than when I started three pages back.

The ride down is bumpy; we start out well enough, calm azure sea and cloudless sky diffusing into one; the white island beaches and their leisure and pleasure seekers are left in the wash of Atlantic breakers; the stop-over has been on a literal, littoral speck in the ocean.

The Super VC 10 is next to empty having disgorged its load of tourists; we are asked to sit up front to balance the load; there seem to be more flight attendants than passengers; my heart pounds, sticks in my throat on this last leg of my journey; from here on, all that has been familiar will be gone.

Great banks of storm cloud meet us headlong, seat-belts are fastened, engines rev, the plane banks and begins to really fly for the first time since leaving winter; glimpses through the cloud reveal a change of scene; the southern Atlantic turns brown and muddy; we are flying over the great ocean currents that pick up the mud of the Andes way out beyond the deltas and carry it up the eastern coast of South America to join the Gulf Stream; the mud of the Andes carried east for thousands upon thousands of miles by the Orinoco and the Amazon and which, gradually settling, classifies the whole South American coastline from Belem to Trinidad; and with the mud goes gold and silver, and copper and lead, and diamonds maybe.

Descending at last, the plane breaks through the cloud cover and we are over land again, a deep green, dark leaf-green land of trees, mangrove and snaking red and brown rivers; nature gives way quite suddenly; now regular fields of cane and rice, tin roofs, villages, tracks, roads, bigger villages, smoke, canals, koker dams, donkey carts, the first lights of dusk from a town somewhere over to the left, the setting sun behind us, banking again and the red sun now on our left; we are floating in almost silence, approaching my New World; the engines suddenly scream again, the darkening ground rushes up, a bump, a squeal, the splash of spray as we chase through new rain puddles awash on the tarmac.

Georgetown, Timehri airport; "Welcome to Timehri International Airport" in unlit neon tubes; a pair of white and green DC3s parked angularly, nose up, ready for a morning flight to one of those places no 'international' could hope to go; red, black, yellow and white arrows, and green flags; a thread of a dozen passengers winding carefully past rain puddles towards the terminal complex, and still being splashed by a passing luggage cart pushed by two grinning uniformed jokers; night has fallen suddenly; there has been no dusk.

A small concrete foyer, white and green paint, flaking, wooden slatted Customs benches, undefined smells, language familiar but distinctly different, the recent humidity now wafted by a gentle outside night breeze and aided by great ceiling fans still turning; portraits of prime-ministerially avuncular black faces on the Customs Hall walls; my New World; the compressor in an Ice-Cold Coke machine in the corner shudders into action, successfully competing with the familiar snippets of language.

CHAPTER THREE

EPEIROGENESIS

Guyana epitomised the New World in so many ways.

This New World of mine was part of an ancient growing land; the geologically ancient continental shield was what formed its core, its beating heart in the interior, but new land was also being constantly built out by delta and claimed from the Atlantic Ocean. Denuding the old to feed the young.

The ancient people were still there, the noble American Indian, but ignobly held at bay in that same heartland. The new people had arrived uninvited and unwanted, or had been brought themselves, not wanting, to populate the new land, to work its economy for the greater good and greater glory of the greater race back home.

> And the New People had encouraged the New Land to grow more, had built the koker dams and drained the swamps, and the Race Back Home looked upon It and saw that It was good and productive and made lots of money and afforded a strategic protection.
>
> And the Masters rewarded their Slaves with Freedom and made them up into Servants, and gave them Law and Education, and reserved for them places in Heaven, and eradicated malaria.
>
> And the New People were encouraged to introduce New Plants to grow for Foods, and New Animals for Food and to keep as pets and to keep down the pests.
>
> And the Ancient Land gave up its Secrets and its Timber to feed and shelter the New Animals, and their Keepers.

The terror that was the native marsupial mouse was eradicated by the brave European cat. No more would the soil's nutrition be wasted on unproductive mangrove and its symbionta when life-giving rice or Demerara sugar cane could be grown. 'Drink your tea with two spoons of sugar now luvvy!' The soil was being renewed in life and giving renewed life. The slaves, the indentured labourers, the traders, the coolies, the teachers and administrators were all living their newly intertwined lives. And here was I, about to start my new life, my adulthood.

> And seeing that their Work was done and that the Times they were a changing, and that the price of cane sugar was a falling, and that there was no longer a strategic role to play in the South Atlantic, and that the place was generally Fucked up, the Masters became bored with their game and left for Home, and gave It over to the Servants.

And now they were salving their conscience by sending a twenty-one year old pupa to aid them for two or three years. What a wealth of knowledge and experience I had to share!

The country, by rights, should have been a total disaster, an ecological write-off, a prime example of the havoc that humanity and the pseudo-science of economics has wrought on its only home, but much of this I was too young to see then. What I saw, in my youthful black and white, was a poor country struggling to come to terms with the rich modern world. I saw people striving to do their best for themselves and their children, though often against the odds. I saw strength and tenacity, understanding, love, humour and harmony. I saw a country of great beauty, of unsurpassed natural wonders in the interior. Guyana was a country of almost infinite variety in its fauna and flora, yet how many species were being extinguished before they even had a chance of being catalogued? It was a busy country; it was full of Caribbean soul, noise, music, fun. It was a harmonious conglomeration of peoples, the forerunner of the multi-culturalism which is now so avidly embraced by all people of culture.

Guyana was a people country; its soul was its people. But as pawns in a European chess match, how could these people, why should these people take responsibility for the changes wrought?

Guyana was schizophrenic. It was a Caribbean culture set in the South American continent. Had it ever been Spanish? Was it Dutch? Perhaps British? Portuguese? Ethiopian, Gujarati, Tamil? Hopei, Macushi, Wapishiana!

The coastal plain was entirely of man's own making, and certainly most of the population was to be found there, inhabiting the narrow strip of reclaimed land just thirty miles deep. It was almost as though the new people had to keep their homelands in sight, to keep in touch with their roots. This Guyana was moulded totally around its people; it was a very cultured and cultural Caribbean land.

The great interior motherland, the South American part, was still nearly pristine, for few had ever ventured there, a legacy of the white man's policing, the voodoo-fear of the noble American Indian. White settlers had pushed through 300 miles of jungle, up rivers and falls, in search of cattle pasture, and found it at last in the deep southern savannahs of the Rupununi. That was about the only settlement in the interior, apart from scattered Amerindian villages and the pork-knocker landings. The cattle men had burnt and cleared the jungle between those small patches already cleared by the Macushi and Wapishiana. Expatriate profit moved in on sustainable subsistence.

The children of slaves had had little to do with this part.

I wasn't sure exactly why I had come back after all these years, but these were people I'd worked with, spent idle time with, explored and adventured with. I trusted them. I enjoyed their company. Reason enough?

Adventurers during the rule of the Spanish, Dutch, French, and latterly the British, had had but two things in mind. First, the search for the lost golden city of El Dorado and second, the search for the great inland sea, Parime Lacus, on whose shores El Dorado would be found. On their way south, they found gold and diamonds in the Essequibo River, the Mazaruni and the Cuyuni, and in many other streams. But the gold and precious stones were only ever won in small quantities, and the city of gold and Parime Lacus eluded them.

The rivers and ways were left abandoned to those of lesser fortune, escaped slaves turned prospectors, and the shopkeepers who mortgaged them rum and pickled pork for the right to work on their river dredges. Small communities were established on river landings, often at rapids or waterfalls which broke the river journeys and below which the diamonds and gold had accumulated in eddies and whirlpool caverns on the river bed. This was a land in which there seemed to be a mutual respect between explorer and the explored; there was no rape or pillage, but rather a sustained winning by seduction of meagre livelihoods. A few, taking a little from out of a vast land.

The shopkeeper became king. He was employer, sub-contractor, landlord, publican and keeper of the whorehouse and purveyor of the barrels of preserved pickled pork belly that lent their name to the prospectors, the pork-knockers.[1]

This is a story of pork-knockers, Brazilians, Indians and the adventures of old bent Tom Askew. The place is Orinduik, a small village on the border with Brazil.

[1] The story goes that in order to test the barrels of pork for freshness, one should rap or knock loudly on them and see how many worms come to open the door.

PART ONE

CHAPTER FOUR

THE CAPER

Orinduik is on the Ireng River. The river there is already about eighty kilometres old having been born in the ageless moss forests of Mount Ayanganna; it is maybe fifty metres wide and there is a superb series of falls and rapids as it cuts through a series of hard silicified jasper beds. You can get across easily enough in a small canoe, if you know the water and jasper bed falls well enough. Enamuna is a small settlement on the Brazilian side, a couple of kilometres away from the river, and from there a rough four-wheel-drive track runs south to Boa Vista, the capital of Brazil's Roraima State. There is an even rougher trail running north and north-west to nowhere in particular, roughly paralleling the Ireng valley. We will come to that later.

It was about ten o'clock at night. I'd had a bellyful of roast alligator tail with crisp dry cassava bread to soak up the grease. The healthiest part of the evening repast had been fresh mango to cut the earlier fishy and reptilian flavours. A glass or two of rum melded with the mango and life took on a much rosier hue.

Harald and I swung in our hammocks, belching and rumbling in unison, a sort of peristaltic duet in F minor. I was half listening for sounds outside, waiting. The ghost of Bob Marley wailed out from the party next door, but he had been wailing all evening and had now become just another part of the background. Bob, accompanied by a cacophony of croaking and clacking and cricketing creepy crawly night things.

The intensely aggravating high pitched whine of Japanese motor bike engines exploded into the cricketing night, and then just as suddenly died immediately outside the hut. Footsteps crunched on the gravel track and 'Go Tell It On The Mountain' was drowned out for the second time by a loud scratching and scrabbling sound, a feathered and furious barking, and flapping of wings. Petal, Harald's pet powis[2] was announcing visitors.

Midnight, Tall Boy and Don James pushed through the beaded curtain at the doorway. Don had taken the brunt of Petal's overprotective nature and was rubbing at a long scratch down his left cheek. Harald had tamed Petal from a fledgling chick, after he had roasted her mother; she thought she was a mother hen, albeit a rather huge one, and would protect her adopted brood of open range organic chicks as if they had been her own, with her very life if necessary. Harald re-introduced her to the newcomers. She had met them before and should not have attacked, but then this was another time, another place, and powis are not renowned for their intellectual capacity; they are purely instinctive creatures. It had taken her at least a week to get used to me and I had any number of flesh wounds to prove it.

"Harald, when you goin' to cook that damn bird?" Tall Boy looked back through the doorway with hungry eyes. "I could soon put it out of its mad mothering misery for you. There's no need to wait for next Christmas you know."

Midnight cut in in enthusiastic agreement. "Yes man, good idea, and then you might be able to catch one chicken and wring its neck for our Sunday dinner."

Harald, however, was quick off the mark being nearly as protective of his chicks as was Petal.

"What you would want with chicken now? I got a lovely red dragon fish stewin' up here in the fire, with fresh mairawiri peppers, Tom can back me up on that, eh Tom?"

Tom indeed was more than ready to back Harald up on that account, anything to see that pot of food finished before it came to be reheated for breakfast.

"Oh look, it's great... it's just lovely, marvellous... unbelievable tucker..." I rapidly ran out of suitable superlatives, "and it doesn't have any bones."

This was some greeting! I'd seen Midnight Maurice a couple of times through the years and on various continents, but for Tall Boy and Don, well it had been nearly twenty years since I had met them and it was not long, therefore, before the old emotions took over.

"Gimme five!"

"Slip me some skin!"

---

[2] a bush turkey, ten kilogrammes and exceptionally tasty when not too tough.

"Gimme five man!"
"Slip me skin man!"

Rum was poured, then chased. Another bottle was opened. And suddenly the years vanished and the party next door was drowned out and sunk without a trace. And even the reptile stew was finished. Man, they must have been hungry!

I am met on the wrong side of Immigration by a chap from the High Commission; my name is held aloft on a card, though there can't be many like me in this crowd of a dozen; I will never remember him, I will have no recollection of him in fact; I am sure he will never remember me; we shake hands, his attention elsewhere; he has a function to attend and stops only to inform me that I will be met outside Customs by someone from the Mines Department - 'tall black chap, beard,' and having fulfilled his task, that is all the contact I will ever have with my overseas representatives; I am obviously not diplomatic material!

Immigration, Health and Customs are relaxed; I've been shot through with half a dozen assorted vaccines before leaving civilisation; I produce my letter of appointment, and am stamped through; I have the impression that the sooner everybody gets off duty and home tonight, the better it will be; the mood is Old Year's Night; the new year is now only a few short hours away.

Maurice 'Midnight' Tyler and Harald 'Spanner' Sukhdeo.
"Heh man, you gotta be Thomas." It is said with a 'Thee'.
"Tom," I say, "with a 'Tee'."
"Maurice, " he says, "Maurice Tyler. With a 'Tee'."

Tall black chap with a goatee beard; our man from the High Commission has proved worth his weight in gold.

"Got a Rover outside," Maurice says. "We can go straight into town; these all your bags man? You're travelling light; how's the flight? She was on time for once, heh, we nearly missed you all; we got you booked into the Park for a couple of weeks; got a house buildin' but not quite ready yet you know;

soon as it is, we'll move you all in there."

"Great; yeh; that's right; heh, it's okay; I guess so; sounds fine; oh yes, that sounds really good." I am starting to judge the breaks in the conversation and get a word in edgewise.

"Here's Harald; heh, Harald, bring the Rover round man, let's get going, we don't have too much time."

The accent is expressive, sing-song, a little like Welsh in a funny kind of way, I think; an assortment of cars is pulled up in front of the terminal building; most of the passengers, it seems, are being picked up and for each one arriving there must be at least a dozen in the reception committee; I can imagine what chaos there must be if a full aeroplane ever lands here; bags are passed over, kisses planted, there's a lot of hugging going on; welcomes are obviously very demonstrative in this people country.

I stand by my bags, an island in a whirlpool of activity.

Maurice is somewhere out front; a rather sorry looking Land Rover pulls up and double parks in the No Parking Zone alongside a fifteen year-old Austin Cambridge taxi; I lean against the crowd and make it past the taxi touts.

Harald grabs half my load. "Where de hell Maurice gan to now? He seh he wanna go Georgetown quick an now he limin' wid some girlfriend, tekin' a finey in de bar I don doubt."

There follows a sound I am to learn quickly, an indrawn breath through closed teeth and pursed lips known locally as 'suck-teeth'; it is a sound that implies total exasperation; the exasperation may be warranted, or it may not; 'suck-teeth' can be, and is, applied to almost any circumstance or situation.

Maurice reappears with, "I thought I'd lost you-all then." He offers no further explanation.

I remember Harald had kept the engine running and in the weeks that followed, I became convinced that this particular Rover, regd PD 142, should be kept running even during servicing and refuelling. Harald was the only one I ever knew who could get it started. He was a natural born mechanical engineer. I figured the way he spelt his first name indicated Scottish ancestry though his second name, which was Sukhdeo, and his complexion were about as Scottish as a generous sporran. I imagined a wayward sea captain cast ashore by pirates in the Bay of Bengal. His Celtic connections might have been rather distant, but to me, he was as Scottish as the Glens and the Glenfiddich malt that coursed through his bloodstream. PD 142 had seen quite a few years of sterling service in the interior, and had then been put out to grass in Georgetown, to run the odd errand as a reward for all its hard work in the past. Harald knew it like a truant child. I and most of my fellow geologists loathed the old brute and would have gladly seen it to the bottom of the Demerara River with a pair of cement boots.

Midnight - Maurice Desmond Nathaniel Tyler - and Harald 'Spanner' Sukhdeo were the first two Guyanese I had met, all those years ago at Timehri.

Harald had proved more than just a good mechanic, he was a great mechanic; he was resourceful and inventive. In this country of either no spare parts or outrageously expensive spare parts, he could fashion his own blue long-tailed widget and fit it where only a red one had ever fitted before. But more than this even, he was also a passable cook which was the rarest of qualities in a Guyanese bushman. I have never been able to eat anybody else's alligator tail! Harald had joined me as a so-called camp attendant for my first bush season, and had stuck with me throughout.

As for Midnight, he and I had run a couple of drilling programmes together. We were firm old friends who had shared many good times, in Georgetown and out. Midnight had been the one to suggest I come back here, for the fun to come.

Tall Boy and Don James had worked for me as foreman and prospector on a couple of occasions in the Mazaruni Basin, and both had been with me on the Ayanganna[3] Expedition.

Tall Boy, or Osborne Rankin to use the name his mother gave him, was a two metre plus shining black giant of a man. He came from Buxton on the coast, but he had spent most of his life in the bush, prospecting, labouring, working on the diving dredges. He looked as though he had spent his life in the bush and had the philosophy to go with it! He had some really useful contacts in some most unusual parts of the interior, and he was as strong as an ox. Mount Ayanganna had been where we developed our strong mutual respect.

---

[3] Mount Ayanganna, 2040m monolith covered in moss forest and one hell of a place to forge lasting friendships.

And last but not least, there was Don, an Arawak Indian originally from the north-west. He had a certain uncanny ability with a batel[4] and a set of diamond sieves and could read a trap in a creek from half a mile off. He said he had a nose for it, but I could never see anything too remarkable about that particular facial appendage. His English was good as he was brought up in Georgetown; also, he had worked with pork-knockers on the Potaro and the Mazaruni, so he was great for liaison with some of the more isolated Indian communities there. And lastly, although he was only about half the size of Tall Boy, he could pack an equal load.

We were all assembled, glasses topped up.

"Is everything set up with Riaz?" I asked the room at large.

Midnight grunted a reply to the effect that yes, everything was set up with Riaz, and had been set up with Riaz over a week ago now, and that Tom with a 'tee' should have known that.

"Okay, let me put it another way. When did you last see him? Over a week ago, eh? And what kept you in Boa Vista so long? Watching over his old lady maybe. We've got a lot riding on this guy Riaz. We don't know him. Well, I don't know him at any rate, and from what I've heard, I ain't too sure I want to. He's the type would sell his mother." They say I'm a bit of a worrier!

"Quit worrying' Tom, it's too late now anyway. Look, we got it all sussed out and we'll leave tomorrow night. Two days and we're in Chi Chi. Two days to dynamite and suck out the caves. Two days more and we're back here, home and dry, and nobody need ever know we've stirred. They'll keep the bacchanal goin' next door, non-stop. We'll give ourselves a week to sober up, then ship out."

It all sounded so simple. A six-day caper to swap a couple of boxes of plastic explosive for a couple of packets of diamonds. I should have known better, though mind you, the first part of the master plan seemed to have gone off without a hitch. Diamond was cheap in the Mazaruni Basin. Officially, stones had to be sold through the government agent at the government's own fixed price, less a quite substantial cut for the government agent. The price was about enough to prevent immediate starvation, and just enough to promote chronic alcoholism. (The alcohol was available through the government agent

---

[4] A batel is a sort of conical gold pan like an upside-down coolie hat.

of course). We could afford to pay a small premium and make some very good friends, and some very good profits, but the agent and the agent's agents must never know.

Midnight had heard of a new diamond find in the Upper Mazaruni, about twenty kilometres upstream from Imbaimadai, up a south bank tributary near the Chi Chi Falls. He had been told that the stones were rather special, the first recorded South American pink gems, and could therefore be worth a small fortune. So far, six pink gems, each over four carats had been recovered, but the creek was small, half dry and choked with tacoubas and the prospector, a local character name of King Harry, was having problems cleaning out some caves. He needed a few sticks of tovex to waste nature sufficiently to get at the cave system beneath the falls. Dynamiting was considered okay as a general procedure, but it couldn't be carried out easily without the local shopkeeper knowing, and hence the government agent finding out - and that would mean bye-bye to the Chi Chi pinks. So, the plan was simple. We could smuggle in the tovex, and smuggle out the stones.

"Riaz has the stuff?"

"Quit worryin' Tom." This time it was Don James. "Riaz has the stuff. It's in two crates, about forty kilos all up, and another box of det cord. We got detonators, crimps and fuse. We could start a revolution if that is what we wanted."

"Come to think, maybe that's not such a bad idea." This from Harald, the revolutionary Celtic philosopher.

"He's got the crates in the schoolhouse with senhorita Josephina," Don continued.

"Now that's quite an explosive combination, Riaz and Miss Josephina." Harald cut in again.

"The dets and fuse, Don, they're not from our official supplies, are they?"

"No Tom man, that would be too risky. Corporal here, he knows exactly how much we got, an' besides, if anyting went wrong, you bet they trace it quick right back to we. Best if everyting trace back to Brazil side."

There was not much we could do, or had the energy for, till the next morning, so good use was made of the time we had to plot and plan and empty another bottle of D'Aguiar's Special Reserve. It rained during the night. A bone-chilling breeze blew from the south across the savannahs and Bob Marley sang "Don't Rock The Boat" and "Sun is Shining", though it was not of course.

That night I relived my memories, my first impressions of Georgetown. It was not for the first time either. Funny, but I knew that when I eventually returned there, so little would have changed. It would be more tired, but then so was I. The paint would have peeled more, there would be more violence in the air, less laughter, but these were the subtle observations of a seasoned traveller. In essence, physically, it would all be the same. The Park Hotel and the Cambridge opposite would still be plying their same trades according to their own principles, and would outlast me for sure.

What strikes me most on my first journey in PD 142 is its suspension, or rather, the lack of its suspension; I am so relieved I haven't brought Grandma's best china service in my hand luggage!

It is about thirty miles from Timehri to Georgetown, down a B grade road; we follow the left bank of the Demerara; there are villages every mile or so, really it's one long string of village, one, sometimes two or three houses broad, with the river to the left and cane fields to the right; the names are unfamiliar, quaint, some distinctly foreign, others not quite foreign; Soesdyke, Golden Grove, Diamond, Houston; the journey this evening takes about an hour, when to do it in safety should take perhaps double that; steam gives way to sail; I think to myself that the internal combustion engine, likewise, should give way to less sophisticated modes of transport - donkey carts, hand carts, bullock carts - but not in Guyana; might is right on the road from the airbase.

I am suddenly tired; I can see little in the beam of the headlights, visions and sounds of chicken feathers scattering in the slipstream, splashing out of potholes; we talk a little, Maurice and I, small talk; I am squashed uncomfortably between Maurice and Harald in the middle seat with my legs splayed around a selection of gear levers and brake handles, hoping that they won't be needed, worried about what Harald might grab in an emergency; Harald keeps up most of the conversation, which revolves around how he is going to 'party for so', how this girl or that 'won't stand a chance', and last year's conquests of the heart; mostly I am trying to decode all the smells and sounds of my New Tropical World, like the newly-blind man in his sightless universe.

I think now I must have spent most of the journey just dreaming. Nothing over dramatic could have taken place for I remember there were no exceptionally fierce braking manoeuvres - but then PD 142's brakes were not exactly in the peak of condition!

We pass through the outskirts of Georgetown; I can see a little more from the occasional streetlight; wooden houses in all states of repair, some bright with new paint, others barely worthy of the description shack, jostling one another for space; open windows, curtains or cloths billowing out in the night air; people are everywhere, sitting in doorways, in windows gazing out on their world, ambling, chatting or hand-holding in the street, congregating around the open double doors of rum shops, singly buying last-minute necessities in the local store; this is a people-country.

Can you understand? Living in 1990s suburbia, how can you understand?

I had lived in Georgetown for three years, but one of my clearest memories now is of that first night. Ever since that night, few experiences can rival it, though, funnily enough, nothing of real significance occurred. I just grew up, that is all. I was at my most impressionable right then, a child with a new toy; perhaps it was this dreamer's first encounter with reality. I had relinquished my diet of soap opera, The Archers, a story of everyday country folk and I was now swimming beyond the mainstream.

We pull up outside the Park Hotel, a three storey colonial style wooden building on stilts; an impressive polished hardwood staircase leads impressively up to the foyer on the first floor; everywhere is polished wood; large fans turn lazily in the ceiling; but for the lack of punka wallahs, I imagine I could be somewhere in the Raj because all the hotel staff are of East Indian origin, the descendants of indentured labourers imported after the abolition of slavery to grow rice and sugar cane; the staff are impeccable in dress and politeness, but slightly distant, I can feel it; perhaps they are judging how best they should relate to their new guest.

Maurice takes his leave; it is now about nine in the evening and he obviously has things to do! Harald and his trusty steed are to come back, not the next day, but the day after; my first day at work, after all, is to be the January first public holiday, quite an auspicious start to a career in the Public Service don't you think?

My room on the upper floor is so huge that it looks quite bare; there is the polished wooden floor and, centrepiece, an antique heavy wooden bed with an enormous circular contraption in the ceiling from which to hang a mosquito net; dark, smooth-black wood, and hospital-crisp white linen and sheets; a small fan in one corner turns but has hardly any effect; my window looks hotel-inwards, overlooking a kitchen roof with appetisingly steamy vapours extracting beneath my nose.

I don't want to eat; I am tired, but it is hot and I can't sleep; I go out to explore the rest of the building and come inevitably to an open veranda lounge area, and there I spend the next hours lazing, stretched out in a Berbice chair[4a]*, gazing out over Main Street and nursing rum punches of unimaginable quality; in this Raj, am I clinging to the last vestiges of my past life?*

I learn that the Park is just a five minute stroll from the city centre, but also that I should not venture out alone; I am not a demanding guest; I am eager to learn, and my character thus is adjudged worthy of honest advice; I guess my tip to the young man with a bright future may also have played a small part! I gaze out over Main Street. I gaze amazed.

Main Street is a double width road lined with thirty metre high tropical hardwoods and broad exotic figs, and with bushy bougainvillaea and other shadowy areas in the central reservation; immediately opposite my veranda is Georgetown's most famous illegal whorehouse; the young man with the bright

---

[4a] A Berbice chair has extendible arms over which one can drape legs.

future is Bikram; he tells me that it is run by a syndicate of six lawyers; I am unsure whether the legal profession should decline or gain in my estimation.

Certainly I have never since been surprised by any revelation regarding the law and lawyers, fuel for my eager cynicism.

I could say that this most notorious of establishments, which had the robust and classy name of the Cambridge (named after the local Austin Cambridge taxis perhaps? I doubt it!), provided me with my first evening's entertainment in Guyana, albeit at arm's length!

The Cambridge Hotel is slightly seedy-looking but not too run down; there is a large double green door and an even larger black doorman, through which and past whom I can catch very occasional glimpses of a dimly lit interior; a sign outside advertises 'chicken-in-a-basket'; music blares out over more human sounds - 'Don't chain my heart', an open invitation to see in the New Year at the Cambridge Hotel.

The Park Hotel is two star; I wonder how many stars the Cambridge has, and were they awarded for corporal or corporeal distinction.

A constant procession of clientele, girls and their managers are in and out, up and down the street; one or two girls solicit in the street outside, but surreptitiously, shadowy, no doubt they have neglected to pay their dues to the establishment; a police car cruises by, ignores the girls but stops by a group of young men who clearly have management potential; I wonder if anything changes hands, but I can't really see clearly; the meeting seems quite open and amicable.

Most of the clients are none too steady on their feet, especially coming out; there is a smattering of tourists, but then I guess there must only be a smattering of tourists in the whole country; much of the business appears to be fulfilling local requirements.

As the more drunken leave, groups of two or three young boys in beanie hats peel out of the bushy shadows to follow their intended victims into the side streets; one puts an arm lock around the victim's neck and throat, from behind; another relieves the victim of the weight of his watch and wallet, and a quick getaway is effected by a third on a push bike; it's a game, known as 'choke and rob'; the streets of Georgetown are not very safe for the lone reveller, but there is an 'honesty-among-thieves', a pecking order, because no choke and rob is carried out on arriving chicken-in-a-basket clients, just on those departing.

In the early 70s, choke and rob was a fairly unsophisticated form of mugging, a little frightening perhaps, but not exactly life-threatening. It rapidly developed, however, into terrifying and vicious street crime as the country's economy crumbled and inter-racial strife intensified. It mushroomed until it became a tool of politicians and of the army they commanded. On my first night, I just looked on with a certain naive amusement. I had little sympathy for either victim or conspirator.

I sleep before midnight, my room is cooling at last; I wrestle with my mosquito net and see in the New Year dreaming their annoying whining dance, and wake well bitten; I examine the net to see how mosquitoes the size of a sixpence got through to their evening meal.

The next morning is bright and already warm when I surface from my internal pit; I shower cool, and dress cool; the young man with the future, Bikram the evening drinks waiter, is in the breakfast room; crisp, hospital white linen tablecloths are laid out on polished dark wood tables; I eat fresh pawpaw with a squeeze of lime and toasted slices of an unusual sweet bread; I drink coffee with sweet evaporated milk; I try the eggs, but they come sloppy and, to me, quite inedible; the salt and pepper are served in small glass jars with miniature wooden spoons - an English salt cellar soon becomes damp and clogged in the humidity; I am starting to feel hot, even in the lightest clothes I own; the atmosphere is becoming muggy; I have no one to talk with, Bikram is busy clearing up for lunch (Bikram works twenty hours a day it seems) and I go back to my room to continue my acclimatisation in private.

As I open my door, I hear a faint scuttling sound but can not quite locate its source; my window is open but the fine lace curtains are hanging unmoving in the humidity; the small fan has been turned off; I look under the bed, I fling open the tall wardrobe door, I move stealthily over to the bathroom; a cockroach the size of a small rat and looking like Kafka's Gregor scuttles past my foot and into the main room; I turn and he is gone.

My door opens again and a maid comes in.

"Am sorry sah, I didn realise you was comin' back. You wan me for finish fixin' your room now? Or I gan come back later, is no trouble sah." She is a formidable middle-aged, spreading black lady with tight black hair, not greying yet; you could land a whole battalion of shock troops on her chest; she tells me her name is Patsy; Bikram and his friends call her Big Patsy; she takes control and fixes my room; I'm convinced that Gregor must have thought it was her coming into the room when actually it had been myself, and that was why he had made himself so scarce and in such a hurry.

"Eh - eh! Is dis your fus time dis side here sah? An how you likin' it now? Is may be a bit warm for you dis af'noon, but she gan cool down after she rain an den you gan got out an about a bit. You go down Main Street by de sea walls, down by de big hotel down dere. Is very nice down dere sah, by de sea walls." Big Patsy draws breath. "Is where you come from sah?"

"Oh, I'm from England," I pause, then quickly add, "but I'm not a tourist, you know, I'm here to live for a few years, to work in the Mines section."

"Eh - eh! Is dat so?" Patsy is thoughtful as she straightens her back from fixing the sheets. "London, eh? You mus know me cousin den Maggie George she name. She's live in Brixton, number seventeen Railway Parade."

I am slightly taken aback, floored in fact; I have no idea that this type of conversation is perhaps one of the commonest forms of small talk here; everybody has a relative, or a friend, or at worst, a friend of a friend in London, and cannot understand how I, an Englishman, cannot possibly know of them as well; I guess, though, that it's not just a question of scale, a hundred thousand people in Georgetown compared with ten million in London; it goes deeper than that; people in this country do know one another; I feel it; they know their neighbours; they make it their business to know the people who just moved in down the end of the street; they are the type would go round, knock on the door, offer them a welcome; lonely grannies don't die here, left to rot for days before their neighbours realise something is amiss.

"Actually, no, I don't know her. I'm not from London you see. I'm from further north, Yorkshire."

"Ah well, I got anudder cousin, Winston. He's from Islington, I tink he say das in de nort. Yo should know him den?"

Patsy doesn't wait for, or even seem to expect an answer; she offers to throw in her job at the Park and be my housekeeper, and if she isn't suitable, she has a daughter she can recommend, or a cousin, or her friend; she has her man who can garden, and be my bush camp attendant; I put her off with vague answers... find... excuses.

CHAPTER FIVE

NIC BRINGS NEWS

At first light the rain was still drumming noisily on the tin roof. It is generally quite easy to extricate oneself from a hammock, given the motivation, and the bottle of D'Aguiar's Special Reserve proved more than adequate for this task; it had me dying for a pee. Outside, fortunately, the rain was easing now and the only trauma was in negotiating the pools of mud left behind from the overnight downpour. I relieved myself round the corner of the hut, gazing down at one of the most beautiful sights on this earth. Seriously though folks, the river and falls at Orinduik are one of the unsung wonders of the world; I can't imagine what you thought I meant!

The rain finally stopped but on the north side of the village, the jungle trees dripped on; a quiet mist rose slowly from the sinuous line of the river, as though from a thousand genie lamps. But to my left, the gently swirling mist changed to a wild and turbulent spray as the river broke through the first of the jasper bars and everlasting peace gave way to perpetual thunder.

There are maybe twenty huts in Orinduik village, strung out along the river bank. On the east side there is a gravel airstrip, long enough for a Twin Otter, an international customs post, army barracks, and police station all bristling with flags and aerials, the paraphernalia of modern frontier civilisation and 'places of importance'. There are two shops and a rundown guest house. Surrounding the village are small fields of cassava and corn, the staple foods of the region, and little groups of fruit trees, informal higgledy-piggledy orchards of pawpaw, mango and lime. A few pigs and chickens scratch between the huts. Small groups of skinny cattle range on the savannah, boasting the O brand of the neighbouring pastoral station.

A few of the village men are employed as vaqueros on the station, but most of the villagers live a subsistence lifestyle, barely removed from the status of 'hunter and gatherer', moving their fields year by year and occasionally cutting new ones out of the edge of the mother jungle. Only one generation ago, they would have fished and hunted without equal but with the advent of shotguns and gunpowder bombs, the fish and game are now depleted and the little hunting parties have to roam increasingly far from home. There is no school, except for the school of life; there used to be missionaries and a missionary school but the soul saving is now all conducted from head office in Lethem. There used to be tourists, either staying at the station, or day trippers on the weekly scheduled round flight from Georgetown and Lethem, but there were never very many of them, and now there are no more. The government guest house these days is used only for occasional itinerant officers. Orinduik is well and truly off the beaten track.

There is a road through the savannah, south to Lethem. Well, it's more like a rough trail and its hundred and fifty kilometres are rarely fit to be travelled at this time of year, except on horseback or by trail bike. I had arrived by plane a week before, ostensibly to collect a rare red and green banded jasper for a lapidary workshop in Georgetown. The rock hounding cover meant I could legitimately use explosives for blasting, but only under close surveillance from the authorities who in this country tended to be of nervous disposition. The 'authorities' in fact were totally paranoid, and I therefore had to account for every last inch of fuse and each individual detonator. So the cover was ideal; nobody could possibly accuse me of misappropriation or misdirection of explosives.

The sun was now rising and the mist was evaporating. I let the warmth seep through my skin. Soak it up; later it would be unbearably hot and humid out in the open. I turned back into the hut, lit the kerosene stove and filled a kettle of water for coffee. I looked around for where Harald must have hidden the sugar - not from me, from the ants - and found it at last in an airtight jar atop a scrubbed clean wooden bench, the four legs of which were sitting in four little kerosene-filled tin cans. I brewed the coffee in an iron pot. The effect of the aroma was almost magical; within seconds it seemed, the hut was alive with semiconscious beings holding out tin mugs and all grabbing at once for the one pot. Fortunately for them, the pot was deep. Breakfast was eggs, freshly harvested from under Petal's mothering gaze, and fried, and yeast bake left over from the day before.

There was a light tap at the door and a round face complete with a Vidal Sassoon pudding basin haircut appeared through the curtain. It was Nicodemus, one of the two Sand Creek Wapishiana lads who were along for their muscle.

Nic took a deep breath.

"There's a message from senhor Riaz. He say to come over, right now this mornin', but be real quiet an' meet him, somewhere quiet maybe, but close by. He say there's maybe some trouble. I tink is women trouble maybe, but they got a policia comin' up from Boa Vista. Domingo he tink maybe is he is the trouble an' not no woman."

A second Sassoon pudding basin appeared behind Nicodemus, grinning confirmation of this observation. Domingo rarely spoke in public.

Harald sucked his teeth and made to brew more coffee.

"Bloody hell, I told you that man was no good. I just know it. What did I say last night? Damn and blast." I could feel erudition creeping on. "Perhaps Midnight should handle this shit. He knows this glandular Portuguese gigolo son of... "

Midnight cut in to save me further public embarrassment, "Calma calma, Tom man, it's okay. Look, maybe is no big ting. It mightn't be a bad idea to tek a trip over, eh? You ain't been tha side before. Let's take a look see at how the land lyin', see how she stay. See how that mud track lookin'. We could mek out we goin up river to search for the jasper. Domingo got a woodskin bout three mile up, so we could be over and back in, well, three maybe four hours at the most, and we'd still have plenty time left over to finish off sortin' out here. We don't all need to go. Anyway man, what else we would do today except get drunk again? Maybe this is the right thing for us after all. Could promote longevity of we livers even."

There was a general murmur of agreement. Midnight made sense for once. We could easily make the trip today without arousing any suspicion on this side of the border. We would have to hope we didn't meet anyone on the Brazil side of course, except the idiot Riaz. Nicodemus could cross openly at the village, then get word back to Riaz that we would be at the north fork creek crossing between ten and eleven. I hoped this wasn't going to be a serious problem, but then in Brazil, 'woman trouble' has always meant serious trouble.

Don James and Harald were left behind with a list of jobs, packing food, sharpening machetes, weighing and dividing loads for the back-packs. We would have to move all our gear up to the canoe later in the evening. Tall Boy would try to look as though he was busy trimming the jasper blocks on the rough saw, and packing them for transport to Georgetown when the dry came and the 'road' reopened.

Midnight, Domingo and I made for the edge of the jungle and set off along the right bank creek trail. The trail was a well used one as it led to small fields out some distance from the village, and then continued as a fishing and hunting route up the main valley. Domingo accelerated ahead and soon was lost to the two old blokes. The jungle swallowed us up in its own kind of muffled silence; the river was sluggish, and strewn with fallen trees and sunken tacoubas[5]. The trail followed closely along the river bank, detouring only to avoid massive buttressed mora trees and to get around the mouths of small side creeks. The ground was uneven and muddy, criss-crossed with slippery roots. The only sounds were our own, and the occasional warning bird call. Bright luminescent morpho butterflies kept pace alongside, flirting, flitting through the sunny breaks beneath the canopy, and then there was the flash and splash of a kingfisher. It was still cool in the jungle shade and we made good progress. After half an hour, I could hear the sound of rapids. Tell-tale clots of white foam floated languidly downstream on the red water. The foam became foamier, and swirlier, and in a few more minutes we were at the foot of more rapids and shouting to hear ourselves speak.

Domingo had hidden a small woodskin canoe in the bush, and as Midnight and I arrived, had already retrieved it and was baling it out ready for the crossing. We wasted no time in getting across, using the current to advantage, and then paddled a hundred metres up a tiny blind creek on the Brazil side. The creek was jammed full of tacoubas but we were able to weave our way between most of them as the water had flooded back from the main stream. We cut and pushed our way through a strip of secondary undergrowth and came to a clearing.

The Brazilian side of the Ireng is in complete contrast to the Guyanese bank. The jungle has been razed, hacked and burned to oblivion in the names of progress, population pressure, poverty, avarice and ignorance, none of which are excusable. The river banks have been overrun by secondary vegetation, razor sharp grasses, stinging ivy, broad-leaved weeds harbouring all manner of creeping, crawling and slithering things. Butterflies breed like crazy; there were literally hectares of shimmering light made by thousands upon thousands of the beautiful insects, and their caterpillars chewed

---

[5] A tacouba is a log.

through the mountains of weeds and, incidentally, through the few poor surviving crops which had replaced the primary jungle.

We now had to pick our way through the cut and burnt fields, negotiating stump holes and fallen trees, their burnt and blackened stumps, and the poison-ivy which vied in competition with stunted cassava bushes and rows of sorry corn. We headed directly away from the river; there was no path and progress was slow. There was no shade here either and the tropical sun was already high in the sky and burning uncomfortably on the backs of our necks.

We arrived at the north fork creek crossing hot, sweating, thirsty and irritable. It was already half past ten but there was no sign yet of senhor Riaz.

CHAPTER SIX

NIC BRINGS MORE NEWS

The heat and sweat were quickly fixed with a dip in the creek; the thirst was assuaged with a mouth washing draught of tepid water from a plastic bottle. The irritability remained, gaining momentum. I had never met this bloke Riaz but I was beginning to take quite a dislike to him as well as just not trusting him.

There are roads of sorts through the newly cleared land north and west of Enamuna. The early clearing had been carried out northwards along the Ireng valley, maybe five years ago. This land is already poor, its nutrients leached, and it is now good only for a little buck corn and some ground root crops. The vaqueros are pushing west instead - one would have thought they should have learnt their lesson, but such are the pressures. The track north is hardly used any more; the main route runs westerly. There is a sandy creek crossing just past the fork and it was here that we waited for senhor Riaz and his trouble, whatever that might happen to be.

At half past eleven I washed and spat another mouthful of tepid water from the bottle. Shit man, you couldn't even drink from the creeks anymore!

At half past twelve my ears pricked at the sound of an approaching engine, a diesel. We held back, which was a fortunate decision as it turned out to be the Enamuna policia in their Roraima Blue Toyota. They took the west fork.

Midnight and I sat at the top of the creek bank collecting what little cool air there was and chucking things and making ripples. Meanwhile, Domingo was more constructively engaged. He had wandered off some way down the creek poking a stick into the water looking for dinner asleep and buried from the heat in the muddy bottom sediment. A nice fat haimara[6], perhaps, would certainly not go amiss.

I gazed transfixed at an army of ants on the march. Not too hot

---

[6] Haimara, as tasty and steaky as best Scottish salmon.

for them yet! Adamant Company has his collective mind set on a large juicy worm, six succulent segmented centimetres of annelida amazonica, lightly sautéed on a bed of sun-baked clay, garnis-au... suddenly divine intervention steps in, literally, and Wally the Worm turns and sheds off the remnants of predators as he worms his way blindly back into the coolth and safety of mother earth. Adam and his mates are not impressed, bloody slime ball of a worm.

Hah, now this was more like it, much more interesting; might even be a match. Septimus Scorpion scuttles onto centre stage as the next potential luncheon platter. Crunchy carapace of clawed arachnida, cooked to perfection with a crisp side salad of unclassified tropo leaf. In a classic pincer movement, a dozen privates from Platoon A break ranks and leap onto Septimus' lashing tail. "We'll hold him down, you chew his head off lads." But it was not to be without casualties. Anthony and Arbuthnot are sent to ant heaven, Alistair and Andrew, on secondment from the Highland Bagpipe Regiment get the wind knocked out of them. Amelia is sent flying, Amy and Angelica get stuck in the butt, Arthur and Archie are trampled underfoot. Annie gets her gun but it's no use... heh, this is no good, Septimus is getting away... divine providence uses a long pointy stick this time... two dozen fresh troops replace the vanguard at the sting in the tail, and their mates chew through Septimus' legs, immobilising him at last. The Emperor Tomus Askewinus points his thumb downwards and the sting is severed and the rest of the nasty little critter is jointed and carried off triumphantly to the larder. Now that was real entertainment!

At one o'clock, it was bloody hot, I was bloody well sweaty again, I was bloody thirsty, there was no more bloody tepid water in the bloody bottle, and I was damned irritable. The butterflies were resting, the ground was steaming, there was no shade, the flies were too bloody friendly, my eyes were full of sweat, a kingfisher called...? Weird sense of humour, I thought, at this time of day! Domingo replied with an owl hoot - weirder yet - and the kingfisher Nicodemus appeared like magic in the undergrowth before us.

"Senhor Riaz, he's in trouble," pronounced Nicodemus wisely.

"You don't say," said Midnight, "and with us man. Where the hell is he?"

"Senhor Riaz, he says he's in trouble, an if he's in trouble, then we too, we's in trouble. That's what he say," said Nic.

"Just slow down Nic," I now said, "and tell us what the trouble is will you? If Riaz's trouble is our trouble, then we should know what is the trouble we's in." This was getting worse than slapstick I thought. I attempted to elucidate by means of an intelligent metaphor. "A broken leg is one kind of trouble; if someone is threatening to break your leg, then that's another kind of trouble".

"Somebody threatenin' to break he leg," said Nic.

I gagged.

"Just his leg?" laughs Midnight, "I think I'll break his skull man."

"Sure, break every bone in he body," continued Nic, now warming to the subject. "Is woman trouble. Senhor Riaz, he say how he get a woman into trouble. He been seein' the woman in Boa Vista an' now he find out she's the policia mulher, an' now the policia come here to Enamuna come lookin' for he, goin to brok him up. But he lucky so far because the policia, he not know who is Riaz, or what he look like."

"He must have some idea," I said, "a name, something. He's come to Enamuna. There must be some reason for that."

"Senhor Riaz, he tink the policia, he trace the truck. He don dare go near the truck because he see the policia lookin' at the truck an' writin' in he book." Nic continued in a conspiratorial whisper, "Senhor Riaz, he lyin' low with the schoolmistress. Somehow, he got senhorita Josephina on he side."

"Don't you mean on she back?" rasps Midnight; his demeanour had suddenly changed from jocular to blackly serious.

I glanced over at Midnight. He had turned a distinct shade paler, which for him was no mean feat. He wasn't called Midnight for no reason at all. He looked as though he was about to blow a fuse.

Nic carried on regardless, imparting his heady news. "I tink senhor Riaz tell some story in the village that the man who mess with the policia mulher maybe some man from Guyana side, who visitin' in Orinduik. An' I tink maybe he also tell how is a black man that play hokey wid she."

My mind flashed back across twenty years to Timehri airbase. "Tall black chap with a goatee beard?" I bit my tongue as I said it.

Midnight blew his stack. "Is me!" says Midnight. "They're turning it on to me. I black. I bin to Boa Vista. I bin to the delegacia de policia there to get papers for your damn truck. That damn truck registered to me. That bastard Riaz, he's turned it on to me. Jus let him come here now and I'll brok his skull in trut!"

I tried to make a joke out of it - Midnight was blazing. "Heh, calm down Midnight. Knowing you, there might even be a grain of truth in all of this, eh? You were supposed to be back from Boa Vista four days ago. What kept you, eh?"

The joke had little effect. Midnight muttered something under his breath that sounded a lot like 'bitch". I surmised there may have been something going on between my dark friend and Miss Josephina, but decided to leave that subject well alone for the time being. "Look, maybe there's no problem," I continued. Let Riaz stay around here; he just drops his cut, that's all. I can handle the tovex; we're not using electrics so the fusing is straightforward, He'd do a cleaner job, no doubt, but I'm sure we can manage it between us. And it's one less dead weight to carry. Nic and I will go into Enamuna and get the stuff. Simple!"

"That can't work Mister Tom," says Nicodemus. "Senhor Riaz say he not givin' over the explosives till the policia he go away. I tink he tief them. I tink maybe thas his main trouble, not no woman."

Midnight was still on fire, neither was he listening to Nic's latest dissertation. "Well, I ain't goin' to be no sacrificial lamb man. It might be different if I did know the woman, but I ain't even had that pleasure man. Not yet. And now that bastard Riaz puttin' he hands all over my sweet Josie."

I had surmised correctly!

"Whoa there Dobbin. Let's not go off at half cock and screw up this whole deal over a piece of skirt. We've got to think this thing through, logically, one - two - three."

There was a long and heavily pregnant pause whilst Midnight continued to smoulder.

"Think man, think."

Our pork-knocker friends, King Harry and the Grey Shadow, were expecting us to arrive at Chi Chi or Imbaimadai no later than Wednesday next. We couldn't get a message through to them now, so we couldn't delay. If we were late getting the tovex to them, they may go ahead and do the job alone, make their own ANFO, and probably screw up the whole cave system. They would collapse the lot because ANFO could never give a tight enough bang, and bang would go the diamonds!

"We've got to be out of here by tomorrow..." Midnight smoked on.

"... the day after that at the latest," was my humble contribution. Then a masterly plan started to formulate itself in amongst my abused grey cells. "Why don't we just nick the stuff, like Riaz did?"

CHAPTER SEVEN

SABOTAGE?

Midnight and Domingo crashed back the way we had come. They would have to take the canoe downstream, closer in to Orinduik. We had wasted too much time today so we would have to take more risks now.

Nic and I headed straight for Enamuna. Nic knew his way around. I had no idea what I would do if we were seen; what the heck, if it happened let adrenaline take over, I figured.

Enamuna was a new government-inspired settlement. It was set back from the Ireng as though not wishing to be too close and therefore possibly influenced by its Guyanese neighbours. Whereas Orinduik comprised egalitarian wood and corrugated iron, Enamuna was a street of smart stucco and tile surrounded by an abysmal shantytown. The stucco and tile section bristled with aerials and showy flags and other signs of worthiness. The school was at its northern end, set back from the street, and with a playground area of swept laterite gravel in front. Detached from, but immediately next to the school was the schoolhouse, built, complete with shady inner courtyard, for the incumbent schoolmaster or mistress. Down the road were six or seven similar official-looking houses for the other town dignitaries, guests of government and so forth, then the church, the town office and courthouse, and at the southern end, the delegacia de policia. Across the road, and down a little from the schoolhouse was a coffee shop, what Nic told me was the customs office, and a small army barracks that looked, for the time being, deserted. The abysmal shantytown hardly bears description. About the same size again as the stucco street, it was home to maybe ninety five percent of the village population, tatty and totally insanitary, it is simply too depressing.

There were three Toyotas, all short base Landcruisers, in the street. Two were parked outside the delegacia de policia. They were relatively new, liveried in Roraima State Shiny Police Blue. The third Tojo, parked twenty or thirty metres on our side of the shop was more your typical bush truck, bordering on senility, vigorously rusting and that immediately recognisable shade of sun-faded Toyota matte jungle green. A topless, orange coloured VW bush-buggy truck, engineered for utility rather than stunning good looks, stood outside the schoolhouse, and another was outside the third house in the street. A five car town!

I stood leaning behind an empty shanty shack right on the edge of town and surveyed the scene. There was no way we could move in any closer without being seen, not before nightfall and that was still several hours away. There was the buzz of a small aircraft and Nic and I both instinctively shrank into the uselessly narrow shadow of the shack as the plane passed low overhead on its approach to the strip. Light planes were often more common than cars out here.

"How many planes on the strip Nic?" I asked.

"Three this mornin' Tom," Nic replied. "I heard another come in and leave about eleven o'clock, and another around noon and I didn't hear that one leavin' yet."

A rapid mental calculation told me this was a five plane town! Almost as many planes as houses, I thought. The vaqueros must be meeting in town for some reason. Weird, I thought, usually they would have chosen somewhere bigger, more central, Deposito or Limao.

A bell sounded and two dirty little half dressed kids ran out from behind a shack just a few metres away, and headed off screeching like a pair of misplaced mynah birds towards the school. It seemed to be a sign. More kids appeared and they all made off towards their afternoon mecca. The siesta hour was over and suddenly the shantytown in front of us was humming with activity. I caught a fleeting glimpse of a tall graceful female figure, the schoolmistress for sure, crossing from the back of the schoolhouse to the main school building. A diesel engine burst into life outside the delegacia, and one of their Toyotas raced off towards the airstrip presumably to meet the latest arrivals.

A small man, with a weasel face and thinning slicked back, greasy black hair skulked out of the front of the schoolhouse and crossed the street towards the truck which was standing near the shop.

"That's senhor Riaz," Nic whispered.

I didn't really need him to tell me, and whispered a grunt in reply. Riaz was examining the truck, but from a distance; he seemed to be assuring himself that all was normal as before.

"Midnight's truck?" I queried, though knowing the answer already. "What's he doing now?" Riaz had been looking up and down the street intently, then, all of a sudden, he had made a dash towards the truck and flung himself through the driver's door, and had ducked down behind the wheel. We could not see any more. "I wonder if he's trying to tamper with it. Midnight didn't give him the keys, did he Nic?"

"I don't know, but I don't tink he would have Tom. Don say they put the explosives in the schoolhouse because the truck can't lock up. They tell the senhorita was tins of food and supplies for the Englishman. I pretty sure was Don heself had the keys last."

"Well, I think he's up to no good," I observed rather obviously. "He could be trying to hot-wire it, or more likely disable it somehow. Nic, you take a walk past but don't show too much interest. Just see if you can see what's going on... and keep your head down; we don't want him to recognise you."

Nic was already on his way; left alone, I started to feel very exposed and vulnerable. I peered into the packing case shack. It appeared to be quite empty, so I slid in through the door and prayed it would stay that way. The shack stank not very pleasantly, a sort of mixed odour of rotting things. The only furniture comprised two damp and green-grey mouldering cardboard boxes. The floor was beaten red earth, turned to mud where the roof leaked, which was mostly everywhere, and spattered onto the furniture. I remained standing, able to spy through a crack in the wall which gave me a view down half the street.

I couldn't see Nic whilst he kept to the school side of the street, but I could see Riaz' reaction when he realised someone was approaching. He sat bolt upright in the driver's seat, and stayed very still. I didn't think he recognised Nic because after only a brief look he ducked back under the dash to continue what he was doing. Nic crossed over the street right alongside the truck to get a good look. He hesitated behind it, as if looking for some coins, then disappeared into the coffee shop. A minute later and he came back out; this time he stopped right by the side of the truck, rolled a cigarette and lit up, then ambled back up the street. Riaz had ignored him completely.

"That was a great ploy Nic. What did you see?" I asked.

"He's doin' some wirin' with the ignition. He has wirecutters and strippers. I tink he's up to no good Mister Tom." Nic was never backward in stating the obvious!

I let my imagination run riot. An explosives expert with wire strippers and an ignition system...! Not that it made any sense; I could not see what he would have to gain from wiring up the damn truck - unless it was all part of an elaborate bluff.

"You sure it was just wiring Nic, nothing mechanical? No wrenches or other tools?"

"Jus wirin' Mister Tom," Nic was adamant.

"I'm getting paranoid," I thought aloud, "he's probably just disconnecting the flash heater leads; Harald will get the old brute going again no problem... "

Meanwhile, Riaz had finished his dirty work and had made off somewhere round the back of the shop.

I was not sure what to do next. I wanted to get inside the schoolhouse, check on our crates, account for everything in them. Only then would I be able to set my mind to rest, but it was not going to be that easy. I was scared to move through the town in daylight; I would be picked out as a gringo stranger from half a mile. The shack stank and Nic and I crept outside into welcoming fresh air.

The police truck arrived back from the airstrip and stopped in front of the town office. Four men got out, stretched themselves, then went straightaway inside. The police truck drove slowly, and it seemed deliberately, towards us, but only as far as the school, then turned and returned to its post in front of the delegacia.

CHAPTER EIGHT

MILLIE

I made up my mind. School would be in till five thirty. It would be dark by six thirty, but then the schoolmistress would be back in her parlour. I had to find the crates and I had to find them now.

"I'm going into the schoolhouse now," I said. I picked a handful of dirt and scrubbed my face and arms with it, then mixed it with sweat from my shirt. I took off my hat, of which incidentally I was particularly fond, and kicked it into the ground in front of me. "You come behind Nic. Whistle if you see anything - and roll me one of those disgusting cigarettes will you?"

It was turning out to be a long hard day. I felt filthy, sort of sticky, and figured I must smell nearly as badly as the shack we'd just vacated; I should pass for a Brazilian all right, at a distance.

It was two hundred metres to the school; I felt reasonably invisible among the shanty shacks, just kept my eyes down on the ground in front, listened to my heart thumping, and tried not to choke on the cigarette. I muttered 'Bom dia' to a group of people who were sitting drinking outside a liquor stall, but they gave no reply nor sign of recognition and I felt a boost of confidence. Alongside the schoolyard, where there is a narrow built up sidewalk, I nearly stumbled on the verge, and once again felt very exposed as if a hundred pairs of bored but imaginative eyes were examining me from the school windows. I could hear Nic's footsteps crunching behind me on the laterite gravel.

I was past the school now and outside the schoolhouse; I stopped and waited for Nic to catch up. The stucco and tile street here was deserted though I thought I saw a movement behind the beaded door to the coffee shop opposite. Couldn't be the breeze because there wasn't one! Nic moved up behind me, between me and the door to the schoolhouse. He pushed it with his shoulder and the two of us backed silently into the cool tiled interior.

I had not even had time to turn around when the house was suddenly filled with a terrific commotion, screaming and screeching.

Nic and I froze.

"Quien es? Quien es?..." Another screech and a whistle.

I shut the door quickly, hoping beyond hope that no one outside had heard. I spun around and faced up to a huge hyacinth macaw. We were in a narrow corridor which led through to the inner courtyard. The macaw was perched high up in the far corner, its natural destructive instincts tempered by a heavy duty steel chain around one foot. The chain was at full stretch as the bird leaned out towards us, chomping at the bit, so to speak. Oh for a sprig of millet! The rare bird screeched on in its own peculiar form of Portuguese dialect; I couldn't hope to understand it, or obey its directives.

There was a bowl of fruit on a low table half way down the corridor. I grabbed a mango, and defying imminent and possibly permanent disfigurement, proffered the fruit to the free claw. The enormous purple bird screeched a final screech and drove its huge beak like a jack-hammer into the fleshy fruit - and clasped its free claw firmly round my wrist.

Millie Macaw chewed on the fruit. Pieces of mango skin flew and mango juice squirted in all directions, but mostly over me, and dripped up my arm like sticky goo. Millie Macaw had no intention of releasing my wrist, in fact, tightened her grip to get a better purchase on the fruit. I eyed the beak circumspectly. The beak of a full grown macaw, and this Millie was full grown for sure, is a most wondrous thing. I had witnessed one undoing the wheel nuts of a Landrover - move over torque wrenches; I had heard tell of them rivalling bolt cutters when faced with inch gauge steel chain. I knew what Millie here could do to my fingers or hand, and involuntarily shuddered at the prospect.

I tried gently withdrawing my arm. Millie's grip tightened even more as she started to do the splits. She stopped chewing on the mango and eyed me suspiciously.

"Quien es? Quien es?... screech... ha ha ha."

I gave back my arm and the bird dug back into the fruit.

The sweetest part of a mango is next to the stone. It is there that the flesh clings to the seed. One of the great unsung pleasures of life is to suck the mango stone, to suck off the flesh from all those stringy bits. The string gets stuck between the teeth, but it is well worth all the attendant pain and dental floss. Millie Macaw knew all about the sweet mango stone, and she did not have to worry about flossing afterwards. She was almost preening the sweet flesh from between the hairs of the stone and looked set for the duration. One thing was sure, I could not hang around waiting for her to satiate herself.

Nic came to the rescue. Quick-thinking Nic came barrelling towards us, flailing his arms wildly and emitting a high pitched screech which, in my befuddled brain I figured was some sort of mating call. He had a handful of grapes from the fruit bowl, and from half way down the corridor, proceeded to bombard the bird. The mating call, evidently, was not that convincing. The bird had merely looked up and momentarily paused from its work of eviscerating the mango. Then a perfectly aimed and particularly ripe red grape hit her square on the end of her beak and exploded in her face. Ah ha! - this was more like fun; she opened her huge wings, let go my wrist, swung back onto her perch and started spinning around it delightedly till her chain wrapped itself around the perch as well, and she came to a shuddering flapping halt - look no hands! - upside down. An indignant screech and the remains of the mango dropped on the floor with a splat. Nic fired a final salvo of grapes - the seedless variety of course; I nursed a sore wrist and what was left of my wounded pride. The bird screeched her indignity and, by degrees, extricated herself from her unfortunate predicament.

"Quien es? Quien es?"

Nic retrieved what was left of the mango and offered it back to the bird, this time at arm's length. Millie accepted it most graciously and peace reigned at last.

The whole incident with the bird could not have lasted more than a couple of minutes, but it felt like a lifetime and surely the whole town must have heard. And the mess! My harmless little reconnoitre was already turning into a disaster!

There were two doors opening off the corridor, one on each side. To the left was a sitting room - three chairs, a bookcase, a cupboard with fine china displayed - with glass patio doors leading directly into the inner courtyard. It was all very neat, probably rarely used, pristinely clean, almost like a display showroom, and no crates of weeping gelignite to spoil the overall ambience. The room on the right of the corridor had more of a used look, but was also impeccably tidy. It was the schoolmistress' office. One complete wall was lined with books; there was a desk with a comfy-looking five star swivel chair, and a pair of filing cabinets. On the desk was a typewriter, electric, the latest model, with a half finished letter. I just managed to control my curiosity. There were stacks of school reports and files. This room also looked very pleasantly onto the cool courtyard, and also, contained no crates.

One thing did grab my attention though. There was an ornately silver-framed photo on the desk, a photo of the schoolmistress in her younger days, smiling on the arm of a slightly older man in full dress uniform. He was short in stature, an easy comparison accentuated by her pair of gangling long legs; in fact in many ways they looked like chalk and cheese and yet their eyes told of some family resemblance. They did not look like lovers. I had seen the man only once before, and then at a distance, but I recognised him immediately.

Time was passing. I knew I could bluff it out if Riaz was to come back, but things might be more difficult with Miss Josephina. Nic and I therefore split up to search the rest of the house; Nic took the north section and I took the south, which turned out to be the 'guest wing'. There was a dark, pokey little bedroom with a small washstand, a single wooden chair and a hammock. The guest obviously didn't follow his hostess' fastidious standards, for the place was a totally insanitary mess. Clothes, strewn over the back and seat of the chair, overflowed to the floor like a pile of volcanic ejectamenta. Cigarette butts were ground into the floor and rattan carpet, and stubbed out in the washbasin. The air in the room was stale and smoky. Empty beer bottles, most of them lying on their sides, were arranged as if in a halo on the floor around the hammock. There were two crates within easy reach of the hammock, against one of the walls, but they did not contain explosives, just premium beer, cerveja premia. Next door was a storeroom, with a deep freeze. No crates, just a rather dubious looking side of steer.

I met Nic on the fourth side of the quadrangle. He had been through a bathroom and a kitchen and, like me, had found no sign of what we were searching for. The two rooms on this fourth side of the square were the senhorita's bedroom and a living room which had a lived-in look in contrast to her front display. Both rooms were tidy though, despite being well used, and everything in them smacked of a tidy and perhaps unimaginative mind. I left Nic with the onerous task of inspecting the bedroom with its private closets and cupboards and whatnot; few are the men from Sand Creek who have ever had the opportunity to linger amongst the lingerie of such a fine lady's boudoir! I had no doubt that the stout fellow searched most assiduously, but it was all to no avail; my own search in the lady's living room was no more successful. We had drawn a complete blank.

I took a deep breath. "But Don did say the crates were here, in the schoolhouse, didn't he Nic? I wonder if he meant the school itself, or, is there another storeroom somewhere?" I was really just thinking aloud.

"No more storeroom here Mister Tom," said Nic. "They got a storeroom in the school but Don say was in here, in the house for sure. I already look at the back but they ain't got nothing there either."

We walked back across the courtyard. I was feeling really dejected now. It was nearly five o'clock and I knew we should have been finished and out of there long before. Back in the corridor. Damn, I'd forgotten the mess.

"Quien es? Quien es? ha ha ha."

I almost took a swipe at the bird, then saw its beak again and thought better of it; I was about to deliver an almighty kick to its perch instead when the penny dropped. At the base of the perch, tastefully arranged but now bespattered with assorted pieces of half masticated mango and grape, and maybe the odd chunk of human flesh, were three wooden boxes, crates by any other name. One well placed match, perhaps, and a more vindictive mind might picture an enormous hyacinth macaw flying higher and faster and further than any of his or her species had ever flown before!

I had thought earlier of slipping Millie's chain so she might be blamed for the awful mess. Now, however, my less vindictive side took control. Tom the bird fancier imagined a macaw beak crimping detonators, and shuddered at the thought.

"We can't let the bird off," I said to Nicodemus. "We'll just have to clean up this mess. How long before school comes out?"

"Half hour maybe Tom. We got time, let's do it..." Nic was already disappearing towards the kitchen and storeroom.

I looked over the crates quickly; I obviously couldn't get too close to them, but from what I could see, the seals seemed to be intact. So, Riaz' little scheme with the Toyota was more than likely all bluff. I racked my brain; it would be nigh on impossible to separate the macaw from the explosives without creating an almighty shindig and alerting the whole household. Riaz would have to be got rid of, and the lady Josephina would have to be otherwise distracted. Hmm, Midnight might be able to keep the schoolmistress busy, but we would need a third party to remove Riaz from the scene, or, yes, perhaps we could arrange for the local constabulary to show some interest in him. The bird ruffled its feathers as if I needed a further reminder; oh jeez, why was life so difficult? It might just be easier to bowl in at the dead of night, commando-style, and chloroform the bugger!

Nic came back with mops, bucket and brushes. The bird seemed to take a keen interest in the clean-up proceedings and stopped its screeching, and then started preening itself contentedly. We both worked like mad and it still took us nearly the full half hour to remove all traces of mucilaginous mango and all the other assorted Millie memorabilia.

We got ourselves out of the house and I resumed the posture of Brazilian peasant. We had barely crossed the street when the school bell rang. We squatted at the side of the road opposite the schoolyard and watched and waited while the school emptied, about forty or fifty children in all, all ages, all quite dirty and bedraggled. All the kids, without exception, turned one way towards the shanty town.

Senhorita Josephina finally appeared, turned to lock the door, turned again and was walking towards us. It was the first time I had really seen her so close, in the flesh so to speak, though I had had her described to me from many and varied angles. She certainly lived up to those descriptions. I guessed she was in her late-twenties or early-thirties. She was tall and elegant. She had long black hair and a medium-bronze complexion, the kind that glows in the late sunshine. She had a very fine, sculptured face and, even from this distance, striking deep and dark brown eyes. Her figure was good, very good in fact, and quite obvious in tight jeans and white open neck shirt.

"Wow, lucky lucky Maurice!" I thought.

She was coming closer, about to cross the street directly in front of us. I could feel the blood rushing to my face and fixed my eyes on the dirt in the road, and pulled my hat down as far as it would go.

She spoke at us, rather than to us, and in Portuguese of course. I could only understand the odd word but the gist of it was, "Get lost freaks. I've been watching you. What are you watching my children for?"

My eyes were drilling into the dirt at my feet. Nicodemus said something guttural in reply; I hawked and spat into the gutterless road, and we both moved away, trying to appear unhurried and unconcerned. But I could feel those beautiful deep and dark brown eyes turned onto us, questioningly, burning into us as we shambled off, following after her children, towards the shantytown.

"Who are you? Perverts? What are you doing here?"

CHAPTER NINE

TROUSERS AND FLEAS

Midnight and Domingo crashed back the way they'd come. They were in a hurry; the day was already half gone.

Midnight was nursing a chronic case of wounded pride. He had taken a real shine to the Enamuna schoolmistress, and to have his pitch jeopardised by Riaz' lies, well, it was just too much to stomach. Just let him get his hands on Riaz' throat, he'd tear out his tonsils.

Domingo, in comparison, was characteristically phlegmatic about the whole situation; he was along for his bush craft and muscle it was true, but he was also on the team for his unquestioning Wapishiana loyalty. He and his younger brother Nicodemus had worked for Mines Department geos for years, as had their father and a variety of uncles and cousins before them. They felt a part of the establishment and were totally dedicated, but to individuals rather than the establishment itself. He led the way at a cracking pace, back through the abandoned and sunburnt cassava fields to the river.

Midnight was feeling hot and bothered, hungry and tired. He kept up an almost constant stream of grumbling as he jogged and stumbled along, and struggled to keep up with Domingo. He became dizzy in the heat and short of breath. The horse flies were about and making a meal of him. He had started with setting complex and involved plans on how he would take his revenge on senhor Riaz, but his imagination was soon put aside with the overwhelming physical effort that was now required of him. He fell behind.

Domingo seemed to leap over the felled and charred tree trunks and stumps; Midnight laboured over them now, and began to seriously regret the excesses of the last few days.

Domingo reached the thick secondary bush bordering the river and plunged through without pausing.

Midnight lost sight of Domingo; in truth, he wasn't sure where he had last seen him. The ground was sandy; he imagined he could see tracks but he wasn't sure. He looked for fresh machete cuts which marked the trail they had cut in the morning, but could find no familiar signs. He halted to catch his breath and listen. The flies at the river's edge seemed to have acquired plague proportions and were particularly large and virulent. He could hear nothing except their malignant whining and the gentle sucking of water below - or was it his blood?

Domingo could, and invariably did, move through the bush as silently as a hunting cat. He could not even hear himself. He was acutely aware, therefore, that the massed brass band behind him which was Midnight, had stopped playing. The trail to the river was hardly visible as we had not wanted to advertise our presence that morning, and he soon realised the boss was lost. He stopped and let out a series of piercing whistles; the brass band shuffled its feet, tuned up, and played 'When the Saints Come Marching In'. The ground heaved and reverberated.

Midnight had been standing as quietly as he could, trying desperately to listen for Domingo, trying desperately not to snort and splutter as he was attacked by the myriad of flying biting bugs which were coming at him from all directions. They were in his eyes, even up his nostrils, and stuck in his moustache and...he gagged as he swallowed living protein. There were some old camp frames at the edge of the bush, and a small fireplace. The sandy ground there was perfect for harbouring jigger fleas[7] which bore under your toenails to lay their eggs. Midnight could feel himself involuntarily scratching and saw the sand heave with fleas beneath his feet.

Domingo's whistling had come just too late. Midnight bounded off again with renewed energy, or it may have been sheer desperation, not following any trail but just leaning against the bush blindly. He was stung and scratched all over; he felt as though his whole body was on fire. His shirt was torn and flapped uselessly on his back. At one point he slipped down a steep bank and found himself waist deep in a stagnant pool. At least it was a little cooling on his skin. He waded through, his canvas jungle boots now heavy with the muddy ooze, climbed back up the opposite bank and practically collided with the whistling Domingo. He got no sympathy from that quarter, just a gleeful and infectious grin.

"I thought I needed a wash," Midnight laughed, "but it looks like somebody put mud in the bathtub, eh!"

"You see the haimaralli[8] in the pool boss?" Domingo asked, still

---

[7] Pulex penetrans - the name says it all.

[8] A haimaralli, is an aggressive and highly poisonous water snake.

grinning from ear to ear. "You sure he didn't bite anyt'ing?"

"Nah, I ain't seen none. I could have sat on an anaconda[9] and not know it," replied Midnight. "For now, I covered in blasted jigger fleas. Where's the river?"

"Just down here boss, look the woodskin there."

Midnight now led the way, on the run, pulling off the tattered remains of his shirt as he ran, and jumped headfirst into the backwater. He stripped off the rest of his clothes and spent the next fifteen minutes picking off and drowning fleas. Domingo sat and watched a while, with the grin permanently attached, then went about his own business retrieving the canoe and baling it out. It hadn't rained so the canoe obviously had the odd leak.

Midnight, eventually satisfied with his flea picking, pulled his trousers and boots back on, and the two men set off down the backwater. The water level had dropped a few centimetres since the morning, enough to reveal significantly more of the sunken tacoubas, and for much of the distance they were out of the canoe, wading and hauling it over the trees. At the point where they rejoined the main river, Domingo pulled over to the bank, scrambled up and grabbed a handful of leaves from a nondescript piece of greenery. He threw the leaves back down to Midnight.

"Here boss, rub this on your foot. Will chase them jiggers for sure." Domingo always spoke with a grin.

"Well, thanks Domingo, old chap," says Midnight, with just a trace of sarcasm. "You could have told me this stuff was growing here."

"Sorry boss, I didn't see it before." Midnight's sarcasm was lost on Domingo, and he was put firmly back in his place.

"Thanks Domingo man, thanks," says Midnight, this time more genuinely; he was starting to scratch again.

Domingo got back in the canoe and saying no more. paddled out into the mainstream, eyes now intent on the water, watching for rocks and tacoubas, and let the current do most of the physical work.

Midnight sat as still as he could in the unstable little craft, eased off his boots and trousers yet again, and proceeded to rub the dark broad leaves over his legs and feet, squashing the juice out between his toes, and started to relax at last.

---

[9] An anaconda (eunectes murinus), is a non poisonous water snake,which becomes aggressive when hungry.

The stream carried them along quite strongly at first but after a few minutes was reduced to a languid flow; the two men got on their knees and took up their paddles. Unused to this, Midnight's first few strokes would have capsized them had Domingo not been in the stern to right the situation. By degrees, though, Midnight's skill improved and they were soon moving along at a rate of knots.

"It's just like riding a bike. You never forget," said Midnight.

Domingo grinned but I wonder whether he would have understood the comment.

They passed three points on the river, using what little current there was, then pulled into the Guyanese bank a couple of hundred metres before the village clearing. The bank was high and overhanging. They grabbed lianas and climbed up; Domingo then cut branches and laid them over the canoe to hide it, and the two of them high tailed it to the hut.

Harald screamed when Midnight entered the hut.

Don creased himself laughing. "Heh, is the bare bum brigade!"

Tall Boy came dancing round the table. "Tek me, tek me darlin'."

Midnight had left his trousers floating down the Ireng River and was now standing centre stage, stark bollock naked, modestly holding his boots in front of him.

"She mus have been some fire tail, boy," said Harald with a poker face. "I hear tell them Brazilian gal does eat meat for breakfas, dinner, an tea. Did she keep your trousers for a trophy?"

"Ow, how you all cruel so!" says Midnight. The only thing got inside my trousers is damn jigger fleas, if you all must know. Man, I wish it had been one of them Brazilian beauties!"

The ribald banter, aimed squarely at Midnight's somewhat abashed bum, imagined trophies and various penetrative parasitic pests, continued unabated whilst the unlucky fellow rummaged for another pair of trousers and climbed, decorously, into them. With Midnight back inside his trousers, the atmosphere in the hut took on a more serious tone.

"So where's Tom?" Harald asked. "I hope he ain't tinkin' of bringin' no jigger fleas in here too. We seen enough meat for one day"

"Well, you all will be spared that at least," replied Midnight.

"Tom's back in Enamuna with Nic," and he continued to apprise the others of what had transpired at the north fork crossing.

Harald, Don and Tall Boy listened intently, exchanging meaningful glances as Midnight brushed lightly past the subject of his good standing with Miss Schoolmistress Josephina and Riaz' dastardly rumours. For the rest, they sat quietly and absorbed the news that Midnight and Domingo had brought the woodskin down to within shouting distance of the village, and that they were all to make ready for a hasty departure. Tom and Nic were going to 'nick' the explosives and would come back directly to the village as soon as they had done so. And thankfully, Harald, Don and Tall Boy had not moved any of the gear up to the upper falls yet, so there had been no wasted journeys.

CHAPTER TEN

RIAZ

Riaz considered himself to be a man of accomplishment. He was not a very clever person, nor a very nice one; he had no degrees, nor was he wealthy, but if accomplishment included being a self-taught street-wise hustler, then he certainly was a very accomplished man.

He was born in the barrio porto at Belem, a little over forty years ago. His mother, who was seventeen, worked in service and didn't really expect or want him along; she named him Ernesto after a past and perhaps earnest lover. She was a pretty mestizo girl and had had many past lovers. Belem is the major port at the mouth of the Amazon, and the capital city of Para; Ernesto's father could have been one of a score of transients, but by the look of him, was probably part Chinese or Japanese. Ernesto didn't think much about such details, Brazil being a land of the most intimate admixture; he didn't feel unduly out of place.

At the age of seven, young Ernesto was a seasoned street kid. He abandoned the name his mother had given him and became Arrozito, a diminutive for the kid who 'always had rice'. He slept well under cardboard cartons or packing cases down by the docks, lived well off the good graces of seafarers, and stole food when he couldn't beg it. By the age of ten, he was what most westerners would consider as 'worldly', again by the good grace of the seafaring community. He learned smatterings of foreign languages. Another year or so and he had figured out that there was more of a future in the management of others like himself. He was now a fully fledged senior member of Belem street life.

By the age of twelve, Arrozito was bored with big city life and yearned to learn more of the places he heard stories of in the bars and street cafes. He jumped a ship heading upriver, careful to make sure it was reputably flagged. He had known of other boys like himself stowing away on Greek and Korean ships and being found floating out to the ocean two days later. The ship he chose was English, bound for Iquitos; five days later, the captain put him off at Manaus.

Manaus had grown out of the confluence of the two greatest rivers in Brazil, the Rio Negro and the Solimoes, the very birthplace of the Amazon itself. For four hundred years it was at the spearhead of Christianity in Amazonas but was little more than an outpost. And then almost overnight with the advent of the model T Ford, it became the running gear, a veritable power house of modern development, a boom town based on latex. It became the jungle centre for ostentation and over-indulgence, the home of rubber barons who washed their dirty laundry in Europe; how paradoxical to think that a town founded on the rubber trade could have grown out of a centre for the Catholic Mission! The rubber wealth did not last, however, and by the early nineteen-sixties Manaus was still very much a frontier town, depending on the rivers for virtually all its communications with the outside world. It was declared a tax-free zone, which to many was its sole attraction. There were no roads to go anywhere; the Trans Amazonica and Pan American Highways were mere pipe dreams. It was a town totally cut off from the mainstream of Brazilian life and politics, but the fact that it was so cut off helped to develop its own unique character and, to put it as nicely as possible, its political autonomy. It has since developed as a major trading centre, a hub for Acre State, northern Rondonia, Amazonas and Roraima, as well as the eastern provinces of Peru, and its population has more than doubled in the last thirty years. The old people of Manaus are its unique character.

Arrozito fitted in well in Manaus society, with the market economy and its people; he hustled, worked the streets, sold cigarettes outside the cinema and pushed soft drugs to American and European hippies. When he had to leave town for his own good, he shortened his name and went bush, worked on logging camps, then graduated to prospecting for gold and working on the river dredges, but nothing too strenuous, or for too long at a time. He grew up. He was a garimpeiro through the late seventies, then a claim staker in the gold rush of the mid eighties. He never stopped hustling. He trusted no one, and no one trusted him. He had no friends. He was not a clever man and most of his plans for fortune fell through, one way or another. And yet, despite this lack of obvious success, his peers did nevertheless recognise him as a very accomplished man. He never got rich, but he never lost any fortunes either. He was the archetypal small time crook.

He did have enemies though. During his time as a garimpeiro and claim staker, he had learned to use explosives and had gained quite a reputation in the field. He became involved with the vaqueros and the road builders pushing the Pan American Highway link from Manaus to Boa Vista on the Rio Branco. The settlers had raped the Indian women and pillaged the Indian villages; the local Indian tribes had declared war on the settlers; Riaz had traded guns and dynamite to both sides which worked for a while, but not for long. He certainly did not make many friends that way, but gained a certain local notoriety. He also grew an extra pair of eyes in the back of his head!

Riaz had followed the settlement push northwards, lured by the same tales of gold and riches that had motivated the early explorers and had ended up as a small time crook, part-time garimpeiro and occasional gun runner in small town Boa Vista, I'm not sure in which order. He also managed a side business pushing marijuana and cocaine to a trickle of off-beat tourists.

Two weeks ago, Riaz had been given a lead that a group of Englishmen[10] were in town and were in the market for explosives. He had met the two Negroes and their Indian friend. They said they were prospectors and needed some specialized explosive such as tovex for underwater use. Riaz, street-wise, knew instinctively that this was no ordinary prospecting trip that was being planned. The haggling began.

Riaz did not like to admit that it might be difficult to obtain such specialized stuff, but he did happen to know the army used it and figured he could lay his hands on some. He told the Englishmen it would be no problem, for him, but the price, well that might be more than they were willing to offer.

The Englishmen told Riaz that the price was out of their hands. They were being cut in by someone else, a percentage.

Then there was little that Riaz could do, they would have to go back empty handed, or find someone else if they could. Unless maybe they cut him in as well?

Okay. The deal was done, cash down and five percent. But he would have to help arrange transport as well!

Okay. The deal was done.

---

[10] For Englishmen, read Guyanese.

They had not told him about the other Englishman, the English Englishman. The Indio had let it slip. Riaz, always with his eye to the main chance, figured he should increase his cut. After all, whenever foreigners were involved, his price invariably went up. This was the first law of Brazilian micro-economics!

He had arranged for the truck; the Englishmen insisted on registering it, they were scared of the law. The Englishmen had gone on ahead; he had insisted on that.

He had planned to rip off the tovex that same night but it had rained cats and dogs and they had given him a small advance and he had spent too much time drinking cachaça[11] in a less than respectable quarter of the town, and playing cards with his friends. The next night had turned out much the same, rain, cachaça and gambling, but the cash advance had been very small and on the third night the rain stopped. He had 'acquired' the tovex; the method by which he had acquired it necessitated its immediate removal, that night, in the dead of night, as far away as possible from Boa Vista. He did not stop till he reached Enamuna. He was not too happy with himself, though. He had nearly bungled the job when at first he got the army barracks muddled up with the stores; and he was pretty sure the truck had been seen parked at the back of the magazine, maybe they had even got an idea of the registration under its layers of amateurishly prearranged caked mud. Neither had he had enough time to clear certain potentially incriminating evidence from his shack. If the policia linked the truck to the Englishmen, and linked the Englishmen to him... come to think of it, it had seemed rather peculiar at the time that there were no guards patrolling the compound, nor even much activity in the guardhouse; the magazine had been left open, and really quite well lit; the tovex had been stacked right in front, on a trolley of all things. He had not believed his luck at the time.

So he was not all that surprised when he saw the Boa Vista policia in Enamuna that next morning.

Riaz dropped another empty beer bottle onto the floor beneath his hammock. He stretched an arm to the chair and felt for another cigarette. There was one left, he lit up and inhaled the smoke deeply. No sign of the Englishmen yet. They had sent word for him to meet

---

[11] Cachaça is a local fermented sugar cane drink, very strong stuff.

them at the north fork but it was hot and he felt lazy, and when he had gone to get in the truck there were no damn keys, and then he had seen the Boa Vista policia cruising down the street and had had to make himself scarce again. And then, well, it was the siesta hour, and the bitch had not even offered him food. Why couldn't they come into town? He drew on the cigarette again, his chest contracted as he coughed and went into spasms. He heard the school bell go and heard the schoolma'am leaving through the back of the house.

"Unfriendly bitch," he said to himself. She didn't speak to him, she hardly looked at him; anybody would think he wasn't welcome staying here. At least she was keeping to her end of the bargain.

He felt mean, he felt that the Englishmen wanted to con him. Let's face it, he often felt the whole world was trying to con him. He took a last pull on his cigarette, then swung his legs out of the hammock, kicking into the chair and strewing clothes on the floor. He flicked the cigarette butt expertly into the washbasin to phizz under the dripping tap. He put on shoes, collected a little bag of tools from under a filthy shirt, relieved himself against a courtyard pot plant and slipped out of the schoolhouse.

There was little activity in the street. One or two urchins were running from the shantytown, late for school. A police truck roared off in the direction of the airstrip. Funny, he thought, there had been quite a lot of activity over there today. He made doubly sure that it was all quiet, then crossed over the street to the truck - another cautious look - and jumped in. He pulled a bunch of leads from under the dashboard; they all looked the same to him. He stripped a couple of the wires back and shorted them out - if it did nothing else, it might confuse the blasted Englishmen.

He caught a movement in the street, with his sixth sense, and sat up. The Indian boy was approaching on the school side of the street; he recognised him instantly, he was the one who had brought the message that morning from the Englishmen. He was not sure whether the Indian boy had recognised himself in return, but surely he must have seen him. He would have to bluff it out. He ducked back under the dash and held his breath. The Indio crossed the street and came right towards him, but for some reason paid him no attention. But surely, he must have seen. The Indio went into the shop; only an English Indio would have done that, Indios were supposed to do their business at the other end of town. The Indio came back, rolled out a cigarette. He could have killed for a smoke right then. He fiddled with some more wires, hiding his face as best he could. Maybe this Indio did not know about the truck, maybe he would take no notice. The Indio walked slowly back towards the shanty. Riaz breathed a sigh of relief, got out of the truck and slipped into the back of the shop, and bought himself a new pack of cigarettes.

Riaz smoked nervously from his new pack of cigarettes as he followed the Indian back up the street, keeping out of sight behind a row of shacks. He saw the Indian meet the Englishman, but did not dare to go close enough to hear what was said between them. He would not have been able to understand anyway. But the presence of the foreigner, and this surely was the foreigner, meant he was obviously dealing with something big. The Englishman looked younger than himself, but maybe not that much. His beard was very grey and his lanky hair was thinning from his temple. Well preserved perhaps. He did not look much though, not exactly your formidable opponent. Yes, they would pay more all right, when they discovered the Toyota was not going anywhere.

The police Toyota came back into town and dropped a group of fat vaqueros off at the town office. Riaz spat and lit another smoke. Riceiros! Must be a meeting, politics maybe. The truck continued up the street towards him, stopped right opposite him. He froze in a thin strip of shadow. The policia was looking directly towards him, right through him. He stayed motionless, not even daring to breathe and returned the policeman's stare. The truck turned and went back to the delegacia. Riaz felt as though he had never existed, was a mere figment of someone else's wild imagination. He pulled deeply on his cigarette and the magic left him as the smoke hit his rotting lungs.

He wondered what they were up to, the Englishman and the Indian. He was a little surprised when they both started back into town. Where the hell were they going now? He made his own way along in front of them, watching with his second pair of eyes, back towards the shop.

He heard the Englishman stop at the schoolhouse; he went in through the back of the shop and sat down at a small metal table with a glass of beer, to wait and watch. He saw the Englishman and the Indian enter the schoolhouse. He heard the schoolma'am's parrot scream and smiled to himself. He had wanted to wring the bird's neck, stupid bloody animal. In fact, he nearly had done so last night.

He nursed a small new scar on the fleshy part of the back of his hand, just behind his thumb. Damn bird! They were taking too long a time, the Englishman and the Indian, what the hell were they doing so long? He began to get nervous and chain smoked as he watched through the shop door curtain.

He was not too sure of the relationship between the Englishmen and the schoolma'am. The tall Negro and another Indio had been waiting for him when he arrived at Enamuna, and had taken the crates and put them in the schoolhouse. He had not been too happy about that and had insisted on staying close to them. She did not like the arrangement, though. She had hardly passed a civil word; in fact, she had only grudgingly accepted the status quo when he had hinted, in private, that the policia might be looking for a black Englishman, and something about contraband. He had guessed she had something going there, or would like to, the lascivious bitch. He had used the excuse to move the crates himself from the storeroom to where the damn bird was perched; they would be safer there, and, being so visible, they would be well hidden. He had congratulated himself on this brilliant line of thought. If she tried throwing him out, he would inform on the boyfriend.

The bloody parrot had stopped its screeching. The Englishman would think the explosives were in the storeroom, he would be bound to search when he could not find them there. But then maybe that was not what he was after. Riaz ordered another beer, this time drinking it straight from the bottle. It was airless in the shop, muggy, and he started to doze. The shopkeeper swung in a hammock behind the counter and he dozed too. There were no other customers.

It was starting to cool a little; the bead curtain in the doorway moved gently as a light breeze came in from the east. Riaz jolted awake spilling flat beer on the table and over himself, and saw the Englishman and the Indian leaving the schoolhouse. They were obviously empty handed. They came towards him but did not enter the shop. He was on his feet, a little unsteady but ready to bolt through the back. The shopkeeper eyed him suspiciously. Riaz did not like the shopkeeper, too fat, too smooth, too rich. The Englishman and the Indian sat on the roadside outside the shop. He saw the schoolma'am walk over to them and heard her call them freaks and perverts. He laughed to himself, and swallowed another mouthful of beer - ugh, flat, warm beer.

The shopkeeper watched Riaz watching the schoolmistress and the strangers, but said nothing.

The Englishman and the Indian moved away up the street and Riaz, thankfully now, moved off after them, again leaving by the back and walking behind the row of parallel shacks. The schoolmistress was intent on the two strangers, she didn't notice Riaz.

As Riaz followed the Englishman and the Indian along the trail towards the river, he began to realise that he was losing control of the situation. He did not seem to have the bargaining chips he thought he had. The Englishman must have found the tovex. He had fixed the truck, or so he thought, but was that enough? He would have to play a good bluff to get the price up.

Nicodemus and I headed straight down the trail towards the river and Orinduik. Nic had spotted Riaz watching us from inside the shop.

"He's still with us Mister Tom," Nic said.

"Yes Nic. I think he's been with us all afternoon," I replied. "I thought I saw someone in the shop when we first went in the schoolhouse. He must have been watching us all the time. Still if he has been watching us so closely, he won't have had the time to get up to any nonsense. Let's go back and get the others. Heh, did Miss Josephina really call us perverts? I wonder what she thought we were for goodness sake. Freaky maybe, but perverted, never. I'm really quite affronted, how about you Nic?"

"Sure Mister Tom," says Nic, "I'll go in front you if you like."

PART TWO

CHAPTER ELEVEN

INSURRECTION AND TREASONABLE ACTS

The three men waited in silence in the comandante's outer office.

Two of them, in uniform, sat in straight-backed wood and rattan chairs which had been placed along one wall. They passed their time making eyes at the comandante's secretary who sat at a desk facing them, pretending to be much too busy to notice, but who was nevertheless making a few surreptitious observations of her own. The men exchanged lascivious winks and nudges when they thought she was not looking, and shot sweet and meaningful glances when they saw she was.

The third man stood, staring out at the praça. The office was on the third floor of an imposing twenties building, the Manaus police headquarters on rua Tamandare, near the cathedral. All the buildings on the street stood as monuments to the rubber barons, unchanged since 1920, Italian marble and glitz. The windows had been thrown open to gather the cooling afternoon air, and the noise of traffic and the whistling of a traffic policeman wafted into the room from below, but not obtrusively so. The man at the window looked impatiently at his watch, and started to pace, obviously annoyed with the world in general. The two uniformed cabos smiled to themselves but wore serious chameleon faces whenever the comissario glanced in their direction.

The comandante's secretary looked nervously at the heavy and ornately carved double doors which led into the inner sanctum and gave the paradoxical impression of cavorting Italian nymphs and cherubs guarding the entrance to some pleasure grotto. "I'm sure the comandante will see you as soon as he is free, comissario. Perhaps you would like some more coffee while you wait?"

Comissario Alfredo Color smiled thinly and, quite out of character for a moment, raised his brows questioningly to his two men, "Coffee?"

Coffee was agreed and the secretary unfolded her good-looking legs, climbed out from behind her desk and went out to get the drinks. Her every measured move was closely followed by the two corporeal pairs of eyes; comissario Alfredo Color, however, was much too preoccupied with his own thoughts to take any notice of her or her legs.

Color had been transferred to 'Insurrection and Treasonable Acts' from the Vice Squad just over twelve months ago. He was an ambitious man, if not a particularly bright one. Vice had been a very cushy number in this town, and being an ambitious member of the squad he had been able to keep well on top of his quota of arrests and still have plenty of spare capacity for a private income. As a result, in addition to the odd embarrassing disease, he had picked up a rapid series of promotions, to second-in-charge. At that point, however, he had started some serious stepping on toes. There was never a shortage of arrest material, nor of graft, but he became convinced that the only way of advancing further in the police force was to take a sideways move. An opportunity was presented and grabbed but as it turned out, this was probably one of his worst career decisions. Less than a month after he left Vice for Insurrection, his old chief was caught, quite literally with his pants down, and promoted out of Vice and into Administration leaving something of a vacuum behind him which Color no doubt felt he could have most admirably filled. Be that as it may, Color had spent the next twelve months with his head buried in files and filing cabinets, and in charge of his new 'squad' of two desk corporals. He must have stepped on some mighty important toes! He never made it onto the streets. There were no arrests, he had never even got close to making an arrest. Worse yet, his capacity for backhanders was reduced to plain zero and he was progressing nowhere fast, not at all a good situation for a man of such ambition to find himself in. The last twelve months seemed to him like an awfully long time. He had become irritable and officious in the extreme. He was not a happy man. He had never been a particularly likeable man and over this short space of time had become particularly disliked by his two desk cabos, and most other people with whom he had dealings.

Most of the problem was of his own making. There was no doubt some excellent potential in the state for his new Division, what with constant problems between the Indian tribes and the settlers and logging companies. He even had a limited brief in neighbouring Roraima State though he had never actually been there. Color, however, was just not the right type of policeman for his new job. He lacked its basic qualifications, subtlety and couth. He should have taken a mediator's role but instead he always took sides. He did not understand Indians, could not begin to relate to them. He did not appreciate their problems, what white Brazilian did after all? The Indians were just a frigging nuisance. And on the other side of the coin, to the vaqueros, he was a city slicker who couldn't know or understand the first thing about life or survival in the bush. Color was a city street cop, pure and simple, and most of all simple.

Yet it had been his old street contacts and knowledge that had come good for him in the end. He was convinced now that he was onto something big, certainly something bigger than his pathetic three man Division could handle, and, if he played his cards right, it could be his passport out of his present miserable predicament.

Right now the whole world was turned against him. He hated it, he hated everything that was holding him back, he hated having to use unfabricated evidence, he hated files and kept them locked away in filing cabinets, he hated administrators, he especially hated desk clerks in uniform whom he considered universally lazy, or stupid, or both and who held the spare keys to the filing cabinets and all his secrets.

The comandante's secretary came back high heeled into the ante room balancing a tray of coffee cups and handed them around.

"Is the comandante aware that I am here, Miss?" Color asked her, maintaining a distant and very forced politeness. "He does know of our appointment?"

"He has someone with him, Sir, and cannot be disturbed. I am sure he will not be long now," the secretary replied, avoiding the comissario's questions. It was a well rehearsed line that she had used on many previous occasions.

There seemed little the comissario could do; it was obvious that the secretary had not the slightest intention of disturbing her boss. Color wondered who it was in there with him. He had distinctly heard some muffled grunting coming from the grotto (my description) behind the double doors, but had not been able to make out a conversation as such. He had telephoned that morning requesting an interview, and had been told five o'clock. It was now well past six and his two men would be putting in for overtime if he knew them at all! He turned his back on the room again and resumed staring out of the window. The sun was now low, and by coincidence at a perfect angle to reflect the room behind him in the mirror of the window glass.

The comandante's secretary was relaxing back at her not-much-modesty panel desk with her legs outstretched. Color's cabos were staring transfixed, and all but drooling, as her skirt sensually and slowly, and possibly quite unconsciously inched up along her thighs. Color's paranoia blossomed. He felt superfluous and unwanted, and suddenly very angry. He spun around glaring at his whole world. The girl blushed and squirmed in her seat, which had the opposite effect to what she wanted; her skirt squirmed even further up her legs to her stocking tops. The two cabos sat, straight-backed and poker-faced, each holding their coffee cups gingerly over their respective laps. One of them, the taller of the two, managed to raise a hand to wipe some very noticeable dribble from his chin.

The situation was ripe for embarrassment and there seemed no magic remedy to defuse it. Color focussed his mondial glare at the girl and the girl eventually managed to get her skirt back down to within a respectable distance from her knees. Color drained his coffee in a single gulp and the girl got shakily to her feet and offered to relieve him of his cup. As she did so, she pressed a hidden button under her desk.

The grunting or whatever it was that was coming from the inner office and which had been gradually and imperceptibly increasing in volume suddenly ceased, and as suddenly became acutely tangible by its very silence. The secretary coughed and collected up the cups, clattering them as noisily as she could. Further muffled sounds issued from the inner sanctum, not precisely definable, shufflings, metallic zippings and clippings. The secretary left the room; the two cabos sat, staring at the wall; Color stood, arms akimbo, staring at the double doors.

The brass doorknobs turned and the doors were thrown open. A rather large man, with short cropped blonde hair and a distinctly Gothic air, and wearing full colonel's uniform, came out. The three men in the outer office instinctively stood to attention and saluted...and held their salutes. The colonel comandante, for his part, completely ignored them as he pompously ushered his guest past. She was wearing black fishnet stockings, the hems of which were slightly twisted, and a very revealing short canary yellow dress... and very little else. She tottered in front of the colonel on three inch stiletto heels. But at least for her part, she did acknowledge the other three policemen... with a smile and a raised digit.

"You'll remember her, seu Alfredo, she used to work out of praça Sao Miguel. Nice little bird. No doubt she will have flown through your capable hands a couple of times!" The comandante finally acknowledged his men's presence as the outer office door shut on the 'nice little thing' in high heels. "Well, you'd better come through and tell me all about it."

"Sir!"

The comissario followed comandante Malcenski into his office, leaving the cabos to resume their seats and silent thoughts outside.

"Do you remember that gutter rat Riaz, Sir?" Color began. "He's surfaced again and I believe I could be on to something important. I need more men, and well, budget, Sir." Color believed in coming straight to the point.

Malcenski, preoccupied with his own thoughts, leafed through his appointments diary, and made notations here and there.

Color went on, "I believe it could involve foreigners, Sir. I've heard from the street that Riaz has been contracted to supply high explosives, perhaps even some plastic, ostensibly to a group of prospectors."

Malcenski snorted derisively, "Riaz, that shitty little animal! Why don't you just pull him in and have done?"

"We could do that, yes Sir, but that would be an end to the matter. If we could give him some more rope, though, we could find out who or what is behind all this." Color had an annoying tendency to talk down to his superiors.

"Yes, yes, of course, of course," said Malcenski brusquely, "I wasn't born yesterday you know! So, you want a case budget. How does the foreign connection come about?"

"The prospectors, if that is what they are, Sir," continued Color, a little more deprecatingly, "are from Guyana, and maybe payrolled by a Yankee or a Britisher. From what my sources tell me, Sir, they could be troublemakers, communists, or environmentalists at the very least. They are certainly very friendly with the Indian tribes."

Malcenski looked thoroughly bored with his comissario and wished he had never had him transferred out of Vice - but then, on second thoughts perhaps it had not been such a bad move, hmm, next Tuesday should be free. He noted "3pm, Lolita" in the appointments book and looked up at Color again. "I don't see there's much I can do at this juncture, if that is all you have. It's all rather thin, don't you agree?"

"I need men, Sir."

"You have men. You have those two goons out there. What's wrong with them?"

"What's right with them, Sir? The only reason I brought them with me this afternoon was to keep them from making some unbelievable cock-up, and to illustrate to you the total resources of my Division! Sir, those two goons, as you call them, out there are it! Riaz is back in Boa Vista, so I'll have to go after him there. Those two are totally incompetent, worse than useless. I don't think they've ever travelled beyond the city limits"

Malcenski sighed. "My heart bleeds for you, seu Alfredo. I give you two of my best desk men and what do I get in return? Hah, nothing but complaints and more complaints. Well, let me spell it out for you. I have no men to spare. Get it? None, zero, nix. You must work with what you have. You have cabos Perez De Silva and Pedro Romero, and you'd better make the best of them, totally incompetent, lazy, stupid or whatever." He paused, half smiled, and scratched the top of his blonde crew cut. "I'll tell you what I'll do; as a special dispensation, I'll give you a travel budget and an authority to draw on funds from B.V. You might like to buy yourself a map! But no more men...and you'd better make sure you don't step on too many toes up there, you know what they're like. The chief thinks he's a little Napoleon!"

"Thank you, Sir, perhaps... if you could reconsider...a temporary transfer, or exchange, for De Silva and Romero... to Traffic, Sir...?"

"No, comissario Color, no, no, no. You have who you have, and you work with what you have. Make sure you take very good care of them! I will repeat myself for the last time: I have no more men to spare. Good day, comissario." Malcenski pushed back his chair and stood up.

Color saluted and left without a further word.

CHAPTER TWELVE

CARACARAI

They had been driving for fourteen hours, since well before dawn, De Silva and Romero taking shifts at the wheel of the Amazonas Police Bright Glacier White Toyota Landcruiser. Color had sat in a rigid silence for most of the journey in the front passenger seat, and what little conversation there was had taken place between driver and back seat passenger. Not that there had been much to discuss. The most interesting subject of conversation between the two cabos would undoubtedly have been women but they didn't feel comfortable debating such matters with Color sitting there like a stuffed prude. Soccer, also, could have been discussed as it was Sunday and they were missing the big match, but, try, as they did, they could not pick up the commentary on the radio. They were way out of range. Quite annoying really.

They were driving the Pan American Highway, a two lane mud road aimed down the centre of a hundred metre wide swathe of bulldozed jungle, as straight as a Cat D10 blade. The clay of the road alternated between a dazzling white and a clinging red and the Glacier White Toyota quickly turned chameleon. V-shaped drainage cuts arrowed from the rutted and corrugated laneway into the deep green of the jungle.

The highway had originally been built on good solid foundations and surfaced with smooth laterite gravel. Much of the surface, however, was washed away now, leaving little tell-tale black sand trails in the drainage ditches and the strong foundations also had proved about as lasting as the politicians who built them.

Neither Perez De Silva nor Pedro Romero really had a clue as to how to drive the road. Alfredo Color was too proud to admit that he could do little better, but nevertheless made it quite clear that he was not at all impressed with either of his men's driving ability. The only way to drive corrugations, in fact, is to put your foot to the floor and ride over them, otherwise both you and your faithful steed will be reduced to a shaking mass of jello in no time at all. And if you can't drive fast, get over that vibro-hump, you end up driving so slowly that you get stuck fast in the first boggy patch you come to.

Mind you, if you drive too fast, and hit a patch of laterite gravel, well then it's a little like performing a ballet on black ice!

Pedro Romero was the slightly taller of the two cabos and was also the braver driver. His legs seemed to reach the pedals just that little bit more easily. He had progressed to the stage of trying out various pedal combinations, but still could not quite get the hang of it. He had run off the road, completely, twice. After the second occasion, Perez De Silva had insisted on taking over again, but they were five kilometres down the road before any of them realised that they were heading in the wrong direction! What was more, Perez drove like the short wimp he was and, having amazingly turned the truck around without incident, it took less than half an hour for him to get it hopelessly bogged to its axles. It took them a further hour of cursing and digging, and even then they had to commandeer the help of a passing bus, to pull themselves out. Comissario Color had felt most embarrassed for himself, never more so than when one of the bus passengers laughingly pointed out that the four-wheel-drive hubs were not even locked. Another peasant joked that the government officials seemed to be as stupid as their stupid-looking hats. Color's pallid face turned chameleon to match his mud spattered truck. Pedro Romero had resumed the driving.

Fourteen hours to reach Caracarai. Fourteen hours of monotonous green jungle, patchworked with desolate clearings, hectare upon hectare of smouldering stumps, regrowth trying desperately to reassert itself, carbon and weeds interspersed with the human tragedy of roadside shanty living. They had passed through one town, Paraiso, but had not dared to stop in case they could not find the courage or strength to get started again. Color prised himself from the Landcruiser gingerly, unsteadily. He felt as though his whole body was shaking, a little like stepping off a ship after a long ocean voyage. It should have taken them only half the time to reach this far but Boa Vista still seemed a week away at this rate; they would have to rest up here and finish the journey the next day.

They had arrived at the Rio Branco ferry crossing. The river was broad and fast flowing, turbulent with whirlpools, and crossed by a rickety cable ferry which could take two buses or trucks, or half a dozen smaller vehicles at a time. The ferry looked so frail, no match for the great river. It had just docked with two buses fully laden with their roofs piled high with cases, boxes, assorted bric-a-brac and livestock.

The river level was quite low, and the bank down was steep and badly eroded and gullied. The first bus laboured up the slope towards them, now sliding perilously sideways, now gripping again, slipping, spitting out clods of mud and gouging new gullies, and eventually lurched over the lip of the bank at an horrifically unstable angle. Color stood watching with a mixture of horror and amazement for none of the passengers had even bothered to get out.

Perez the Wimp swallowed hard, tapped Pedro the Fearless on his braided epaulet and whispered, "Good luck chum," and got out of the back seat.

The second bus followed the first, wheels spinning crazily and churning yet more ploughshare ruts into the so-called roadway.

Pedro the Fearless swallowed hard, crashed the Toyota into high ratio which was another first for him, and then proceeded to execute a totally uncontrolled three hundred and sixty degree pirouette down the slope and onto the ferry deck. For some unknown reason, having performed this stunning feat, Pedro Romero seemed quite unwilling to get out of his seat in order to stretch his legs. His eyes appeared to be fixed on the opposite shore and what looked from this angle, in the rapidly reddening western light like an even more impossible bank ahead. He seemed rather embarrassed and squirmed uncomfortably on his seat.

Meanwhile, however, behind him, yet more heady drama was unfolding as Pedro's erstwhile mate, Perez, and the comissario made their respective ways down to the ferryboat by foot. Imagine one city slicker ex-Vice cop with city shoes, and one incompetent desk cabo, on the muddy muddy banks of the Rio Branco, six hundred kilometres from city base. They would have been more at home on a downhill ski slope in Alaska. Color, in the lead, his precisely creased trousers and polished shoes spattered with mud and caked with heavy clay, descended in perilous fashion waving his arms like the wings of a headless chicken. Perez, following in his master's footsteps, trying so hard not to laugh, momentarily lost concentration and ended up on his arse, legs in the breeze, and roller coastered into the back of Color... Color went headlong, arse over tit for want of a better description, and didn't stop till he reached the Rio Branco.

I would have liked to leave you with that simple image, but then you may have formed the wrong impression. The raging torrent of the Rio Branco could have swept the comissario away and out of all our lives in the one tragic incident, out of the Northern Hemisphere, across the Equatorial line and back to the south. His body, bloated, and half consumed by piranha and alligators might have been washed up somewhere between Caracarai and the mouth of the Amazon, but let's face it, it would not have impinged further on this story.

But that is not what happened, for our comissario lives on in the tale; his tragedy is yet to come. Color got more than a little wet, it is true, went up to his neck in fact, but... the ferry docks at a calm spot in the river, naturally, and therefore he was never in any danger of being swept away. Furthermore, South American rivers, contrary to popular belief, are not all infested with man-eating fish and reptiles; no more so is the Rio Branco, and consequently Color was in little danger from that direction either. In fact, the spot where the ferry docked doubled up as a local outlet for excremental materials and general garbage and most self-respecting piranha or caiman, therefore, would not have been seen dead within ten kilometres of the place!

What happened was this: The ferry was crewed by two men, the captain and his first mate. Since the captain was engrossed in watching the antics of Pedro Romero, he was blissfully unaware of Color's predicament. The role of hero of the hour, therefore, fell to the first mate who was a pleasant, unassuming and very rotund phlegmatic Negro character, name of Enrique. Enrique propelled his round body across the deck, grabbed at a large boat hook and thrust it at Color. Color, who was only up to his neck in water because he was sitting on his bum, was caught deftly by his starched uniform collar and swung unceremoniously onto the deck, much like the landing of a prize specimen fish.

Color was angry, embarrassed and affronted, and not for the first time that day. He felt belittled and insulted. He was wet and cold, and getting colder. His clothes stuck to his skin, and the excremental mud was irritating and rubbing in some most awkward places. In essence, he was a very pissed off and rather foul-smelling policeman, so much so he could barely bear to stay so close to himself. He did not even say 'thanks a lot' to the first mate who had so gallantly rescued him; Enrique's bit part ends right here almost before it got started.

De Silva sheepishly boarded the ferry, still unable to control the laughter within him, and approached to enquire after the state of his comissario's health; it was only Color's final image of his own abrupt dismissal from Malcenski's office the day before that prevented an immediate and violent reaction on his part. A violent tongue, however, can be infinitely more biting than any fist; not one word was said that can be recorded here.

The ferry was loaded up and, on its chains, chased the sunset to the west bank where Pedro managed by some miracle - he would say some fancy foot work - to keep the Landcruiser upright on its journey to the top. There, Color made an instant executive decision to break the journey, putting himself up at the police post whilst his men scrubbed down and washed and polished the Glacier White paintwork and slept in the truck.

The final leg of the journey on to Boa Vista went without a hitch. North of Caracarai our Manaus Treason Squad, or MUTS for short, passed from an Amazon that was being destroyed by the twentieth century Brazilian Vaquero to the savannahs created over twenty centuries or more by Indian Land Management.

The country they passed through on this second day was softer somehow, more at peace with itself, as though it had come to terms with Nature and that this was all part of a sustainable evolution. It was not natural, to be pedantic, but it sure looked fine. The cattle were fewer and fatter, the savannahs greener, the tree-lined creeks lusher, much much lusher.

This is not to say, however, that the MUTS were aware of the contrast. Their minds were on more important issues. De Silva and Romero had already learned much about the bogging properities of thixotropic Amazonas red mud, and how to lock four-wheel-drive hubs, but still had to concentrate all their collective efforts on driving the laterite gravel and corrugations.

They managed between them to keep the truck pointing north for they had absolutely no desire to spend one more night in the bush, improving the diets of a dozen particularly voracious breeds of mosquito. Color remained silent the whole way, his nose stuck out of the window breathing in fresh air. He was given no reason to criticise and as a consequence, was positively seething inside.

They arrived at Boa Vista soon after the siesta hour, tired, hungry, thirsty and still resonating from the corrugations. Color made his second executive decision for the trip and checked into a comfortable pension just one block from the town centre; then, in a fit of uncharacteristic generosity, he checked his men in downstairs, with instructions for the laundry.

CHAPTER THIRTEEN

A BATTLE OF WITS

The comissario who ran the show at police headquarters in Boa Vista was a small and slightly dishevelled looking detective called Antonio Juarez, Toni to his friends. He had a dark complexion, but facially his features were more European than African. His character, however, was more African than European, very jovial and outgoing; he was altogether a rather nice sort of bloke, for a policeman. The dishevelment was by design, calculated to confuse the opposition, and no doubt resulted from watching too many Columbo movies. He made friends easily and, like his alter ego, was also a prodigious judge of character. He intensely disliked insincerity, pomposity, pushiness, superiority and suchlike abominable human traits, and being a very sincere person himself, did not care who knew it. As a result, he was sorely misunderstood and distrusted by those with such traits of character, which included all of his superiors, not least the comandante Malcenski in Manaus. Hence Malcenski's very unkind reference to him being a little Napoleon. He was very much in charge of his shop but he was certainly no tyrant; he was not only well liked by his men but also very highly respected for his innate abilities and common-touch approach.

Color sat opposite him across the desk as Toni Juarez mentally ticked off on his fingers - *pushy*, yes, *pompous*, certainly, *insincere*, hmm limp handshake, so probably yes, *superior*, the way he treats his men absolutely! And a bloody liar! "So, Malcenski offered you three of my men and another vehicle did he?" said the little Napoleon.

"And an open budget," pushed Color, warming to the situation and waving Malcenski's authority in the air. "This case is a very important one," he added, pompously, "and, need I say, it is also very sensitive. I am not at liberty to divulge all the details to you," - now in a distinctly superior tone - "at this stage, just treat the whole thing with total confidentiality..."

Juarez' patience was stretched to its limit. He knew Color was lying about the men and the car; Malcenski would never have given him such carte blanche, and anyway, how could the man be so stupid?

Any confirmation was only a phone call away and he would hardly be likely to delegate his staff and resources without such back up. But what topped everything was Color's idiotic contention that he, Juarez, did not know what was going on! Who the hell did he think had tipped him off about Riaz in the first place? Perhaps he really did believe the information had come to him straight from the streets!

He was on the point of taking off on this most sorry of apologies for a policeman, but instead took a deep breath and decided to bite his tongue for the time being; he was keen himself to find out what was behind this explosives business, and even the great Antonio could, on rare occasions, stoop to being a two faced son-of-a-gun. He knew Riaz had been double dealing between the vaqueros and the Guaiara Indians a couple of years back, but he thought he had learned his lesson and had given that line of business away long ago. Color's ideas, however, appeared obstinately fixed on the insurgency angle; Antonio Juarez wouldn't bother expending more energy on trying to broaden this blinkered approach. Better to let things run for now, keep in touch and be around to pick up the pieces. Whatever happened, he didn't want any more trouble with the Guaiara, and most of the vaqueros were just itching for any excuse to restart the war. What a bloody mess that would be!

"We know where Riaz is. We've kept a watching brief on him for the last week, not round the clock or anything like that - it's not really necessary because he's a very predictable sort of animal," Juarez said quietly. "I'll keep a man on that till he makes his next move, then take it from there." He paused, waiting for some sort of reaction and was rewarded with a supercilious smug sort of half smile. He went on, "Oh yes, the army has been informed of your request, and, I must say, it took a great deal of persuasion to get them to agree to it. I think they may have preferred him to get his hands on some of the really old sweating gelignite they have lying around, and maybe get blown up in the act. However, they have agreed, and the tovex will be there and perhaps even labelled 'please steal me'. They tell me it looks more like a high cholesterol Polish sausage than the traditional stick and fuse that he's used to; I just hope Riaz is able to recognise the damn stuff... and I also hope they remember to let him escape."

The smug half-smile adjusted itself slightly, trying to work out whether these last comments had been made facetiously or whether they were serious. Color was not well known for his sense of humour and had little appreciation of sarcasm or its sister satire.

"Just so long as our friends in the military have followed my instructions to the letter, I am sure that everything will work perfectly according to plan," he said. Inwardly, he was congratulating himself on having successfully twisted this little country cop around his little finger. The smugness positively oozed as he considered his success in the matter of men and car; he had hardly hoped to be so fully accommodated. Obviously this little Napoleon, as Malcenski had called him, had recognised his city colleague as his natural superior in such matters of national importance.

Juarez picked up a pencil and started doodling on a scratch pad. Then he put the pencil between his teeth. Next he drummed on his desk top with the fingers of one hand, and finally proceeded to play a brief accompaniment on his teeth with his pencil, all the while grinning inanely at his guest. It was past six thirty and time for his usual drink with the rest of the lads down at La Oficina.

"I will let you know as soon as there are any developments, Color," he said, "you can be assured of that."

But Color seemed totally impervious to the hint and just continued to sit refining his most superior face.

Juarez continued, "Of course there's no need for you to hang around here. I will arrange to have you and your men picked up from your pension the moment we hear."

And still Color made no move to go. Juarez was now distinctly thirsty and starting to feel more than just a little ratty. It was a long-held tradition that he and a number of his close colleagues would spend an hour or so, after leaving the office, in La Oficina, a pleasant low-key bar just two blocks away. There they could sit on a veranda overlooking the river and indulge themselves in a glass or three of fine wine, cut by the speciality of the house which was a particularly excellent marinara vinaigrette, and chew over the day's events. The beauty of it all was, they could tell their wives or girlfriends quite truthfully when they rolled home late that they had been unavoidably detained at the 'office workshop'. The wives and girlfriends knew all about the ruse, but it was an unspoken rule that no one should break this little piece of magic. Visitors and guests, of course, could be invited along to La Oficina, and on many occasions were, but Toni Juarez drew the line at inviting supercilious twits like Alfredo Color.

"Well, I have to be getting on with my other work, Color, if you would excuse me," said Juarez.

No move, just the merest flicker of the eyelids as Color raised his brows to look even more steeply down his nose.

Juarez stared at the end of Color's nose, at a tuft of coarse black hair growing out from its bulbous end, and whistled softly, and scratched his own nose sympathetically, thoughtfully. "Would you like me to arrange a car to take you back to your pension?" he said, as slowly and deliberately as he could, as one might to a small and slightly backward child. "I can assure you it would be no trouble, no trouble at all."

Color, at last, was moved to respond, in clipped superior tones.

"I think that I would prefer to await developments here," he said, "where I can keep my fingers on the pulse, so to speak."

Juarez' jaw dropped. He was so taken aback, in fact, that he practically dribbled onto his desk. He had met some obstinate stuck up twits in his time but this one took the biscuit.

The clock on the wall said nearly six fifty. This was getting beyond a joke, ridiculous! Duty called. Time for the big hint. Toni Juarez stood up abruptly, swept a pile of files into his desk drawer and made a deliberate show of locking it. He turned to his filing cabinets and locked them also.

"Well, I have to be going now, Color, administrative duties you know, can't wait... I'll inform my desk sergeant that you will be leaving soon and he will arrange a lift for you if you so wish. Not that the streets here aren't safe to walk at night or anything like that you understand... "And with that, and yet without looking further at his tormentor nor giving him the courtesy of a farewell handclasp, he left his own office, deliberately clicking the door latch and pulling it shut behind him. He barely managed to stop himself from turning out the lights.

Color was left gaping alternately at Juarez' empty chair and the door through which he had disappeared. "What a most peculiar sort of fellow," Color said aloud to himself. "Too much inter breeding perhaps." And with that, having, he considered, just won a great battle of wits, he left the office also. Taking a lesson from Malcenski's book, he walked straight past the desk sergeant without acknowledging him, but with a most exaggerated flourish. He returned directly to his pension, to a meal alone and to watch the latest news from Brasilia via satellite, alone, and to an early and empty, except for himself, bed. He was dog tired and fell asleep, with his boots kicked off but the television droning on.

CHAPTER FOURTEEN

LA OFICINA

Toni Juarez made sure that Color got safely back to the pension, then turned and walked briskly in the opposite direction, down to the river esplanade and his favourite watering hole. A light breeze was blowing from the south, heralding a storm. It would blow away the fumes and the sultry atmosphere that had been building up for some days now, he thought.

"Here you are at last, seu Antonio!" Juarez was greeted at the door by his offsider Santos. "Right on cue to get in the next round of drinks." Santos looked more closely at his chief's face. "Heh, don't look so miserable, cheer up, he can't have been so bad."

"Oh but he was, my friend, he was..." Juarez paused, then continued more thoughtfully, and just a little moodily, "and worse... God only knows what sort of policeman they're breeding in Manaus these days... but it sure explains the crime figures. The man's a buffoon, but look, it's not so funny for us. He's the type..."

"... might forget to get the next round in?" interrupted Santos with his tongue hanging out and an empty glass proffered beneath his chief's nose.

"Hah! Point taken, my friend," Juarez brightened. "It's just that people like him really bring me down. Okay, I won't be so serious. Let's drink. A carafe of Oficina Roja?"

And to the barman, "More of your worst, Juan, blood of the saints and martyrs."

And the full carafe was already in Santos' hands before Juarez had even finished ordering.

Juarez and Santos sat looking out over the river, nursing a half full carafe. The sun had finally dipped over the savannah and a wall of dark cumulus storm cloud was rolling in from the south, from the Amazonas heartland. It was eight o'clock and the others had all gone home to their respective wives, girlfriends and beefsteaks. Toni Juarez did not believe in sharing his thoughts and concerns with all his men, but Santos was different. He had offsided for Juarez for three years now and their mutual respect and trust were well bonded.

"So, you think this Color character could be a bit of a problem Toni," said Santos, using the familiar now that they were alone.

"Yes Sao," said Juarez, emphatically, "I do. The more I think about him, in fact, the more problems I see. He's basically a brainless pachyderm, you see, and that's what makes him so blasted dangerous. There's no doubt he would side with the vaqueros if anything were to happen, and I've no doubt also that the vaqueros will do their level best to make something happen, the first excuse they can find. So, you and I, Sao, we've got to keep Color from providing them with that excuse." He broke off to sip at the blood of saints and martyrs and to pick at a bowl of the mixed seafood, searching for a favourite morsel, eye of squid or toe of clam perhaps.

Santos took up Juarez' thoughts. "I can see why you're worried, Toni, especially if as you say this Color bloke is such a thick skinned twit, but what I still can't understand is how anybody could be so idiotic as to believe this caper has anything to do with the Indios, Guaiaras or whoever! Riaz' contact came from the Guyana side, even he must know that much, and there hasn't been any connection there since the Rupununi Uprising... and that was over thirty years ago! It just doesn't..."

Juarez interjected, "Oh look, a man like that doesn't think logically like you or I, Sao. He only thinks in terms of excuses, angles, bigotry. No, my friend, he only got on so well in Vice because he was surrounded by other idiots the same as himself. Malcenski knew the score and he gave him this job where he thought he could do no harm. Hah! It looks like that one just backfired on him!"

Juarez stabbed at a calamari ring. "Anyway, Sao, it's information time old friend. Did anything happen with Riaz this afternoon? From now on, we've got to keep well in front of Color. Shouldn't be too difficult, but we must make damn sure that we do!"

Santos gulped the remaining dregs of the blood of saints and martyrs from his glass. "Hmm, something did happen this afternoon, yes, as you said it would Toni. The same three came visiting again, the two blacks and the small Indian. You know, I'm not sure how they got put on to Riaz in the first place, maybe his English you think? Anyway, that's not important for now. They did most of their talking out back but I could see all right. The older, bearded one was in charge. Now, here's a piece of luck. Riaz got himself a truck, an '83

Tojo - and you'd never believe it, legitimate! He actually bought it, paid money, cash, for it! So, Riaz and our bearded friend take off, leaving the real tall Negro and the little Indian guy behind at the shack. I figured to follow the truck, but look, I needn't have bothered - they came straight over to the delegacia to register it! You believe all this Toni? Terrorists?"

Santos refilled both their glasses.

Juarez made no answer to the rhetorical question; he held his glass, sipped, and looked at Santos over its rim, then stabbed at another marinara prize and swallowed. "Name?" he asked.

"Tyler," Santos replied, "Maurice Desmond Nathaniel Tyler, from Georgetown. I've put out a low key request to Brickdam[12] for information. They came across yesterday from Lethem, legit, second time for the week. All three crossed together - they've been making no attempts to hide themselves at all. The tall black guy is Osborne Rankin, from Buxton - that's near Georgetown - and the little Indian guy is Donald James, from Morawhanna. I've requested background on both of them as well, maybe we'll hear tomorrow, or by the next day. I didn't want to make a big deal out of it. I mean, shit man, these guys look so honest they might even believe Riaz is legitimate himself."

"What! That bastard." Juarez could be quick with his wit. "But you're right not to make a mountain out of this, Sao." He paused thoughtfully, then asked, "Morawhanna, that's in the northwest isn't it, near the Venezuelan border?"

"That's right, Toni," replied Santos, "but some of these guys move around a fair bit, so I don't think we need attach too much significance to that just at the moment."

"No, no, we'll not complicate matters unnecessarily until we hear from our friends in Brickdam. Let's keep it all in the police, though, because if Foreign Affairs get a hold of any of this, they'll likely blow it sky high."

"Literally maybe," grinned Santos.

A drum roll of thunder sounded as the storm in the south gathered momentum and drew closer.

"You said it! It's bad enough with the military in the game, but I think I can keep them under wraps; the colonel owes me a favour."

---

12 Brickdam police headquarters in Georgetown.

"Anyway, that was just about all that happened, boss. They registered the truck, then Riaz dropped Tyler off at a little pension, not far from here actually, and Rankin and James were already back there to meet him. I stuck with Riaz, but I know the man at the pension well and he'll tell me if and when the Guyanese make a move. Riaz went straight home but I figured I should leave one man on him for tonight."

"Who?"

"Rodriguez."

The thunder was suddenly upon them, playing a stirring overture. Heavy rain drops symphonically smashed onto the roof tops. The fumes of civilization were washed away.

"Yes, he's okay. Not that Riaz will be going anywhere tonight in this! Where did you say the pension was?"

"I didn't, but it's just one block from the central praça, you'd know it, Pension Mira Vista it's called. Totally respectable place of course!"

CHAPTER FIFTEEN

DREAMS OF AMAZONS

"Pedro, Color's gone out, let's go see what this village has to offer,"

Perez De Silva kicked Pedro Romero in the side to wake him up. "All this pension has is bread and water, let's go and get drunk elsewhere."

Romero opened his eyes, yet they did not move. He stared at the white-washed ceiling overhead, with its one naked low watt lamp. He was dreaming:

he is on a road gang, thumping the creases out of the hard top with a jack-hammer; he is sweating and hot in the midday sun, there is no shade and the creases in the road get bigger and bigger; he is naked, suddenly, shivering uncontrollably, his teeth chattering; his whole head, his inner ears are resonating to the clicking of cicadas louder even than the crashing of the hammer and just as persistent; he is running now down the road which is jack-hammer smooth, running, rhythmically, resolutely, over hills, ever uphill; there are sand dunes and he is an ant clambering up them, forever up and across them; and their fractal corrugations; and the fractals of fractals; and he sinks defeated into the sand; he is lying on a downy bed, his whole body vibrating gently, pulsing warm and tingling with pleasure...and he is staring up into the face of a beautiful girl; he's never seen her before, she is a true Amazon, pure strength; her face is her eyes, she has deep brown shimmering eyes, he is shivering now with desire, he is running his hands over smooth hills of smoothest skin yet she is for ever just out of reach; and as he reaches out to her, her face fades into the shimmering filament of the electric light globe, finally.

"Come on, man, wake up!" and De Silva delivered another, harder kick in the region of Romero's kidneys.

"Ah, shit, waddyawan?" The disappointment on Romero's face spoke for itself; he kept his eyes fixed on the light as if hoping beyond hope that the girl would come back. "What you want to wake me for? I was having a dream."

"Yeh, I can tell," said De Silva, looking pointedly at a prominent protrusion under the sheet. "It looks like Percy there was joining in! Look, fix yourself up. Color's gone up to the delegacia. He just poked his nose in here a minute ago, but I pretended to be asleep as well. He just said 'I'm going up to headquarters, be available,' and pissed off. How he expected us to hear with me being asleep and you tossing around like an Olympiad, I can't imagine. Anyway, we have to eat, not even the Lord High And Mighty Color would deny us that, so, let's do it...and if we get drunk in the doing, then so be it, say I."

Romero half groaned, half yawned and swung his feet languorously out of the bed, taking care to keep the sheet in front of him. "You sure know the best time to wake a bloke Perez. How about we go somewhere I can dump my old mate here, put him to bed?" And then suddenly full of vitality, he bounded out and straight into his jeans. "Heh, come on then, what are we waiting for?" And Romero, the slightly taller and more adventurous of the two, was the first to the door, just.

It had not taken the two desk men long to find what they were looking for; although it was hardly fair for Perez to describe Boa Vista as a village, the area they had to search out was little more than one square block. They found it between the main praça and the Rio Branco, less than five minutes walk from the Pension Mira Vista. One side of avenida Roraima was lined with small bars with open, brightly neon-lit entrances and with music blaring. Alternating between the bar entrances were anonymous and dark little doorways, opened only on request, leading to the floors above the bars.

Pedro Romero and Perez De Silva were proving, at least initially, difficult to satisfy. They had started logically enough, at the first open door they had come to, but the food there was not too appealing. They had drunk two beers each in discovering this fact, and in the necessary toasting of each other's health, then moved on down the street to the next set of welcoming lights. They were not ready yet for the dark doorways in between. The second bar served food which was less than appealing, one might say quite appalling, more beer was drunk, respective healths were toasted, but this time more thoughtfully, more cogitatively. It seemed there was less necessity to hurry things along. They discussed their families left behind in Manaus. Both men had young wives and both had small children. They missed their children and wondered if they would find some little souvenirs in this God-forsaken hole of a place. The third bar was distinctly better than the last. Here the two by now fast friends sat under dimmed lights in deep soft chairs rather than at the bar itself. They did not call for a menu, but ate snacks provided, they drank more beer, more than two more, from schooners, they laughed and joked and put their arms around one another and slapped each other on the knee. They missed their young wives and their young wives' cooking and wondered if this God-forsaken hole of a place might have some small trinket to take back in token of their everlasting devotion and appreciation. Our two friends had a little difficulty in extricating themselves from their comfortable chairs, but once nature had called and they were on their feet, they may as well try next door, bar number four. They still were not quite ready yet for the dark doorways in between.

They had to make a quick dash for it to avoid getting soaked in the rain which was now bucketing down.

In bar number four, again plush chairs were chosen in preference to balancing on high bar stools.

"I think we should eat something," De Silva slurred, "I need some protein."

"Two bloody Marys," Romero demanded of the waiter. Pedro was a city boy and liked to show his city boy tastes, "and bring us some nuts."

"Speak for yourself, Pedro old boy, I have my own," said De Silva.

"Brazil nuts!" said Romero.

"Only the best!" said De Silva.

There is often some point, some intangible point when the bonhomie of drinking companions turns inward on itself, perhaps even to the point of moroseness. Alcohol-induced depression it's called. Thus it was with Pedro and Perez in bar number four. The two men sat in gloomy silence for a while with the atmosphere becoming progressively less sociable. It was not that either had offended the other in any way, rather that both men felt equally offended by the circumstances in which they now found themselves, and being fairly typical of all Brazilian men, there could be little worse than an offence against their machismo, however imaginary.

"That Color is a real bastard," announced De Silva to the world in general.

Two black guys and a small Indian were sitting quietly drinking at a table next to them. On the table were stacked a dozen or more empty beer bottles. There were no other customers in the place, but the men took only passing notice of De Silva's commentary. Perhaps they had not heard him clearly?

It was Romero's turn to indulge himself.

"I love my wife. Why should that bastard Color take me away from my wife? How will she manage without me?" He directed this last question to the men at the next table, but received only faint smiles in return. "There's the delivery man, he has his eyes on her, you know that? I'll kill him if he so much as touches her." Romero was on his feet, his voice rising in pitch and volume, his eyes brimming with tears of self-pity. He went over to the other table, unsteady on his feet. "I'll kill anyone who lays a finger on her."

The three smiled back warily, obviously not fully understanding the drunk's problem, a little embarrassed and unsure of whether they might have committed some faux pas, but Romero had already forgotten them and turned back to De Silva.

"I would never cheat on her, Perez old friend," he said, now in a measured, deliberate tone. "I would never do that." Drunks tend to be repetitive.

A further silence ensued whilst the two policemen mixed and consumed more varietal protein-rich drinks. The atmosphere became distinctly conspiratorial. Romero was extremely angry that anyone could possibly think that he would have cheated on his own beloved wife.

"We are going to fix that bastard," said Romero under his breath.

"Who?" slurred De Silva. Of the two, being the slightly shorter, he had the less robust constitution. Perhaps too much protein and not enough bran!

"Color! Who do you think?"

"Sure, let's fix him." De Silva was struggling to get to his feet, ready for any kind of proposed action. "You want we shoot him?"

"No, don't be stupid. We'll fix him, that's all. Should be fun too."

Romero had a very self satisfied grin on his face. A plan was obviously formulating.

De Silva sat on the edge of his chair waiting for further illumination. When it did not appear to be forthcoming, he asked his searching question. "How?"

"You know his wife?" began Romero.

"Senhora Bella, aggh, you can't be serious," interjected De Silva, "how could you contemplate (a bit of a tongue twister, that, but he got it out!)...

"No, nothing like that! Just listen will you? If Color's wife ever found out he'd been a naughty boy, she'd throttle him, yes? So, let's set up our favourite comissario with some of the local talent, and let Bella take over when she finds out."

De Silva sat slumped in his chair, and stared incredulously at his friend.

"Brilliant! Positively brilliant. You're a genius, Pedro. How does the delectable Bella find out?"

"We send the girl in, wait five minutes, then whip in, grab a photo and out before he knows it. It'll be easy." It seemed like Romero had all the answers, at least it did to De Silva.

Two drinks later our two heroes, now arm in arm (for mutual support, nothing more sinister) departed from bar number four, watched curiously by the two black guys and the small Indian.

They knocked at the first dark doorway, and explained that they had a friend back at their hotel who was a long way from home and lonely and in need of special companionship, but who was of a weak constitution and thus was susceptible to colds and influenza should he get his head wet in the rain, not that the friend recognised these qualities in himself, of course, yes they were just two chaps wanting to give their friend a little surprise, for his birthday, yes, that was it, for his birthday... special requests? Well, he, the friend that was, he did have a certain penchant for the larger ladies it was true, yes, he had mentioned that to them on a number of occasions, buxom was the terminology he'd used.

And the two friends were walking out again, under umbrellas provided, one on each arm of Maria, who, to put it as pleasantly as possible, was a rather large girl of indeterminate age and breeding. She was a dark skinned Amazon, size wise, but unfortunately lacked those finer, definitive supernatural Amazon attributes of athleticism, strength and beauty. She was a lady of unnatural fashion, obviously and incongruously so as she had dyed her black hair blonde and painted her brown face thickly with rouge and glitter lipstick. And it would certainly be best if she could refrain from smiling too openly, for she had lost most of her front teeth and the ones she had left were bent and blackened. But despite all of this, she was a warm hearted and personable type of girl. Had our cabos been quite sober, Romero and De Silva might not have appreciated being seen promenading with her through the town, but as it was they fully appreciated the fact that they could lean on various parts of her anatomy for some very necessary support, and anyway it was dark, and raining cats and dogs, and there was no one else out and about to see them.

They approached the Pension Mira Vista with some caution, their finely tuned policemen's senses keenly aware that this was a highly respectable establishment. Maria, in the middle, giggled girlishly, for that was what she was. De Silva tried letting go of one arm, with nearly disastrous consequences. He grabbed back at an indeterminate piece of flesh to steady himself, briefly overbalancing the precarious trio but Romero, being the slightly heavier weight of the two, heaved on his side just in time and set Maria straight again.

De Silva leaned up against the wall whilst Romero peered in through the entrance. The concierge was asleep in a back room. The trio resumed their mutual support roles, aided to some degree by their now furled umbrellas, and crept into the hallway. They made their way through the foyer and headed for the dimly lit staircase which would lead them inexorably to their goal up on the first floor.

Negotiating the stairs, however, proved to be a little tricky, mainly because the staircase was not wide enough to accommodate them three abreast, so to speak. They eventually managed to reorganise themselves, largely by a process of trial and error, to arrive at a suitable topological solution to their problem. Thus, De Silva, who was the most incapacitated by far, went ahead pushed by Maria, bumper to bumper, and Romero brought up the rear holding onto Maria's derrière. The men did their utmost to be quiet, each imploring the others by shushing, but Maria, gripped by the excitement of the situation as well as by Romero's roving hands on her wagging tail, giggled on relentlessly; and the stairs squeaked abominably.

De Silva flopped exhausted at the top of the stairs. He wished his world would stop revolving and grabbed hold of the bannister to stop it from moving.

Romero steered Maria along the first floor corridor.

"That's his room my dear," he said, "just go ahead and give him the time of his life."... tap tap tap..."Oh, don't bother to knock," he added, "no standing on ceremony, you know," and he retired to sit with his green-gilled friend at the top of the stairs, to enjoy the show and to plan his next move.

Comissario Color was dog tired when he got back to the pension. He had managed to swallow a very plain and mostly unpalatable meal of steer and corn, and had gone to his room to watch the news on television and to nurse his indigestion. He had lain back on the bed, fully clothed except for his boots, without even erecting his mosquiteiro, and had promptly fallen asleep with the TV droning on in the background, some presidential debate, crowds of people gathered outside and on the steps of the legislature, he hears his name called out...

the scene is the opera house in Manaus; he is striding purposefully up the sweeping staircase of Italian marble; crowds of people are parting for him to move through between them; he is obviously a very important person, he is dressed in tails, freshly laundered in Paris, France; he strides up the stairs, and up more stairs, past ever more admirers who reach out in vain to touch his sleeve, to the box; el Presidente is there and bows to him and says, 'please carry on Maestro', and walks through his Presidente to the podium, tapping his baton for silence, tap, tap, tap, three taps in rapid succession; the crowd behind him hushes, shushed, he can not see them but he feels their presence, tap, tap, tap, again this overwhelming feeling of power; he raises his baton and the great soprano bursts into life before his very eyes, Kiri Te Stupenda; she is dressed in full armour, heaving breast plates shackled, bow drawn and quiver ready, a veritable Amazon among Amazons; she sings and he makes love to her music, she is the epitome of perfection; she is... she is fat Bella his wife; she sings I've got a crush on you... and she misses top C; the crowd breathes in as one and starts to clap, slowly; there is an undercurrent of vociferous opinion... but it was he, Color Maestro who missed the note and Bella, the lover and fat wife is moving across the stage, coming towards him, her arms outstretched as if in pity, her breasts heaving to protect him, her fisted hands clenching, ready to do battle for him; clap... clap... clap, slow hand clap, a desperate tap, tap, tap, fast baton tap, but his power is gone, the crowd will not be shushed, Bella's face is closing, taking up his whole field of vision; now she is one with the crowd, leading the crowd, pinning him down; he puts out his hands to ward her off; she smiles at him as if he were a truant child and holds out her hands for the baton, 'give it to me my darling,' and the smile turns into a battlefield of broken teeth standing awry like weathered tombstones in an ancient churchyard; his hands meet flesh as her enormous breasts press down on him, crushing him and he pushes back for his very survival and yet still is overcome and enveloped in her flesh; he is crying to return to his mother's womb; he is suffocating under her mountainous breasts; he is pinned by fleshy thighs and he is kissed by a glittering tombstone mouth; and still the crowd comes on, louder and laughing and finally bursting in upon his dream.

Midnight, Tall Boy and Don James had had enough for the night; they had dashed back to the pension through the rain which, still falling heavily, had soaked them through to the skin. They were in good humour though, three quarters eut in fact, and far from quiet as they raced up the stairs. Was this the right floor? Sure, third door on the right.

"See you all in the mornin' folks, we'll need an early start," said Don.

"Wait, wait," said Midnight. "I got a couple of beers in my room left over and goin warm, let's kill them now."

And the three had lurched off to Midnight's room, except of course that it was not Midnight's room.

De Silva and Romero sat at the top of the stairs, literally rooted to the spot as the ensuing drama unfolded before them. De Silva, admittedly, was having some problems in focussing on the ever moving bannister rail, but was nevertheless quite conscious and looking forward to the show being directed by his best and only true friend and buddy-in-arms.

Color was the first to scream. It may be debatable whether he screamed as Midnight opened the door, or moments before. Certainly there could not have been more than a split second in it, and it most certainly was Color who screamed first.

Maria screamed second as the three intruders fell over one another and on top of her. Why Maria screamed is not clear as she had been brought up as a placid type of girl and trained not to be overwhelmed by a small party of four. She was more than a match for this lot. Possibly one reason may have been something to do with Tall Boy's penchant for pinching bare and exposed Amazonian bottoms.

No one else screamed. The rest of the Act was played out in slow motion:

- The three Guyanese righted themselves, though Tall Boy showed a distinct desire to linger awhile. Midnight, slightly perplexed at first, wondered silently where the hell he had put the beers. There was no dialogue; they were trying too hard simply to avoid collapsing in laughter.
- Maria raised her heaving chest and twisted around to look at the perpetrator of the pinch. She cricked her neck and became paralysed in excruciating pain, mouth ajar and awful teeth agrin.
- Color gaped, first in amazement, second in wonder, third in incredulity. He was pinned and defenceless, also rooted to the spot, his arms outstretched to Maria's breasts like pit props in a collapsing mine drive.
- And finally, there was a brilliant flash of light as Romero concluded his part in the play.

Comissario Alfredo Color, momentarily blinded by the flash, never saw the face behind the camera.

Color could not bring himself to admit to the previous night's events to anyone. Maria had fled from his room in total disarray, more than three quarters naked, before he could do more than stare after her vast retreating bottom; he would surely have recognised her in any identification line up but that would have been more than his machismo could ever contemplate.

He eventually screwed up enough courage to go down to the delegacia again; Juarez was as negative and unhelpful as could possibly be, but to keep Color happy had told him of their success in Midnight's identification. This proved to be an error of judgment, a bad mistake in fact. Color's shock on seeing a photocopy of Midnight's passport photo was plain for all to see; he became instantaneously convinced that it was the Guyanese who had been responsible for setting him up with the girl, and that could only mean he was now on the verge of cracking a most powerful international conspiracy.

Midnight, Tall Boy and Don James had already left Boa Vista early early in the morning, taking a jeep taxi to the border crossing at Lethem.

They were half way there before Midnight broached the subject that was on all of their minds.

"Did what happen last night really happen, or was I just dreamin' some amazin' dream?" The three concluded that it must have been something in the Boa Vista water supply, because otherwise, how could they possibly all have had the same dream?

They were over the border and drinking Banks beer in a Lethem rum shop before Color had screwed up the courage to go down to the delegacia in Boa Vista.

It was a further two days before the gutter rat Riaz made his move, in which time Color became totally insufferable and almost caused Juarez to move out of his own office in protest. But eventually Riaz did move, under the watchful eyes of Santos and Rodriguez, and immediately after, hit the dirt road leading northeast towards Lethem in his Matte Jungle Green. Romero and De Silva, who Color had set to watching Juarez' men, were somewhat taken by surprise by the speed of everything; they could not find their boss and completely botched the tailing job.

The Green turned left at Sao Bento. Santos and Rodriguez (in Roraima Blue), who were in radio contact with Juarez and had been on Riaz' tail lights, all the way from Boa Vista, also turned left at Sao Bento. Romero and De Silva (MUTS Glacier White), who had eventually found their boss dining in a rather exclusive restaurant, and picked him up, turned right at Sao Bento, and did not stop till they reached the border post for the crossing to Lethem.

"No Sir, nobody else has passed through tonight, absolutely not, Sir."

A radio phone call to Juarez' bedroom in Boa Vista was equally un-illuminating, and it was a very dejected international conspiracy buster in the White who turned back down the Lethem - Boa Vista road.

The Green, looking even more bedraggled and mud spattered than usual, arrived in Enamuna very early the next morning; the Blue arrived about five minutes later; Juarez flew in on a small chartered plane about mid-morning.

Color and his boys somehow missed the flight; there was an unfortunate misunderstanding and an overlooked message on the part of the delegacia desk sergeant and, "No, I am terribly sorry, Sir, but the only one with such authority is the comissario in charge, senhor Juarez himself. Perhaps, with a suitable route map, Sir, I'll gladly arrange the purchase order, Sir, turn left at Sao Bento, right at Deposito, don't make the mistake of following the track to Maturuca, Sir, but instead make sure you bear north after you cross the Rio Cotingo and you should make it by nightfall, if there is no more rain, Sir."

But there was, and yet they did make it by nightfall, on the second day.

CHAPTER SIXTEEN

PERVERTS AND TWISTED LEGS

"No Nic, affronted! It means, well, you know..." I hesitated.

"What Mister Tom?"

"Oh, never mind, you go ahead."

"Sure, and what is perverts Mister Tom?" Nicodemus did not want to drop the subject.

"Well, they're kind of weird you know, not nice people to know, and I'm sure we are, so Q.E.D. we are not."

"So what we do mek we perverts?" Mister Tom.

"No Nic, we are not perverts..." I tried.

"But senhorita Josephina, she say we is..."

"...I know she said so, but we aren't Nic, believe me. This time, just for once, the schoolmistress got it wrong, right? Just work with that and forget she ever said it." I am not too sure that I can understand what I had just said myself. "You just lead the way, Nic. Lead on McDuff."

"What is mack duff, Mister Tom?"

"Mr McDuff, Nic..."

This was obviously not a good time for English lessons. I let it ride though I knew I should not have done so. Nic would stack it all in his bottomless memory banks and demand clarification at some time in the future when I would have forgotten all about it. He had a habit of doing that, asking what to him were absolutely pertinent but merely deferred questions, but which to me for instance would be totally out of context. Next week, maybe, he would come along and ask me if Mr McDuff was a famous pervert.

I shooed Nic on ahead; in any case, I was not exactly familiar with the path. I let my mind wander but I still felt a little hurt by the schoolmistress Josephina's assertions that we were a couple of deviants with perverted designs on her darling children. It struck me that she had reacted a little too like a frustrated hen who had lost her own brood of chicks. Kids of her own would do her more good than all these proxy children she was saddled with. It was not that she didn't look like the dedicated type, quite the opposite, no, it was just as though she were missing something, love maybe. I could not see these shanty dwellers giving her back anything like love, they were too hard, too practical, too disillusioned after too many years of broken promises and too little progress. To the kids she represented the opposition, authority or something like that.

Or maybe she thought of all the shanty dwellers as perverts, dirty gutter dwelling perverts; there was no shortage of those sorts of ideas in Brazil, but then I would have trusted Midnight to see through that in a girl that he was obviously smitten with. No, when it came down to it, Nic and I must just have looked to her like a pair of dirty old men; it hurt.

Riaz continued to trail us all the way. He was not exactly a smart bushman because even I could hear him trampling along behind. It was really quite amusing in a sad sort of way. You know when you have just been to the butcher and some neighbourhood dog follows you home, he will make sure you know he is there. He will run ahead, turn back, run alongside, cock his leg. He lets you know he is there because he wants something from you. He is simply chancing his luck. Riaz, on the other hand, followed us more like a stray dog would, half out of its mind, knowing it needs you, hunger tearing at its belly, but paranoid, not daring to approach because it knows it will just receive a well aimed kick to its tender parts. I thought of turning, waiting and confronting him perhaps, but my Portuguese was not up to it; nothing would be accomplished that way. I hurried on after Nicodemus.

It was getting towards dusk and I could see the lights of the village over and away to the right. The river was hidden from view but the noise from the falls gradually built up to a crescendo as we headed straight for them and then the river was suddenly there in front of us. There were a couple of canoes tied up at the bank, left for general use. The spray of the falls, however, was less than fifty metres to the right and the current already looked to be pretty strong and fast.

I would have been rather wary of trying out one of the canoes by myself, especially in the evening half light. I think Nic must have guessed what was going through my mind. We take the good canoe and leave the rotten one for Riaz. Maybe he would not try to follow us across, and if he did, then good luck to him.

"We can't tek these, Mister Tom," said Nicodemus, bringing me back to earth with a bump. "If we do, the border man sure to see we. I okay because he know I cross over this mornin', but you not supposed to be this side."

Nicodemus, as usual, was faultless when it came to points of law, having been educated at one of the most law abiding of Christian missionary schools. It could be a bit of a nuisance at times - especially if he felt moral justice might also be involved.

"Then how do we cross, Nic?" I asked.

The river was wide and fast, and populated by some very nasty creatures whose close acquaintance I was in no hurry to make. Nicodemus' reply was what I had feared.

"We swim over, Mister Tom," said Nic.

I am sure I saw his smile widen even more than usual. I am not a good swimmer. I have never been a good swimmer. In fact, my body and bone structure is such that instead of floating, I tend to pierce through the surface meniscus like a javelin and sink like a stone. Surely Nic must remember.

"But it's running too fast here, Nic. Maybe we should find somewhere further upstream," I suggested.

"Too deep upriver, Mister Tom," replied Nicodemus, with awesome finality. "An' they got caiman[13] , an' maybe pirae[14]."

"An' here they got waterfalls an' big rocks an' maybe electric eels[15]," I said, mimicking him for no other reason than because I was feeling pretty bitchy and just a little sick inside.

"Is not far across here. They got a sandbank part way, and then it's just a quick stride between them rocks, that's the only deep part," Nic said, pointing into the distance.

All I could see was the spray blowing back from the thundering falls.

"You want me go over and get Domingo bring the woodskin across further up where the border man wouldn't see?" queried Nic.

"No, I'll make it, just you stay close. I'm not as young and stupid as 1 used to be, Nic." Now I really was being stupid, not wanting to lose face. "I guess it'll be okay if we cut poles." I also did not want

---

[13] Caiman (crocigatus alligdilus) is alligator; they have great sets of teeth.

[14] Pirae (pygocentrus niger) is a larger and more solitary variety of the better known piranha fish; they have superb teeth.

[15] Electric eels (electrophorus electricus) don't have teeth, they give you a 10,000 volt shock instead.

to be left alone with Riaz coming up behind.

We cut poles.

Nicodemus chose our route about twenty metres from the brink of the main falls. He did this, he told me later, because he figured it was about the only place where we would not be seen by the 'border man' as he called him. Had I known this at the time, I would unhesitatingly have said, 'heh, let's risk it, the border man is probably shut fast in his little house having his tea!' But he had not told me and here we were; any mistakes and we would be over the top, and there would be no stopping till we reached the bottom. The falls at Orinduik, by the way, run for just over a kilometre and have a vertical drop of about a hundred and fifty metres. I say 'we', now, but I had every confidence then that Nic would make it across to tell the others of my own sad demise!

The old adrenalin started to pump and the old legs started to shake in sympathy, and still I found I could not stop myself from following blindly and stupidly on. The first part of the crossing was not too bad, the water was only waist deep, and we seemed to be out of the main current. I faced upstream and pushed what little weight I owned against the water, with the aid of my pole, and made progress, two steps forward, one step sideways, two steps back, two steps forward, digging my toes into the sand, one jump sideways, two steps swept back... two, one, two... two, one, two... two... my muscles were starting to ache, most of the pressure was on my back and it was simply not used to this kind of exercise. We got about half way across, about fifty metres on a dog leg, and climbed out onto a shelf of slippery rock, just submerged a few centimetres. I sat on the flat jasper to catch my breath and regain a little strength. My legs had stopped shaking probably because they had run out of energy. Nic pointed back to the Brazilian bank and the fading western light and I could just make out the shadowy figure of a small weasel of a man peering intently in our general direction; I'm not sure whether he could see us as the lights from the village were in his eyes. Perhaps he was listening for the sound of my heartbeat over the thunder of the falls! I could hear that all right!

The next stage of the river crossing was unmitigated terror, well, that may be a little too strong as I am still here to write the tale and, contrary to popular belief, was not actually reduced to a permanently jibbering idiot. At the time, though, I was convinced that I had never been nearer to not 'being' any longer.

We were faced with a narrow channel, not more than five metres across, of churning, boiling water. Beyond that, in the fast darkening light, was an indeterminate mass of black rock. I knew it would be hard, slippery, smooth and totally devoid of handholds or footholds, and I also knew that if I somehow failed to grab a handful of it as I went past, that might be my last view of this world. Nic gave me no time to dwell more on these thoughts. He had had the foresight to cut a length of liana vine from the bank and handed me one end; I fumbled with it, my fingers more and more cold now in the rushing water, and managed on the second attempt to tie it round my waist. I had my umbilical cord.

Nic turned briefly and flashed a smile and plunged in, swimming strongly upstream in the lee of the current. The liana went taught and nearly pulled me in after him but he must have felt the pressure for he immediately struck out across the current. He had time for perhaps only three strokes before the current fetched him back with a crash against the rocks on the opposite side of the channel, but it was enough. He was practically thrown up and out of the water in a plume of spray and I could see him standing, silhouetted against the glow of the village lights, and although I could not have been able to see it, I knew he was also grinning from ear to ear.

My legs were shaking again, but I could not stop myself now. I dived in, keeping as far to the lee as I possibly could. My meniscus-piercing breast stroke seemed to get me nowhere but was nevertheless succeeding in tiring me out, totally. I must have made a few metres, however, because I could feel the vine tugging at my waist again...but I was so tired. I tried to strike out to my right. I fought the water with everything I had, but most of my fight was in trying to keep my face out of the water, simply in trying to breathe because I had forgotten to turn my head downstream. I doubt I even managed a single stroke across the channel. I was swept away, out of control. My right leg smashed against a sharp rock and I felt my knee twist awkwardly. I had lost all sense of direction... my face was full of spray... my mouth spluttering and choking. For some reason all I could do was push my arms up, perhaps in some vain attempt to grab at air... my chest was full of water and I started to slip from darkness into blackness.

My life did not unfold before me. My past regrets did not parade themselves across my battered ego. The liana held and Nic reeled me in and hauled me out, and I lay on my stomach on the flat jasper rock and threw up, emptying my lungs of the Ireng River. My leg was gashed and bleeding profusely, and bent underneath me; I twisted around and clicked my split knee cartilage back into position, and felt no pain, I was too glad that I was still alive...

... and then the pain set in, and somehow Nic steered me across the rocks and lifted me over two or three more narrow channels which would have been child's play to me twenty years before, and then we were over and scrambling along between small rocks and soft sand and keeping our heads down below the lip of the river bank.

I gave a last look back over towards the Brazilian side but could see no signs of movement, no weasel shadows. Both canoes were still pulled up out of the water. I was cold and numb, my knee ached whenever I put any weight on it, and my leg hurt, and I wished, oh how I wished I had taken up Nic's suggestion of getting Domingo to bring over the woodskin. I could so easily have waited and faced up to Riaz if need be. It was not even as if I had ever felt confident of making the crossing, I knew 1 was being stupid. I simply do not know to this day why I tried.

CHAPTER SEVENTEEN

VAQUEROS, INDIOS E GARIMPEIROS

Toni Juarez should have been enjoying himself enormously. It was months since he had given himself an excuse to get out from behind his desk and into the country. Even small town Boa Vista was getting more and more polluted these days with exhaust fumes and the yellow brown smog that often sat over the small town on sultry days before the clouds built up and the rains came to wash it all away, out of sight and out of mind, into the Rio Branco. Out here the air was clean again, or cleaner anyway. Then he looked out of the window, out to the northwest and shook his head thoughtfully. Perhaps not so. In the distance he could see a pall of dark cloud that he knew was born of no meteorological phenomenon.

Fifty to a hundred kilometres away, Brazilian vaqueros were pitting themselves against nature in a last ditch effort to transform what little remained of the rainforest into cattle feed, a slash and burn mentality for which a single year's profits outweighed a million years of subsequent decay, erosion and misery. Whole villages of Wai Wai had been razed and uprooted from the eastern Roraimas, now it was the turn of the Guaiara, Macushi and Arawak in the north and west. It had been going on at this break-neck pace for a mere ten, maybe twenty years without sanction. The vaqueros had destroyed a thousand hectares for each and every one that a thousand years of Wai Wai, Guaiara, Macushi and Arawak had conserved. And yet the country was so vast, so unending, that only now was the impact of all this destruction just starting to be felt, or seen, or acknowledged, or understood, and even so, by so few... and not yet by any who might influence its course. This year's cruzeiro, or cruzado, (or was it the new-cruzeiro?) inflating at two thousand percent in the crushing poverty of Brazil, circa 1990, rules supreme!

Juarez sighed to himself and turned away from the ominous black smoke clouds. He was just a small cog in a minor wheel. He had enough on his plate keeping this year's peace, but, some day perhaps, he would be able to use his influence...

Santos came in. "That was the last of them, Toni. They're all waiting for you now in the town office. I thought it would be better than in here."

Juarez snapped out of his reverie. "Right, thank you, Sao, I'll go straight over. The sooner we get this business sorted out the better. Boa Vista just told me Color is on his way and might reach here by tonight, though somehow I doubt it. Even so, I can't take the risk of him getting to these people first... by the way, Sao, where did Rodriguez go just now? I saw him driving up the street."

"Oh, he thought he saw Riaz sneaking around when we drove back into the village," Santos replied. "He's just going to give him a bit of a scare, that's all. Look, he's on his way back already."

The two policemen went next door to the town office. Four planes had arrived that morning in little Enamuna, bringing a dozen of the most important ranchers from as far afield as Santa Elena, Deposito, Limao and Normandia, a hundred kilometres in all directions. Rumours had been circulating for some considerable time, of trouble with the Macushi, of gun running, and even of a ground swell movement among the local garimpeiros.

Sides in these matters are easy to define; the vaqueros hate the Indios and the garimpeiros, the garimpeiros hate the vaqueros and the Indios, and the Indios, well you guessed it. Juarez understood all this; he did not exactly hate any of the parties, and of course he could not be seen to take sides, but he did have definite sympathies. Right now he had to face up to and convince what to him was the most dangerous group, the vaqueros, that the rumours about the Macushi were unsubstantiated.

The rancher mentality seemed to have grown out of a mostly undeveloped market economy or mechanism which had been taken to its ultimate extreme with no, absolutely no concern for the implicit costs associated with loss of environment, of social stability, of decency or simple humanity. The vaqueros were fat cats who fed at the expense of everyone and everything around them, and who were not about to lose their exalted rank in society if they could possibly help it. By hook or by crook, and any excuse to strengthen their position would do! Think on it next time you eat a can of bully beef.

Compare and contrast with the garimpeiros who had been born and brought up with nothing and had less than nothing to lose. If life got too hot for them, they would move on like the tinkers and gypsies of the Old World. Their impact on this environment was relatively localised, a small unsightly hole in the ground or a washed over river bank. They were basically small scale punk polluters, but it is true that their uncontrolled use of mercury to amalgam gold was having tragic consequences. It is always hard to blame the poor man for using his wits in order merely to survive, but then who had the most right to be poor in this land, the garimpeiro or the Indian?

Compare and contrast with the Indians who had everything to lose, a thousand years of heritage and lifestyle, but aside from their pride in their superb abilities and knowledge of this unique world, were essentially poverty stricken and powerless to resist the late twentieth century onslaught. They had been cowed over the past fifty or hundred years by the slow encroachment of modern Brazil, and now most could only stand without even their pride, accepting the few government hand-outs that were on offer, and the status quo of living in back street poverty. The Indians could only kick out in desperation.

Juarez spent the next two hours with the rich vaqueros, persuading, pleading, coaxing and cajoling them. They had never been approached in this way before, not by this particular arm of authority, and their collective ego was so engorged it might almost have burst. Even from a distance, Color had obviously sown some vigorous seeds of spurious facts amongst these people, and they needed little in the way of further inducement to take up their guns and go out firing. In the end Juarez resorted to outright threat, which did burst in on their egos, and finally convinced them that it was he, and not Color after all, who could and would do them the most damage. Grudgingly, they must also have accepted his contention that the Englishmen did not represent any real threat... and sure as eggs are eggs, they must have realised that Color was very much one of their own kind, a manipulative egotistical bastard, a seeker of self aggrandisement, an exaggerator and a liar who believed in his own lies, and hardly, therefore, a person with whom to do lasting deals.

The vaqueros left the town office and left the town, somewhat subdued, and flew back to their man-made savannahs to kick and spit at the earth, and slash and burn.

Rodriguez had been delegated to tail Riaz, and by early evening had still not returned to the delegacia.

Juarez shrugged. "Hold the fort Sao, I'm going to pay an old girlfriend a visit. You should get us stocked up with rations, then you and Rodriguez should get yourselves some sleep while you can. I've got a feeling we shall be pretty busy over the next few days. Oh, and don't wait up for me, I may not be back tonight."

One hundred kilometres to the south, somewhere between Limao and Deposito, Color, De Silva and Romero were about to spend an extremely uncomfortable and overly intimate night, cramped into their Glacier White short-wheel-base Tojo in the middle of a mosquito-ridden swamp, bogged up to their axles with only an electric winch and a fast-fading battery.

CHAPTER EIGHTEEN

SPITTERS AND KICKERS

One thing was sure and that was I was going nowhere that night. The gash in my leg was a good ten centimetres long, and had torn deeply into my muscle. I had poured in a whole (jumbo) pack of sulphur powder, Midnight had made good use of his travellers' sewing kit, and Harald had wrapped up the wound with layer upon layer of pawpaw leaf and skin which is well known for being a highly efficacious remedy for ruptured muscle tissue. I was beginning to wonder when the witch doctor was going to appear. I lay in my hammock feeling extremely sorry for myself and feeling my leg getting more and more numb by the minute; then Midnight unwound the tourniquet an inch and the feelings flooded back like a million sorry pins and needles.

"That was not a very smart trick, Tom old fellow," said Midnight, "you're not exactly a spring chicken you know. I can't imagine why Nic let you try it."

"Ah look, it's not Nic's fault." I had to defend him. It was no good wallowing in this self pity. "How would he know I'm not up to my old Superman standards? He's only a couple of years younger than me so he must think I'm as fit as him. He hasn't been exposed to forty-odd years of the western world's leading toxins, so how would he know? Hell's bells, I wish I had some kryptonite with me now." I had the feeling that Nic had been getting a bit of the rough end of the stick and I knew that what had happened had been nobody's fault but my own. "Anyway, I'll be fine by the morning," I continued. "I'm not going to let a stupid thing like this stop me now."

"Well... I think you should rest it up for a couple of days," Midnight began, like he was my mother or something.

"We don't have a couple of days, old buddy, so I don't think there's more to discuss, do you?" I swung out of my hammock to go to the can and regretted it the moment my foot touched the ground and the pain flooded in. I stopped and winced and repeated through firmly clenched teeth, "I'll be fine in the morning,"... and I made it to the can.

When I woke the next morning, the numbness was gone, replaced by a feeling akin to having one's flesh roasted on a spit. It seemed I had exchanged the fakir's bed of nails for his bed of red hot charcoal, but at least I could walk. Heh, come on now, everything was just hunky-dory; Harald wrapped me up in some fresh pawpaw skins, Midnight's stitching was intact, nothing was oozing, the sun was shining, our bellies were filled with a last huge breakfast repast of steer, bake and corn, and we were off, Domingo, Nicodemus, Don, Tall Boy, Harald, Midnight and Tom, the Symbiotic Seven.

Speed and stealth, now, were our twin prime concerns. Domingo had already been back over to the Brazil side at the crack of dawn to scout around but had seen no sign of Riaz skulking around. He was by far our biggest problem. Neither Midnight nor I wanted him along any more and I for one was no longer prepared to buy him off.

Nic and Tall Boy, meanwhile, had ferried a couple of loads of gear across the river, after refloating the woodskin which had finally succumbed to its leaks overnight. Nic was happy as Larry. He could not get over the fact that I had brought along such items as a light weight tarpaulin, spare blankets and dehydrated food. He had never guessed, not in his wildest dreams, that any of these things ever existed. He was used to packing fifty or sixty kilogrammes on his back in the old days, when a single oiled tarp weighed in at sixty kilos. For this trip, the loads would be reduced to forty, with the only really heavy items being the explosives. Nic was even happier than Larry!

The plan was basically this:

Nic and Tall Boy would pack most of our gear up to the north fork crossing, two loads each at the most, and wait there for the truck. Domingo, Harald and I would grab the explosives and the truck and high-tail it up to the north fork, where else! I had given up on the idea of enlisting the police to put Riaz out of the way, we did not have the time to think it through or organise a caper like that properly... it just would not work... so Don was dispatched to grab him, gently if possible, and put him somewhere out of harm's way. Midnight, without a doubt, had the best job which was to sideline Josephina while Domingo, Harald and I sidelined the macaw and grabbed the explosives. I was feeling rather envious of him as I saw him swaggering off towards Enamuna and his most onerous of tasks, but then we had been friends for a very long time and I was hardly about to come between him and the love of his life, however temporary she might be!

It was Saturday, not quite mid-morning, and the shanty town surrounding stucco Enamuna was alive and positively throbbing with its five hundred odd inhabitants. Kids, especially, were everywhere and were attracted to our strange little group like flies around a fresh carcass. Half-a-dozen of the small people had attached themselves to Midnight and Don as soon as they crossed the river and would just not go away. Midnight had lost his patience and his swagger by the time the rest of us caught up, and we continued on together. There was little else we could do. By the time we reached the edge of the village there must have numbered a hundred of the pesky little followers and they were drawing an uncomfortable amount of attention to us.

Midnight and I handed out sweeties but it only made matters worse for the sweeties ran out long before the kids did. We had tried the boredom routine. We had all sat silently in a circle, backs to a scrawny tree, and closed our eyes, and stuck our noses in the air, and thought alternative thoughts, and hummed and droned, and still the kids stood around and watched and waited, and waited and watched with never-ending patience for something, for anything to happen. Only the appearance of a hero, a Pele perhaps, would have shaken them from their determination. As it was they merely shuffled their feet and sorted themselves into some sort of rank, the bravest boys standing close in and the little girls remaining coyly in the background.

In final desperation, and after a brief conference, Midnight and I had even resorted to our famous clown and dance-mime routine, waltzing arm-in-arm, I, the short gentleman and he the tall lady, pulling inanely stupid faces and foaming and frothing at the audience. The mime, however, seemed to lose much in the translation, for it hardly raised a smile amongst these hardened youngsters. Making fun of a starving child does little to gain his respect.

So, there we were, well and truly stuck with our audience; we were, it seemed, captive players and the only way of becoming less obvious in this five car town was to split up and thus divide the orchestra from the balcony.

Midnight set out first, and because he was the first and because our young audience was uncertain of what was about to transpire, took with him a score or more of the bravest lads. The rest of us sat on in silence and watched through slit and shaded eyes as he went on his most enviable mission towards the schoolhouse. At the edge of the shanty (he did not approach the schoolhouse directly but went by the same back route that Riaz had used to stalk us the day before), his little band of followers hesitated, not quite brave enough yet, it seemed, to encroach upon the stucco except on school days. Instead, the little darlings evaporated noisily back into the back streets, kicking aimlessly at stones or spitting at sand and gravel with exaggerated bravado.

The main street was not quite deserted. Two policemen were at its far end, standing idly chatting outside the delegacia, but they seemed not to notice Midnight or his faithless disciples, or at least they paid them scant attention. Midnight crossed over the street and rapped on the schoolhouse door, and was admitted rather promptly, as if he had been expected.

Two minutes later, Riaz emerged from the same door, still buttoning his shirt and fixing his belt, and crossed the street to take up a position in the shop, presumably to watch whatever it was that was about to ensue. That was the cue for Don; he took with him a mere dozen of the braver remaining shanty boys, but again, as he approached the forbidden part of town, the boys lagged behind more and more and eventually lost their nerves and kicked and spat and evaporated into their back street world. Even some of the children in our original little crowd now started to spread further away from us, chucking small stones at one another or indulging in what now seemed to me to be their favourite pastime, spitting and kicking at the inert ground. Surely, I thought, there must be a soccer ball somewhere in the village! Don moved quickly and directly down the main street. The two policemen were still chatting outside the delegacia and had now been joined by a shorter, older man dressed in shabby jeans and crumpled shirt, and an even shabbier and more crumpled cowboy hat. Probably a station hand, I thought, though I could not see too clearly from that distance. Don turned straight into the shop.

"We'll give them fifteen minutes," I whispered to Harald and Domingo.

The three of us sat quietly, backs against the same scrappy tree with our hats pulled down over our eyes, hoping the rest of the flies would now get bored with their watching and take up the more exciting local pursuits of spitting and kicking at the unresponsive earth. Some of them sat underneath other scrappy trees, and others kicked, and some spat, and most withdrew to a safe, coy distance.

Fifteen minutes proved more than enough for Midnight; in less than five from being admitted to the schoolhouse, he reappeared with the good lady Josephina on his arm and a smile on his face which extended way out beyond his Ethiopian cheek bones. Evidently, whatever there had been to forgive was forgiven. The lady was dressed casually in jeans and shirt and walked with a spring and a bounce that almost made me gag with admiration for my old friend. How did he do it? He was an old lag like me but he simply must have something that I did not. Just five minutes with the girl and she looked as smitten as him. What I would have given then to follow them, to eavesdrop, to be a fly on the wall and learn the mysteries of his incredible technique, but... well, that would be getting just a little too personal for this story!

There had been no more signs of activity from the shop. Midnight and his hopeful paramour had walked away past the church and the town office, and finally past the delegacia de policia and were headed south out of town. Riaz did not follow them, nor did he emerge from the shop to watch their progress and I therefore assumed that Don was taking good care of him. Midnight, according to the plan, would eventually double back when he was sure no one else was following, and then would come the hard part. He would have to dump his lady love. I had given him half an hour to accomplish this task, and I was beginning to think I may have been a little ungenerous.

We remaining three now made our move, at first heading directly down the main street. This was simply too much for our coy and least brave remaining onlookers to bear and they deserted us without further ado. We were still a strange group, but fortunately had proved to be a particularly tedious one as well.

Harald crossed over the street and made straight for the truck which was looking rather lonely and deserted in its coat of new-blown red dust. Midnight and Josephina, I could see, were crossing the small log bridge at the southern end of the village and the three men outside the delegacia de policia had their backs to us watching the couple. Domingo and I jumped the schoolyard fence and sprinted across to the side of the schoolhouse, taking advantage of the policemen's opportune attraction to the schoolmistress' delectable rear view. The fence-jumping and sprint brought back a second flood of pain and self regret for the morning as the burning sensation in my leg re-errupted. Would I ever learn? I was not looking forward to the days ahead.

The side door to the schoolhouse was unlocked; it let in to a wash-house and in turn to the kitchen on the north side of the courtyard. The kitchen was, I thought, uncharacteristically untidy for the obviously very particular schoolmistress' personality. Coffee was sitting in cups, one on the table, another in the sink, and there was freshly cut fruit uncovered on the table. Evidence of guests?

I took a slice of pawpaw and squeezed lime juice liberally over it, then mashed it to a pulp in a small bowl. I took out my hip flask which contained seven hundred and fifty millilitres of the world's finest medicinal dark Demerara rum, aged lovingly in oaken casks for an average of at least ten years by the LBJ Rum Masters and Distillers to the Queen, and reverently tipped a good fingerful into the pawpaw. I felt a strong urge to tip a second fingerful directly down my throat, for purely medicinal purposes of course, but resisted as the throb in my leg gradually died down again.

Domingo was in front of me across the courtyard and I could already hear Millie raising her voice, and her hackles, at our intrusion. Intelligent birds these! I limped after Domingo with my bowl of chloroform substitute and thrust it into his hands.

"Give her a go at this, Domingo," I said, whilst inwardly wincing at the tragically wasteful use of XM 10 year-old rum.

Domingo tasted a fingerful of the mixture, and winced outwardly, then smiled on and said, "This should work jus' fine, Mister Tom."

Millie was cackling and chuckling, whistling piercingly, and interjecting the odd indecipherable Portuguese phrase. I stopped and stayed as still as I could in the centre of the courtyard as Domingo approached her corridor as stealthily as a bird-hunting cat. Millie quietened down, momentarily, listening for a reaction to her calls. When she heard nothing she tried again, emitting a single awful shriek, but again received no reaction. I could hear her shuffling on her perch, jangling a metal toy or bell. Domingo waited till she was as calm as she could be, then started with a series of guttural utterings and soothing chucklings, and slipped the bowl of doped pawpaw around the door jamb and, I presumed, right under her enormous brazil-nut-cracking beak.

The whole doping process was over in a flash; Millie the fruit lover evidently was unaccustomed to strong liquor and quickly succumbed. Her beak and face feathers were covered in the pawpaw mash, and she hung contentedly upside down from her perch, peering unfocussed into a large polished stainless steel bird mirror. Fortunately she was not a noisy inebriate and simply continued to hang there, cooing and chuckling at her equally inebriated image whilst Domingo and I extricated the two cases of tovex and dragged them down the hallway to the front door.

I left Domingo there and went out by the side door, crept round the side of the house and looked out into the street. Saturday morning, one would have expected at least some sort of activity, but the street through the stucco and tile quarter was eerily deserted. Not even the policemen were to be seen outside the delegacia. Harald was still bent over under the dash of the Toyota and did not even see me as I came across to him and climbed in the passenger door.

"We're ready when you are, Harald," I whispered. "Have you seen any sign of Don?"

"Neither seen nor heard, Tom," Harald replied, with a sort of hissing sound caused by speaking through a mouthful of bared wires, "but I wish I had. I'd like him to bring me Mr Riaz, then I could wring Mr Riaz' neck. The idiot's jus' rip out half the ignition bundle and I'll be damned if I know how long these new splices I've made will last. I've had to wire up all the lights to the ignition circuit, I just hope I haven't got the blasted hooter connec' up as well, else we'll be like a flamin' fire engine when we start up."

"Like the bomb squad, eh?" I asked.

Harald sucked in through his teeth, then said, "Get on with you, Tom," and sat up behind the wheel. "Give her a try?" he asked.

"Never say die," said I . "Shall I get out first?"

Harald refrained from giving me the courtesy of a further reply; the key turned, the glow plugs glowed, and the '83 Tojo 4.2 litre straight six diesel purred as sweetly as the day it was born...and the hooter remained silent and maybe the lights came on, but who cared when everything was going so well. In one minute, we had turned round in the street, loaded the tovex from the schoolmistress' front door, said our goodbyes to a slightly hung over and inverted hyacinth macaw, and left town, headed north, at a dignified and law abiding forty kilometres per hour, Harald, Domingo and I.

In a further two minutes, and at a rather less than sedate pace, we turned onto the western track, kicking up mounds of fine sand...then pushed on maybe two kilometres to a hard gravelly section where quartz had been washed down from a nearby outcropping blow or vein, and where Harald could turn around without making obvious wheel tracks. We retraced our route carefully and then manoeuvred back onto the northern track, crossed over the north fork creek and stopped two hundred metres further along in a patch of secondary bush just off to one side.

Domingo and I walked briskly back up to the creek, brushing sand across the fresh wheel tracks with branches and broad leaves as nobody had driven this way since the last rains. We met Nic and Tall Boy coming towards us, doing the same.

The ruse would be blatantly obvious to any experienced tracker, but might gain us some slight advantage if we were followed by the likes of Riaz.

I looked at my watch; it was just on half past ten and warming up nicely like the day before.

CHAPTER NINETEEN

CAFE ENAMUNA

When Don entered the coffee shop, hot on the heels of senhor Riaz. There were four other people in there:

Two town dignitaries were sitting at one of the small metal tables in the front window, gazing out into the street, drinking from tiny cups of thick strong coffee and smoking extremely pungent, pipe cleaner-thin cheroots. The men had little to say to one another. They were merely passing time, like extras in a movie, looking out into their small world, each individual wrapped up in his own reverie. When Don the Indian entered the shop, however, they at once exchanged the usual meaningful bigoted glances, and tut-tuts, but then realising he was from the other side of the border, relaxed enough to forgive him his foreigner's presumption at encroaching upon their reserved white stucco domain, and withdrew back into themselves.

Behind the disorganised shop counter was the fat shopkeeper and the diminutive shopkeeper's wife. The good wife was conducting a distinctly one-sided conversation, lecturing her husband on some domestic procedure and brandishing a lethal-looking piece of kitchen equipment in order to bring home her bone of contention as forcibly as possible. The monologue paused as Don the foreign Indian entered the shop.

Riaz was sitting at a battered table at the back of the shop with an open bottle of beer in front of him. Don asked the shopkeeper for coffee and then went over to Riaz' table, sitting directly in front of the bottle of beer thus blocking the Brazilian's view of the street. Riaz was clearly agitated but did not move away and instead gave Don the honour of an embarrassed half smile of public recognition.

The two men in the shop window shifted in their chairs so as to gain a better view of the back of the shop, then thought better of it and returned their attentions to the street where the relatively Fair-Lady-Josephina was walking on the arm of Black-As-Midnight Midnight. They exchanged more raised eyebrow glances, resumed their tut-tutting and fancy thatting, drew on their tarry cheroots and ordered more of the thick sweet coffee. For sure, they silently agreed, their morning could become quite entertaining.

Don did not speak until the shopkeeper's wife had brought him his coffee, and returned to her husband's side behind the counter. "Mister Askew says he have to talk with you senhor Riaz," said Don in a low, slow, and deliberately conspiratorial tone. "He wants we go out back, then come round to the border by the south side."

"Por que nao?... Why not he is coming here?" asked Riaz.

Don made no reply, just shrugged his shoulders and sipped from his cup.

Riaz guzzled from his beer bottle, thirstily, amber liquid spilling down his unshaven chin, and continued with his voice increasing in pitch and anxiety.

"Yesterday I say him to come here and he comes yes?...but not speaking with me. I have explosives with me here but I must speak with him. There are troubles with the policia I think. All this he cost me more money. He is the boss, yes?...With the..." Here his English deserted him, "...O barba," he said finally, pulling and rubbing at his stubbly chin.

"Thas the Englishman, yes," said Don, maintaining his slow clear diction, "but nobody is the boss. Look, he wan' to see you because our plans they have to change now. We will be going through Santa Elena now, through Venezuela side by the wes' road, an' out by the kilometre eighty-eight showin' he say."

Riaz was thoughtful, calculating the angles. "That is a big change, yes? I think perhaps this will cost more money again, senhor. Perhaps I finish my cafe da manha[16] , then we go," he said, lifting the beer bottle to his lips again.

The joke relieved some of the tension between the two men. Don had started to explain that we had wanted to meet away from the village, and that I had been looking for him, Riaz that is, yesterday, and had not been able to find him.

The one-sided conversation between the Brazilian rolling pin and the shopkeeper had resumed behind the shop counter.

"Your friend, the Negro, he comes to the school esta manha. Why not the Ingles he come also?" asked Riaz.

And Don had explained that I had been near mortally injured and could not come so far and that was why I wanted to meet him near the

---

[16] Cafe da manha is breakfast, or more literally of course, morning coffee

river.

There was another pause whilst Riaz emptied his bottle and rolled a thin paper of tobacco and considered the veracity of prospector Don's utterings.

The rolling pin was exchanged for a metallic whisking contraption, obviously an instrument of torture to the shopkeeper who busied himself now, his back turned, to his wife's continual tirade.

The two men at the window table again shifted in their seats and once more turned their attention to the interior of the shop. The door curtains rustled behind them and cabo Rodriguez came in.

Despite the fact the cabo was dressed in full uniform, he gave the impression that he was simply taking a morning coffee break from his routine duties. "Bom dia, a senhora, os senhores," he announced to the shop in general, and, "um cafe por favor," he requested of the fat and harassed shopkeeper; then he went to sit at the table next to Riaz and Don in order to play policeman games.

Rodriguez sat sideways, facing both Riaz and Don, and grinned overtly and quite disconcertingly.

"Como estao os senhores?" he said, rather formally.

Riaz panicked. Riaz always panicked whenever the law was within arm's reach. He had been known, even as a pedestrian, to panic at the sight of a traffic policeman, and right then and there the law could not have been any closer without being positively intimate. He turned on Don to save his own skin. His weasel voice squeaked in a string of Portuguese invective as he denied all knowledge of any activity that the gentleman policeman could remotely consider as suspicious or illegal. He did not know this gringo Indio who was sitting with him, in fact had never met him before in his life. Neither had he ever met the gringo Indio's mother, but he seemed able to describe her in some detail and cast considerable doubt on her good character. Fortunately for Riaz, Don could have understood little of the detail of these insults, otherwise I have every confidence he would have laid the petty little crook out flat.

Rodriguez just smiled on, and accepted his tiny cup of sweet and thick coffee from the fat shopkeeper, and pointedly ignored the obnoxious gutter rat's raving and ranting. He tried his broken English on Don, but managed only two or three sentences before he ran out of vocabulary, never mind syntax.

Riaz appeared to be glued to his chair. He could not bear to stay, but no more could he leave.

Cabo Rodriguez smiled even more broadly, enjoying his game immensely, and moved his chair over to the others' table, sitting between them. He asked after Don's health, and motioned to the shopkeeper to bring another coffee for his new friend.

Riaz squirmed and glared at the world, and would have spat but for the presence of the diminutive wife of the shopkeeper and the tools of her tirade.

Don tried a little more to exchange pleasantries with the policeman, but mainly succeeded in hiding behind his language barrier. Then he said to Riaz, "We should go now, senhor Riaz, my friends will be waiting," all the while nodding and smiling at Rodriguez.

Don stood up first, and bowed to Rodriguez; Rodriguez stood up and bowed to Don. Riaz pushed his chair back roughly and had started to stand also when the policeman, still smiling, put a large arresting hand firmly on his scrawny arm. "Senhor Riaz, you should take care," he said. "Do nothing foolish. There are people coming here, coming all the way from your old Manaus, who are very interested in you and what you have been doing. There is one man in particular, a very important man... but he is not nice and friendly like me. He is a danger to you; he will break you. Be very careful, senhor Riaz."

Riaz cringed and struggled to his feet. He made no reply to the cabo, just turned and followed Don out through the rear exit. In the doorway, he looked back, through narrowed narrow-minded and hating black eyes, at the five pairs of inquiring eyes that were turned and fixed on him, and, turning again himself, hawked and spat out into the mud of the back street.

Sixty kilometres to the south, just outside the village of Deposito and near the turn off to Maturuca, De Silva and Romero were digging their by now somewhat discoloured-again Glacier White short-base Toyota out of their second bog for the morning. Comissario Color, the danger man from Manaus, was supervising operations from a charred stump by the roadside; he had taken up smoking again in a vain attempt to repel the millions of mosquitoes and biting black flies[17] that were swarming around his tousled head. He had requisitioned, or rather, appropriated the cigarettes from De Silva and Romero. He was thoroughly miserable and getting meaner by the minute.

De Silva and Romero were past caring. They were covered in shit and blood-bloated cow ticks. They were tired, hungry and thirsty, and were plotting first degree murder as the only means they saw possible to retrieve their cigarettes.

---

[17] Kaboura, extremely persistent blood-loving minuscule and highly gregarious flying bugs that leave a tiny itching blood spot for each bite, nasty.

CHAPTER TWENTY

AYANGANNA DREAMING

By midday, it was clear that something must have gone horribly wrong.

Well it was either that or I had simply misjudged the time that Midnight and Don would need to accomplish their respective tasks. Yes, thinking about it, I could understand Midnight's dalliance in the midday sun but Don was more of a worry... what if he had not been able to dump Riaz?... Then at least, I figured, he had kept the horrid little man from following us. We had seen neither hide nor hair of anyone on either track since we had hidden ourselves away in the bush.

Midday, four degrees from the Equator, is hot any time of the year, and this was no exception. The seasonal humidity also was building up nicely.

Nicodemus was back down the track, at the fork. Harald had the Tojo hood off. He was tinkering with the wires that Riaz had so thoughtfully rearranged for us, and cursing in his uniquely hybrid Gaelic and Gujarati. Tall Boy had gone walking ahead up the track with Domingo. I sat back in the front seat and dozed fitfully, eyes closed and face coated in oil of citronella insect repellent mixing with new beads of sweat, sleep repairing the damage to my stiffening leg.

There are eleven of us in the party, twelve if you count the parrot, and he doesn't like to be left out of these things; the crew is a real mixture this time around, Sand Creek foreman, line leader and cutters, and a back up boat crew from the coast, the Buxton area; they don't exactly fight with one another but they don't get on too well either; I always seem to be in the middle, with Harald the engineer and prospector Don, keeping the peace; the Indians feel they know the river better, they're right, they do, intuitively so, but we have to share the work around and encourage the coastal people to get to know the interior lands as well; they have inherited this country from their slave fathers and must be allowed to share it, though so many of them have never ventured beyond the koker dams.

We leave the boats about ten miles up from the Chi Chi Falls; it's been unseasonably dry in recent weeks and the river above here is just too low now and too choked with tacoubas for us to get any closer; we walk in a broad arc around the clock towards the northwest face of Ayanganna Mountain.

We have been on the line three days now, fly camping, eight to ten miles a day which is not bad considering we have to cut new line the entire distance; we are all carrying full warishis, even I have seventy or eighty pounds on my scrawny back; you take the weight on your neck with the head band, brilliant invention for easing the load; it makes me wonder how the Nepalese Sherpas and the South American Indians both arrived at this same solution; could it have been independently? Mind you, the system is far from perfect, balancing can be a quite a laugh when I try to take a swing at a passing rock... at least the others seem to think it's very amusing and the parrot threatens mutiny on my shoulder; I generally manage to maintain a close-to-upright posture; everybody is packing a load, and that includes the boat crew; this grade of physical activity is a novelty for them; they bitched and grumbled like a pack of primadonnas for the first day, they were too tired to grumble on the second; today they are getting more used to it; a couple of them have never been out of Georgetown before and they are even beginning to grudgingly admire the Sand Creek crew.

The ground has been rising steadily since we left last night's campsite; we are still crossing the basic sill country which explains all this mud; red mud that clings to your boots, cakes itself to the soles of your feet and makes each step like lifting a a dead weight; we are constantly climbing over fallen tree trunks, pushing through secondary undergrowth, tangling in vines and creepers, with lead-weighted legs and overloaded necks; my legs ache with all the feeling I possess in my body; the only rest we get is when the line cutters stop to sharpen their machetes, and they seem to be able to go on forever, blades flashing through the steel-hard wood, a twelve inch soft steel blade pitted against a twelve inch hard-wood tree, three blows and the blade has won; human power tools; it has been drizzling all day and is really quite cool, not at all a tropical feel to the air; we are scrambling between huge talus boulders of sandstone and conglomerate; they are getting ever more huge with every tally as we traverse the final mile to the foot of the mountain; we pitch base camp next to a gushing red-water creek, to rest and gain strength for tomorrow's assault on the peak; the Sand Creek boys are quietly exuberant as they hack down trees for the camp frame; the Georgetown boys are really tired, it shows in the lack-lustre of their eyes, except for Tall Boy Osborne that is... he seems to have caught some of the excitement and sense of adventure; the other Georgetown boys I'll leave back in camp tomorrow; it's a pity I can't leave a huntsman as well; we eat the remains of agouti caught two day ago, with fried bake and a little rice, and drink tea and I sleep a deep and peaceful sleep, drifting into deeper dreams within my dream.

We will have to cut three miles perhaps, and climb four thousand feet; I hardly know what is ahead, my photographs are mostly cloud covered but I do know there will be at least a thousand feet of rock wall to get up and over; this northwest spur is the only route with a chance, the rest of the peak stands sheer out of the jungle with three thousand foot walls; it has never been climbed before and we don't even have ropes, rank amateurs you might say.

There are seven of us in the party; the talus boulders that were the size of houses are now more like cathedrals; we stand in awe; we climb hand over hand on lianas, the line cutters cutting a vertical line, climbing trees to scale the rock wall in front of us; it is cold and thickly misty, a land of near permanent cloud; we are enveloped in moss forest, a weird and wonderful world where spindle-thin trees are dressed in feet-thick layers of sodden, soaking, spongy moss, a frightening and fascinating world of long-forgotten fauna and fabulous flora; my hands grasp for something solid to pull myself ever upwards but all I feel is sponge wringing out its blackly organic water and I pull instinctively away, helpless; my feet reach for a solid branch to take my weight and they push through a canopy of moss into an underworld of mist and moisture, sucking and slewing and full of live and dead things, a truly primordial soup; and still the line ahead and above is cut, machetes now slashing at veils of water and the bright green and yellow tree frogs laugh at our pitiful attempt to invade their kingdom and unseen creatures scurry and slither away at our approaching vibrations; and hours later we push out of the jungle onto a gently sloping plateau at six thousand seven hundred feet, suddenly above the trees and beyond the barrier of the clinging moss forest, now knee deep in a sucking dead bog of black dolerite soil, a nutritionless wasteland where even the great natural Amazonian symbiosis has ceased to flourish, an island of undescribed and indescribable insect and arachnid, survivors all, an example placed by nature as a lesson to man not to disturb the natural order; this is to show you what will become of the entire earth through the death and destruction of old cliched mother nature; there is no more line to cut, just the wasteland to push through, to wade through to the peak of black rock...

... and we look out over the jungle from our lofty learning vantage and we survey as far as we can see, and as far as we can see from the Mazaruni Basin to Kukui and Roraima, to the headwaters of the Ireng to Kopinang and Merume is a sea of green, deep green lushness, of beauty and nature's undisturbed equilibrium; the Sand Creek boys are flushed with their victory, Don and Tall Boy stand a little apart, drinking it all in; we have, after all, conquered Guyana's very own and highest monolith, and after ten minutes of climax will leave it to grab back its own form of peace, our footprints will blend back into the black oozing soil, a very transient visit to plant a nation's flag and claim this wilderness for the future of man... Don and Tall Osborne are talking and coming over to my private island of long-past memories...

It was hot! The sun had come around and was burning on my face and the top of my head. A tangle of bright green secondary undergrowth was strangling the truck and the charred remnants of Amazonas' equilibrium. Don and Tall Boy came towards me, talking animatedly.

I climbed down from the truck, rubbing the sweat from my eyes, and nearly collapsed as my healing leg buckled up under me. "Whoa there," I said out loud, just catching my balance in time, "talk about pins and needles! Hey, did everything go okay, Don? I was worried about you."

"We should leave now Tom," Don said, then by way of further explanation, "Riaz is on his way. I gave him the slip back at the river, but Nic jus' saw him headin' this way, across to the track. We din't want to disturb you before."

I looked at my watch; it was nearly one o'clock already. The sun had left me with a cracking headache. "No sign of Midnight yet?" I asked, only half seriously.

Tall Boy and Don shook their heads.

I was overcome by a crushing sense of inertia.

"Well, we can't leave without him." I tried to be as emphatic as I could, though I knew we might have to do precisely that. It just felt rather hard to gather enough mental and physical momentum together to get going again, especially at this time of day. I would have preferred the lazy option of going back to sleep and back to my old dreams.

Harald thumped the Tojo hood back into place. He was not one for vacillation. "Why not?" he said, with considerably more emphasis than I had been able to muster, "if he keen enough on the diamon' over the Brazilian gal, then he gan follow. I ready, the truck ready, we all here ready savin' the midnight lover boy so, let's go, now."

There was no more to argue over. While I had slept, the truck had been loaded. Tall Boy had left Domingo clearing the track up ahead and Harald had had his fill of tinkering. Even if I could have thought of a counter argument, it would have done little good. Harald had the engine purring, Nic came running and jumped on the back with Don, Tall Boy manhandled me back into the front seat, and we were off.

"Senhor Riaz lookin' down the west track Mister Tom, for now." Nic shouted through the back window, "But soon he gan start lookin' down this way too."

I caved in because after all, I did not have a leg to stand on. I knew they were right. Midnight would have to look after himself, follow if he could, or perhaps just act out a diversion back at Orinduik and Enamuna. The midday-lazy magic inertia was broken and the real adventure had begun at long last.

We had perhaps fifty kilometres of track in front of us, roughly following the higher ground between the Ireng river, which marks the Brazil Guyana border, and the Rio Cotingo which flows south out of Mount Roraima. Roraima itself is the highest peak of the Pakaraima Range, and marks the triple border conjunction between Brazil, Guyana and Venezuela. The track we were following was only partly visible on my aerial photographs; I had been able to trace it just so far, and then only in disjointed sections. I guessed it would eventually bear more to the west, towards the head of the Rio Cotingo, at which time we would do better to leave the truck and walk. From that point we would then have another twenty-five kilometres to cover. I would have to navigate across the watershed border into the headwaters of the Haieka River, keeping my old friend Ayanganna on our right. If we found ourselves too far over to the west, however, we would run the danger of ending up in the Kukui system. Although there would be many good trails leading that way, that could mean a forced detour of perhaps a hundred kilometres (and more than just a few days), and we would have to pass through several villages spreading rumours faster than the pox. The most direct route was the only sensible one, straight down the Haieka and we should hit the upper Mazaruni less than ten kilometres above our goal, Chi Chi Falls. It all depended on our finding the Haieka in the first place.

The vehicle track was rough and rutted, but fortunately not too boggy, and we made good speed. Also, it was reasonably straight except for a few tortuous creek crossings, so I was able to keep a good mental survey of our route. We caught up with Domingo within the first half hour, and after that our progress slowed to the same pace as clearing the track of all the fallen trees and branches. Then it was I had the time to make sketches as we went, and to follow the route more accurately on the photos. So far so good, we were still heading directly north. At the twenty kilometre mark, however, the track turned abruptly west, following the southern bank of a deeply incised creek, and after a further two kilometres it still showed no sign of veering back the way we wanted. I thought mean thoughts; we had to stop while I searched the photos for clues. I was sure I could see the track still running northwards, at least another twenty kilometres from where I reckoned we now were, and in hindsight, I thought I could see the one we were on, heading west towards the Cotingo. There had been no signs of any obvious branch tracks, but I was sure I could not be so far out in my calculations. We turned back and sure enough, in less than five minutes, found the other track leading back down the opposite bank of the creek.

The only problem we faced then was how to get the truck across the creek. There had originally been a rough bridge, one of only a very few on these types of road, but in this instance quite essential as the creek had cut a channel in the rocks at least ten metres deep and the creek banks were no less than vertical. There was now very little remaining of the bridge, save for two half rotten tree trunks still spanning the gap. The supporting timbers were riddled with termites and had been partly washed away into the bargain. Worse yet, there were very few substantial trees left growing along the creek which we could fell, and there were equally few places where the creek banks were level enough to construct a new makeshift bridge, except right at the old site.

Not to be daunted, however, Domingo, Nic and Don wasted no time. They hacked what spindly trees they could find, and lashed them together with bush rope. The rest of us emptied everything we could out of the Tojo and carried it over across the old rotting tacoubas. There was little we could make in the way of new supports, we simply weighed down each side of our rickety bridge with timbers and our load from the truck. We did not dare risk running the engine, the vibrations would have shaken the flimsy structure to pieces without a doubt; instead we winched the Tojo across, by hand, inch by excruciating inch, hardly daring to breathe. Harald fixed up an amazing system of pulleys and shackles that would have made a Clydeside stevedore weep with pride if only he could have seen it, so that the winch practically took the full weight of the front of the Tojo, that is, the bit holding the straight six 4.2 litre diesel. Even so, the bridge bowed under the weight of the truck like a geriatric with overstretched elastic suspenders. But we made it, and I could now at least feel confident that nobody would be able to follow us any further! The final pull had dislodged the remnants of the ant-eaten supports.

Nobody had crossed that bridge for years. So much was obvious once we were on the opposite side. One hundred metres back down the deep cut creek, the track turned again and ran straight as a die, northwards. We were on the right track again, but we had been reduced to a snail's pace, and a not too racy snail at that. There were old charred branches and fallen trees everywhere, tangled in a mass of new growth. It looked as though the jungle had been razed just for the sheer hell of it for there was certainly little sign of any subsequent planting or stock running and there had never been much in the way of passing traffic. It would have been quicker to walk at times. Nic, Domingo, Tall Boy and Don ran ahead in relays, hacking at the encroaching vegetation, heaving aside offending low level and mostly invisible sump-breaking obstructions, and I limped and hopped around as best I could. The Tojo pushed through seemingly solid walls of saplings and small trees which then whipped back up behind us as though nothing had happened, closing the track once more.

The track was also getting considerably muddier as we now found ourselves in more shaly country. Muddier and muddier... in fact it quickly degenerated into a pair of parallel wheel ruts, each one half a metre deep. And then the afternoon rains were back with us once again which did nothing to alleviate matters. Despite all of this, however, Harald kept the Tojo in a remarkable state of balance with one pair of wheels on the verge and the other pair on the baranka, heel and toe on brake and gas, not daring to stop lest he sank into the thixotropic goo... and still Nic, Domingo, Don and Tall Boy had to push on ahead clearing the way with Harald and I forever breathing down their necks.

The rhythm worked well until at last it broke down after a little over twelve kilometres. Looking back on it, something simply had to give and it was amazing to think we got as far as we did. The six of us sat at the side of the track, wet and plastered with mud, with the rain pissing down all around us and mostly on top of us, in various states of exhaustion and manic depression, and gazed, loathing, at the Tojo nose up and bum embedded in one of the deepest and most thixotropically gooshious axle-clinging mud bogs I have ever come across. The engine had to be left running so I, who till then had expended the least amount of physical energy, gallantly offered to cut a drainage ditch from the back of the truck to clear the exhaust of water. My offer was characteristically selfish, of course, as we were still about twenty kilometres from the border, and I hardly fancied giving up my ride yet to start the backpacking. My friends, equally courteous and mindful of my most considerate behaviour, allowed me to indulge myself. It seemed an age before Harald brewed up cups of steaming tea[18], and Tall Boy relieved me of my shovel.

By the time we extricated ourselves from the mud, it was already within an hour of dusk but I did not want to stop. I figured that while the track was still running straight as a die, navigation would simply be a matter of following the odometer and estimating a bit of slack for the wheel spin. I am not at all sure I would do the same again, for the next three hours were simply nightmarish. The hour before nightfall is the hour of the mosquito, the black fly, of just about every pesky swamp-dwelling bug; then dusk eventually scratched into a moonless night and for two hours more we cut, we winched, we slid, in the beam of the Tojo's headlights, and we crashed into hardwood stumps in the shadows. We crossed creeks, poling in the darkness ahead for gravel, the headlights themselves submerged and lighting up an eerie glow under the redwater. It rained buckets. Tall Boy and Don got some rest when they could, under the tarp in the back of the truck, but Domingo and his little brother Nicodemus carried on the whole distance, indefatigable.

At forty-eight kilometres, the track swung abruptly west. Harald did not need to ask, he switched off the engine. The camp frame was up in less than ten minutes, and the tarpaulin slung, and then the rain had had enough and decided to stop for the time being. We shivered in the cold night air, dried off as best we could and ate cold rice and tinned fish because no one could bother with cooking or drying wood for a good fire. Still caked in mud and goodness knows what else, I had climbed into my sleeping bag and was swinging, wondering just what the hell I was doing there and nursing a mug of tea, when a new sound entered my conscious being. We all sat up, as one, listening as the night noises were swept away in the wake of this new sound, the sound of a high-revving engine, and the fire flies resolved themselves into a pair of headlights shimmering towards us along the track.

---

[18] Harald had a marvellous knack of being able to produce cups of tea under the most unfavourable and trying of conditions

CHAPTER TWENTY-ONE

TAILS

Don and Riaz had left the shop by the back way.

Cabo Rodriguez, whose short term mission in life that Saturday morning was to tail Riaz, left by the front, thence to sneak around to the back like the true professional that he was. In leaving by that route, however, he observed that the Matte Jungle Green Toyota truck which had been parked there, unmoving, since he and Santos had arrived in town...and it was the same Matte Jungle Green truck that Riaz and the Guyanese had registered back in Boa Vista of course... had gone. There was not a sign of it except... there were tracks in the street, and it was quite clear that it had left the village going north. Riaz and his little Indian contact, on the other hand, were heading south, in the steps of the schoolmistress and her boyfriend.

Cabo Rodriguez found himself in something of a dilemma. In true professional style he consulted his official rule book, and dashed off to find his immediate superior officer, Santos.

Cabo Santos had his feet up at the delegacia, drinking coffee and smoking something that looked like a dog-chewed licorice bootlace. He had been left in charge of monitoring radio transmissions and had just heard a comedy hour programme listening to his colleagues from Deposito describing some city cops as they passed through. Since he did not wish this idyllic state to end prematurely, and as his immediate superior officer, comissario Juarez had left to follow the schoolmistress and her boyfriend, he therefore suggested that since Riaz was heading in the same direction, Rodriguez could follow on as well. Perhaps they all might even catch up with the comissario and he could then inform him of the matter of the missing Toyota. Rule numero uno in Santos' little blue book read 'how to pass the puck' (Canadian hockey joke!).

Cabo Rodriguez took up cabo Santos' suggestion. He did wonder, albeit briefly, if it could be construed as an order, then dashed off again after Riaz and Don who by that time had turned away from the southern road and were making directly for the Orinduik Falls. It took Rodriguez quite some precious moments, however, before he realised that his quarry had taken this new route. He cut out across the fields after them, and promptly lost the trail... he found it again, he followed footprints... and the footprints ended. Bloody hell, why had he stopped to ask Santos? He thought he heard voices over to his right, but perhaps it was just the wind. He thought he smelled cigarette smoke, but that was carried off on the wind as well, before he could be sure.

Meanwhile, Don and Riaz had arrived at the river and were waiting for Tom. Perhaps, Don suggested to Riaz, perhaps Tom had mistaken the exact meeting place... he should go and look for him. Better yet, both of them should look... you go down the river, and I'll go up.

Midnight and Josephina had left the village by the south track. Midnight for one, had passed the watching policemen outside the delegacia in a state of almost total oblivion, blissful heart-pumping, body-throbbing oblivion. He never thought to look back.

Comissario Juarez, like the true professional that he was, followed behind the couple, directly but discreetly. He was not the type for sniffing out spoor if he could keep his prey in sight.

Midnight soon had his arm round Josephina's waist, to provide support and balance over the rutted surface, and as the road turned further away from the village, his hand somehow involuntarily slipped further down. At least it did until it was arrested and replaced. All dialogue between the two was strictly confined to a bilingual body language, despite the fact that the schoolmistress' grasp of the English language was not all that bad. The weather was very ordinary. Then Josephina in turn put her arm around Midnight, and one thing led to another, and still largely without any open communication, the two somehow found themselves leaning against a burned out stump, locked in a quite passionate if slightly uncomfortable and not at all well balanced embrace, and streaked with charcoal.

Juarez, at that juncture, decided that he should make his presence known before the clinch became so intimate as to represent a potential embarrassment to all parties. "Bom dia irma minha," he said. He approached the couple without breaking his stride, smiling directly at the schoolmistress. "Como estas tu esta manha." He half sighed and breathed deeply from the country air, his arms outstretched to

Josephina. "Is it not so beautiful a day?"

Midnight was stumped, positively slack-jawed. The weather, as far as he was concerned was very ordinary. I just said so!

Josephina on the other hand, showed practically no surprise. She merely smiled back, a little bemusedly perhaps, and purred in reply.

"It certainly is, little brother," for comissario Antonio Juarez was none other than the senhorita schoolmistress' step-brother. The 'little' was more a reference to physical stature than to relative diminutivity. "I did not think to see you again so soon."

Now the step- brother and sister embraced, and poor Midnight had to content himself with a man-to-man handshake as the introductions were more formally made.

"Maurice, please meet my brother, comissario of police from Boa Vista; Toni, this is my friend I was telling you about, from Orinduik, Mr Tyler."

Midnight swallowed, hard, and tried to appear as relaxed as only he or a ventriloquist's dummy would know how.

Juarez took charge of the situation. He immediately grasped the initiative and demanded in predictably Big Brother Latin fashion to know whether senhor Tyler's intentions towards his Little Sister were entirely honourable or otherwise.

Midnight could not exactly fit the outwardly shabby little Brazilian into any of his preconceived notions of a Brazilian chief of police. He felt most uncomfortable and unsure about him, however, and the fact that he fancied his sister like crazy was just too huge a complication. He started to spin Juarez the same story that he had told Josephina, that he and a group of friends were planning to reclimb Mount Ayanganna, twenty years after having first conquered it. The policeman, however, appeared to have his mind on other things and the three walked on in silence a little way.

"So why do you need the specialized plastic explosives, Mr Tyler?" the comissario then asked. "Perhaps it is to make the handholds on the rock face, Mr Tyler?"

The little triangle paused again in the middle of the track. Midnight felt as though he had been ducked two innings in a row. He looked as uncomfortable as any man would staring at an indefinite stretch in a Brazilian country jail. After some moments, however, he managed to collect his wits somewhat and spluttered out that the explosives were needed just in case he and his friends came across a new gold mine on the way. He felt far from convincing and Juarez was equally far from convinced.

It was now the schoolmistress' turn to look perplexed.

"What explosives are these?" she asked, looking at both men, and then as her love-struck neural responses got into gear and the realisation hit her, her voice became querulous and shocked. "Surely not the boxes you store in my house, Maurice, surely not those?"

"Yes, Josie, those boxes... but they are absolutely..." Maurice began.

"How could you? Explosives! And that horrible oily little man Riaz, what of him?" Josephina demanded.

Juarez interceded on Midnight's behalf, his voice soothing and gentle, "Don't worry, irma minha, what Mr Tyler says is quite true. The explosives are completely harmless as they are. You were never in any danger. And as for senhor Riaz, he is a small time crook who I know well, in my professional capacity you understand, and he is of no danger to any of us either." He then glowered at Midnight and added tersely, "I think perhaps we should go back to the village and have a talk about these things. I think I shall require some more explanations."

The three walked slowly back to Enamuna, Josephina in the middle. Midnight provided the requisite explanations. As far as he could judge, he had to be truthful now and hope that Juarez would not feel it incumbent on him to inform his Guyanese counterparts. This did not prevent him from being as economical as possible with his truth, however. He told the policeman about some caves at Chi Chi and why we wanted to help the prospectors there without involving the local government agent. His story was embellished somewhat with hints of corruption and suchlike unsavoury factors, things that would never happen in a civilised country like Brazil, of course.

Josephina proved to be the key. Once Boa Vista's incorruptible Napoleon had been convinced that our little caper did not involve his territory, other than for basic access, his sister Josephina found herself considering the whole affair more in the light of a Boys' Own adventure. Better yet, she was now determined to join in. She slipped her hand delightedly back through her boyfriend's arm.

Napoleon, ever the policeman, did raise the thorny matter that Riaz had stolen the explosives from the Brazilian Army, and that was not exactly something that he could turn a blind eye to, and that it was therefore his beholden duty to recover same explosives, and thereby it might be considered appropriate for him to bring the perpetrators of this heinous, one might almost say treasonable crime to book.

Midnight pleaded in his turn that he and his friends had paid Riaz for the tovex, in all honesty and good faith, and paid him handsomely, and had not believed for one moment that the explosives had been stolen... surely, not from the army!... how embarrassing!... and that he was really most shocked at this revelation and he was absolutely positive his friends would be equally horrified also, and it went without saying that none of us would ever have had a hand in this dreadful business had we but known...

Yet we had received stolen property, Juarez insisted on pointing out this unsavoury piece of unavoidable truth, and, involving explosives as it did, well, such could quite easily carry a two to five year stretch! But of course, where one's family might be involved, and if it was all in innocence, well, there might be some things for which he could develop selective myopia... though there would still be other people he would need to convince.

The three arrived back at the village. Midnight saw at once that our Toyota was gone; Juarez evidently did not for he made no remark and suggested instead that they all take some lunch and discuss the situation further. Cabo Santos brought him a news bulletin, in rapid fire Portuguese, on the state of the road south and the progress of a certain party of MUTS. And there was a message from cabo Rodriguez.

Riaz had searched down the river for the elusive Tom, albeit rather half heartedly. He sat on the flat jasper rock pavement overlooking the falls and smoked and dreamed of how much more money he could make from this deal. The rush of the river and the noise of the falls lulled him into drowsiness and it must have been a full half hour before the realisation slowly started to dawn that the Indio had dumped him.

He headed straight back to the village; the Toyota was nowhere to be seen. He sneaked back into the schoolhouse. The macaw was swinging upside down from its perch and muttering to itself. It looked decidedly the worse for wear, hah, almost as though nursing a cachaça hangover he thought, and laughed to himself, stupid animal. And then he noticed the crates under the perch had gone.

Riaz was a shallow and a lazy man, but this was really too much for him to handle. His normal phlegmatic, apathetic approach to life sublimated like a tovex sausage on a barbecue. He would have murdered Millie there and then, she being the nearest living thing to him, wrung her blasted scrawny neck, except that his overwhelming cowardice had not evaporated along with his phlegm. Instead, he spat at her - it seemed the only thing he could think of to do - and left the schoolhouse in disgust. Santa Elena, the Indio had said, by the west road. Riaz set off in pursuit.

By mid-afternoon, comissario Juarez had got himself organised. There was nothing to be gained from further detaining his sister's boyfriend. Color and his troopers, Santos had reported, were still some thirty kilometres away and in no danger of arriving early. Rodriguez had re-established himself on Riaz' tail, back and forth along the west road like a horizontal yo-yo on a piece of knicker elastic, and was getting precisely nowhere. Riaz was hopeless and helpless. The Guyanese had long since taken off and should be way up along the north track by this time. Let Mr Tyler follow on if he could, and cast the net deeper, perhaps, to catch the bigger fish.

Josephina was also well organised. She would have made an avid follower of Boys' Own. She had thrown, sorry, deftly placed rations for a week into the back of her VW tin can, together with a back pack, boots and a change or two, a traveller's bird cage and a rather cantankerous and sickly-looking Millie, who she never went anywhere without! She let Midnight drive, but kept close on the front bench seat just in case he needed any help with his gear stick.

Juarez followed, once more discretely, in his Toyota. Rodriguez was busy with Riaz, and Santos was fully briefed to keep a close eye on Color and his goons when or if, they ever arrived.

Midnight kept the VW travelling well along the track north. Where a heavy four wheel drive Toyota could become bogged in soft ground, the little VW would simply glide and slide through. Juarez, by degrees, lagged behind and found himself sometimes fighting to keep his truck moving in the right direction, especially when the afternoon rains started.

Just past where the track turned sharp west at the twenty kilometre mark, Midnight, in his rear view mirror, saw the mess we had earlier made at the old bridge, slid to a halt and turned the car. He was without doubt quite mad to try it, but after the most cursory of inspections, (he had no burning desire to leave the schoolmistress' side, get out and as a consequence be rained upon) he pointed the VW at the bridge and planted his foot to the floor. Josephina, who was given no time to take stock, stayed close and screeched as the little car became airborne, and grabbed for anything she could get a hold of. The macaw screeched in unison. Midnight may well have screeched also, judging from what was available for Josephina to make a grab at.

Midnight surveyed his handiwork from the north bank. Nothing, he figured, could possibly follow them across.

Juarez reached the remains of the old bridge about ten minutes later. He did consider giving it a try, but only very fleetingly. He switched off his engine and listened to the faint but characteristic sound of the aircooled VW engine as it faded into the rain and cut bush.

CHAPTER TWENTY-TWO

REVENGE OF THE CABOS

Pedro Romero and Perez De Silva had refrained from committing murder on comissario Color not because they had thought better of it, nor because they had carefully weighed all the consequences, nor even because they had forgiven the rotten bastard, but simply because they did not have to hand what they considered sufficiently artistic means. A slug from a standard issue handgun was much too good for this comissario, oh yes, what they really would have liked was a bazooka, or an anti-tank rocket, or a missile... or... oh, what the heck!

They never seemed to make much progress. It had taken practically the whole day to travel only twenty or thirty kilometres. Both men were dog tired, shaggy dog tired and Color did nothing but gripe at them and criticise...'lock the hubs', 'why do you have the hubs locked?', 'put your foot down', 'don't drive so fast, or you'll lose control'. The journey was becoming a nightmare. They had had no food since lunch the day before. Color had smoked the last of their cigarettes. They were covered from head to toe, and from headlamp to tail pipe in red Amazonian shit and... and... shit, man, were they pissed off!

And there was the bastard Lord High And Mighty Comissario Alfredo Bloody Color, with hardly a mud splash on his fancy black jack boots and just the merest shade of overnight beard growth on his otherwise shiny, stupid bloody baby-face.

No, death was far and away too good a fate for this one.

Pedro Romero and Perez De Silva had become close on this trip. They were working like old partners and each knew what the other was thinking. The question was not whether, but rather...how, when, where, precisely that is. It was not going to be easy, as Color was careful to keep his distance from the dirt and the work. As evidence just look at his pristine bloody, shiny boots. Perez grimaced as he straightened his back from digging under the rear axle transmission case. Pedro, sitting up to his waist in the red muddy water gingerly let the truck back down off the kangaroo jack, to settle on all the bits of wood and twig he had scrounged and pushed under the rear wheels, only to see the wood sink yet further under the weight of the truck and to see the rear axle once more settle and seize.

"Shit, we'll have to unload, Perez, bazookas, rockets, missiles, the bloody lot he's carrying in here!"

Romero and De Silva unloaded the six heavy-as-osmium munitions crates that only Color knew what was contained therein, and for which only Color held the keys, and dragged them over to a tiny promontory of drier ground in the middle of the mud track, some ten metres behind the bogged truck.

"Boom, da-da-da-da-, bkshshcrckkk," mouthed Perez, shooting red-eyed daggers at his loathsome chief who was impatiently drumming his fingers on his leather boots.

"How are we going to get the stupid gorilla over here?" Pedro whispered through clenched teeth. "God, I wish I had a smoke..."

"Brilliant!" Perez could have kissed his mate if he had been a little cleaner. "There's an empty pack in the front."

"Timing has to be right," said Pedro.

"It'll be all in the timing," agreed Perez.

Pedro went back to his work on the jack, this time removing some of the wood. Perez dug a trench to fill a large hole immediately in front of the rear wheels with water, then stuffed the wood for traction under the front. The two cabos seemed to have been re-energised. The scene was set, the engine started, front wheels left deliberately unlocked this time. Perez then made a show of taking a cigarette from the empty pack, thought better of it and placed the pack in the dry on top of one of the munitions crates. The bait was set. Pedro revved the engine and let the rear wheels spin harmlessly in the air whilst Perez returned to the front, cursing him loudly, and lewdly, for being such a dumb bastard.

"Stop that, Pedro, you dumb bastard!" he shouted. "I have to clear the front first."

The stage was set.

Color swallowed the bait and, as nonchalantly as he could, sidled over to the cigarette pack.

Perez flicked the front hub locks on, Pedro gunned the motor, the front wheels gripped and pulled, and the truck jumped forward off the jack. The rear wheels flew through a cubic metre of Amazonian red-shit mud and spun like Lancashire jennies in the Industrial Revolution.

Color was caught and plastered better than any bazooka could have done. At a specific gravity of 1.6 tonnes per cubic metre, 1.6 tonnes, precisely, of red-shit Amazonian mud landed full on him, knocking him back over the crates. The shit had literally knocked the shit out of him.

Not that Perez or Pedro could even have guessed what happened, of course, they were just so jubilant at having devised this new system for extricating Glacier White SWB Toyotas from boggy patches.

"God, I really wish I had a smoke now," whispered Pedro through teeth clenched so tightly that he nearly bit off his tongue. But it stopped him from laughing out loud.

The MUTS finally pulled up at the Enamuna delegacia around dusk. Santos was looking out of the window. He had been expecting them for the last hour or more. Pedro and Perez practically fell out into the street in a state of total exhaustion, like a pair of dead but ecstatically happy drunks. Perez managed to open the front passenger door for his lord and master, who then proceeded to ooze himself out with about as much theatrical dignity as a member of the Black and White Minstrel Show.

By the sheerest of coincidences, just as Juarez arrived back at the north fork creek crossing, cabo Rodriguez was approaching the identical spot from along the west track, on foot. Riaz had finally given up all hope of tracking the Englishmen westwards and was returning, for the third or fourth time to Enamuna, in a state of abject dejection. Rodriguez had stuck with the knicker elastic for the whole afternoon and been rewarded with nothing more than a too long, very hot and latterly uncomfortably wet walk and a pair of excruciatingly blistered feet; he climbed in with Juarez.

"Riaz is just up ahead, making for home I've no doubt. May have bolted when he heard the truck though," Rodriguez said; then asked, "What are you doing back here?"

Juarez shrugged. He also was tired. "There's a bridge down. Tyler made it across in the VW but there wasn't a hope in hell of me getting this beast over. Maybe we could rebuild it and give them a surprise for when they come back, eh? By the way, Santos just radioed to say Color's made it to town, at last."

"Great! Let's get him and his offsiders to cover our friend Riaz then, suggested Rodriguez. "He seems pretty convinced for some reason that the Guyanese have gone off towards Santa Elena, though I can't think why. We've been up and down this road at least three times today."

"Hmm, it's not a bad idea," agreed his boss, "the vaqueros over there are all fairly harmless, hah, brainless too, so he should get on quite well with them. There's not much harm he can do and we know for certain he won't find the Englishmen, or the explosives anywhere in that direction. Perhaps, though, we should pick up our senhor Riaz now so he'll be nice and fresh for comissario Color in the morning?"

Riaz had heard the approaching truck, but at that stage of the day, frankly he did not give a damn. He even thought about waving it down for a lift. When it stopped opposite him, he gaped through the opened blue-rimmed window but did not recognise the cabo from the coffee shop.

"You want a lift?"

"You goin' to the village?"

"Sure, climb in the back," said the driver.

They stopped outside the Enamuna delegacia de policia.

The afternoon rains paused but only briefly through the evening hours, then returned with regathered and fearsome strength to deluge the whole region overnight.

Riaz spent that night hungry, cold and sleepless in a damp bare holding cell. De Silva and Romero did at least feed, but then they passed their night scratching and sleepless in an equally cold and dismal guard house. Comissario Color, MUTS, slept through the night in the guest house adjoining the delegacia, blissfully dreaming on feather pillows of revenge against the world in general, and against his awful subordinates in particular. Juarez, Santos and Rodriguez sat up into the wee small hours listening to the thunder of the storm on the rooftops, discussing nothing in particular, and later dreamt in hammocks of nothing less serious than girls.

Color was handed his present, gift-wrapped, in the interview room before breakfast, and by a masterly piece of interrogative skill and a pair of antique silver plated Royal Inquisition thumb screws, the ace detective quickly persuaded senhor Riaz to turn State Informer.

The morning had turned out to be dismal. There had been unusual hail during the night storm. There must have been at least a hundred and fifty millimetres of precipitation, and still the dark clouds hung over the village, lowering and steadily dumping their load. Wetness permeated into the very fabric of the village, through the stucco walls of the buildings, and even penetrated through to the souls of people. The main street through the village was flooded with a mess of red mud and flowing sand, and at either end of the village, the road disappeared completely from view beneath bilharzia-snail-infested waters. All of this, however, was not yet enough to dissuade our hero, comissario (MUTS) Color, from carrying through his national duty, and in little more time than it takes to swallow a softly boiled egg and for the worst of the rain to pass over, he and his team (would they had been horses, thought Pedro and Perez) were driving out of town. They drove past soaked shanty packing cases, collapsing cardboard boxes and their miserable inhabitants, with Riaz shackled to the back, their precise destination unknown but somewhere in the general direction of Santa Elena, via the west road, purpose; to foil revolution and save the nation.

PART THREE

CHAPTER TWENTY-THREE

THE SCHOOLMISTRESS BARES HER SOLES

The place where we had pitched our tarpaulin was, by good fortune rather than design, on a gently sloping gravelly apron to an area of higher ground. In front of us, to the north, was a plateau of hardcap laterite, the margin of which was outlined for several hundred metres to east and west by an irregular sinuous breakaway between five and ten metres high.

In the morning, we found ourselves camped on a sandy shore, beneath the hardcap cliff and within a stone's throw of a vast watery expanse of inundated secondary bush and failed ranchland which stretched away as far as one could see to the south. That was as far as our good fortune had carried us, though. The campsite had no natural means of shelter, and overnight the breakaway had funnelled a wind through the tarp, and the wind had brought with it a fine, penetrating, spray. Now mostly everything under the tarpaulin was drenched on its windward side, and was unpleasantly damp and clinging on its lee. It was still raining, but easing now.

I shivered as I climbed out of my sticky warm bed and clambered up to the top of the break to find the lee of a tree for my early morning constitutional. My leg felt pretty well healed already thanks to the marvels of either the pawpaw skin or the sulphur powder, or just possibly it might have been both. Anyway, it took my weight okay.

The Green Toyota and the orange VW Tin Can were parked down below, wheel deep in flowing water in what the night before had been the middle of the track. From my vantage, I caught a flash of movement from inside the misted VW, and, having finished with my pressing engagement, whistled a cat call as brightly as I could. The driver's door opened and Midnight appeared. He rubbed his eyes, yawned expansively, stretched languorously and smiling up at me, winked sexily, and stepped out into the knee-deep ephemeral creek which was gurgling under the car.

"Shoots man, Tom," Midnight sucked in his breath and chewed on his words, "you could have said, man."

"Sorry old friend, couldn't resist. Anyway, I didn't want to come too close to you and your galinha in case I saw what the butler saw! Coffee's cooking." My morning was looking distinctly brighter already.

Midnight turned back to the inside of the car and shook something, and schoolmistress' head appeared in the window, puckering up for a morning kiss. Before my friend could oblige her, however, she saw me, and the rain, and the flood, and her pretty mouth turned down just a tinch at the corners. Was it me, I wondered, or the scenery?

When Midnight and Josephina had turned up the previous night, we had all been feeling pretty miserable and tired. Introductions, therefore had been kept to a cursory minimum Hi, how-are-ya? sort of style. We had just a single gas lamp to cast an unflattering circle of harsh light. We had drunk more tea together; they had eaten cold sardines and day-old yeast bake. Then the rain had returned with a vengeance and they had dashed off to sleep cosy and snug in the warmth of the VW. I hoped they had brushed their teeth after the sardines.

Josephina studied me as she and Midnight picked their way up the slope to the camp. She carried her enormous Purple Macaw on a stick held out in front of her.

"I have met you somewhere before, I'm sure of it," she said to me. "Where?" Her voice was distinctly unfriendly, terse, curt, abrupt, all of those.

"The other day, in the village?" I smiled, trying the laid back approach, "you were protecting your brood from a couple of down-and-outs, remember? Nicodemus, over there, he was the other one." Nic was busying himself, sorting and packing, looking very mature and sensible and not at all freakish.

The girl looked on edge, still searching her memory.

"No," she said, emphatically, "somewhere else, another time. Met you or seen you."

"Oh, I should have been so lucky, but I don't think so!" I laughed, now trying to make an outright joke of it though inwardly feeling extremely awkward, "but really, we did not have wicked designs on any of your children," I continued. "You know, Nic was really quite upset by what you called him." I changed the subject. "Anyway, it's time for breakfast," I enthused. People would forget all their nagging doubts on a full stomach. "Harald's been cooking up a storm here, porridge and coffee."

We ate; I avoided looking directly at Josephina. The rain continued to ease some more; I avoided speaking with Josephina more than simple courtesy demanded, but whenever I did move or speak, I felt she was studying me still, trying to place where she had come across me before.

With the porridge consumed, Midnight and I got down to discussing options. The bridge at Saveretik creek was down, and would prevent anyone from following us for at least two days, especially after all the rain we had just had. However, it also cut off our easiest way out. I therefore wanted Harald to try and take the truck out along the track which was now heading west, figuring it would go as far as the Rio Cotingo, then turn south again and join the grid over towards Santa Elena. Problem was, Harald could not go by himself. There would be far too much clearing and it simply was not safe in the circumstances, and therefore that meant Tall Boy should go with him. Now, if Tall Boy was with Harald, that cut down our packing power, which meant it would really be best if Midnight and Miss Josephina, not to mention Millie, also stayed back. Perhaps, they should head straight back to Enamuna, a bit of a walk from the Saveretik bridge it was true, but by no means any more strenuous than walking from where we were now to the Chi Chi.

Midnight seemed all in favour of option number one for there was not a lot of choice, and he went over to tell Josephina. After all, the logic was two-by-four-greenheart-solid. The schoolmistress joined our little private chinwag and promptly demolished my unassailable position with a single explicit verbal blow.

"We go with you," she said, holding Midnight's hand and squeezing tightly, "we both want to go, don't we Maurice darling? We will all share the loads."

"But what about your children?" I tried. "Who will run the school? Surely you can't declare a professional development day at such short notice!"

"That is all arranged, Thomas," - with a lisping thee - "my brother the comissario will send for a teacher from Deposito."

"Hah! Nobody will get through in this," I said holding my arms outstretched to the flood around us.

"He will send by aeroplane, if necessary... and if that is not possible, then one day will make little difference in Enamuna. Nobody there is sitting for his graduation finals! They will not miss me for a few days."

I felt more than a little sad for the schoolmistress galinha who could so easily desert her brood. They held no love for her; they would not miss her. I tried again.

"What about snakes? Pit vipers, anaconda?" "What about mosquitoes and malaria?" "What about your boots?" "What about the bloody papagaia?"

Still Josephina insisted, squeezing ever more tightly on darling Maurice's hand. The traitor readily concurred; sure, they should come along, Josie could easily carry her own load and then some; no, she had no fear of snakes or any other creepy-crawlies for that matter, she was born a country girl, look, she had had a gutful of chloroquine only yesterday; and the boots, well they spoke volumes for themselves poised as they were, level with darling Maurice's shins.

"Well you'll have to leave the blasted parrot cage. Let the lazy bugger walk," I said. It was a last dignified, if feeble, thrust and parry of the vanquished.

The clouds were lifting at last, faint rays of warmth penetrating to the earth. The creek in the track had lived out its ephemeral existence and drained away to the vast swamp in the south. Nic, Domingo and Don were horsing around outside the camp, impatient to get going. Harald had cleared away the porridge pots and packed and was now tinkering with the Tojo. Tall Boy was the only other left in the camp. He sat swinging in his hammock, back turned to us, listening and waiting patiently for someone to come to a decision, any decision.

Midnight took me outside.

"Why don't you want her along, Tom?" he asked.

"Oh, I don't know!" I answered exasperatedly, "Responsibility, I guess... and she might slow us down... and don't forget she is the comissario's little sister!" I found, at last, what sounded to me like a reasonable reason. "She may be able to look after you but the rest of us'll be nabbed the minute we step back this way! The tovex was stolen, remember? From the bloody Brazilian army!"

"Yes, I know, I know. But I'm sure she's okay. If anyone has influence with that Juarez character, it's her. All she wants is a big adventure!"

"And you can't give her one yourself?... Shame on you!" I quipped. I was mad, and obviously could not have been thinking too carefully. I regretted my statement as soon as I had shut my stupid mouth.

Midnight gaped and cleared his throat as if...but made no comment and ambled back to Josephina.

I had run out of negatives and now could do nothing other than endorse option number two...but I still did not like the way the schoolmistress seemed to be continually examining me.

Mind you, option number two was not that different from number one. Josephina's VW was left where it was parked with a message on the dash - 'GONE SHRIMPING'. Harald and Tall Boy threw their bags into the Tojo, and would drive off into the western sunset as soon as the track had dried out sufficiently, but probably not before the next morning. For the rest of the day, they planned to walk, reconnoitre and clear the way as far as they could. The rest of us pulled down the tarp, split up the loads, and I studied the clouds on my air photos, and shot a compass bearing due north.

Don, Domingo and Nic all had full warishi loads, forty five to fifty kilos (a hundred to a hundred and ten pounds), piled high over their heads. Midnight, Josephina and I shared out the rest, probably twenty five kilos apiece, maybe a little more. I congratulated myself on having had the foresight to do a bit of training before coming out, but even with that, my back protestethed. Josephina's self-satisfied smile sagged somewhat with her back, and she needed help to stand up, but there is one thing I will grant her, she sure was determined. Midnight grimaced but did the manly thing and transferred a couple more cans of gourmet baked beans and parrot honey stick seed-treats to his own back pack. Millie travelled on the top of Josephina's warishi; perhaps she thought the bird might add a bit of lift.

Domingo, despite his forty-odd years, did not let us down for a single second. The fact that he had over a hundred pounds on his neck could do nothing to slow him down, and the fact there was no trail had absolutely no bearing on his ability to keep an almost perfect compass bearing. North of the track, the bush had only been cleared for a few hundred metres, and within minutes we were swallowed up in the primary forest. The canopy had protected the floor of the jungle from the excesses of nature, and we were no longer slipping and sliding on sun-hardened rain-wet clay, rather, we were squelching through ankle deep mud and rotting leaves and other forest litter and tripping over the ubiquitous Amazonian root. Domingo did not cut a line as such; he snipped at fine saplings and broad leaves to mark the way only, and we pushed through behind him, one by one, in Indian file.

We walked for two hours, as straight as we could. The ground rose gently but steadily all the way. There were no creeks to cross. There were no outstanding features to recognise. We were clothed in the Amazonian rain forest. We did not talk because we needed all our breath for those more immediate tasks. Domingo stayed in the lead, his younger brother Nic walked behind him also snipping and snapping at the passing vegetation, then myself. I kept Nic in sight all the time that I could raise my head to look ahead. My neck ached with its load. My back creaked and my thighs groaned. I counted my footsteps, each double step, and tried to measure my pace so that I could keep a tally of how far we had come. Seventy double paces to a hundred metres in this type of country, I figured, balancing on greenheart roots, with this load. I wrapped myself in my own very personal cocoon in order to keep count, then I would hear sweet Josie and Maurice darling tramping along behind me, and Millie Macaw scrawking. How could I forget the bloody parrot! From time to time they would lag behind and I, like the impeccably well brought up old gentleman that I was, would slow down in my turn... but only for so long as I could keep Nicodemus in sight. It would be too easy to wander off the line with it being marked as sparsely as it was. As soon as Nic started to pull uncomfortably ahead of me, I would gear down and leave Josie and Maurice and Millie in the capable hands of Don who was bringing up the rear.

In those two hours, we made six kilometres without stopping, and only then did we sit down to rest.

Nicodemus went off in search of water. For all the rain, there was no water to drink. There were no creeks here, just muddy red puddles with films of unknown substances floating on the surface. We sat on leaves placed over logs, to keep our bums dry. Josephina and Midnight sat close and I kept my distance; I felt awkward and turned inward; I could not stand those constantly inquiring eyes. I made a pretence of looking at the clouds on my photos some more, and was naturally none the wiser for it. We were on the watershed that divides Brazil from Guyana, that much was certain, but it was very featureless here, not at all well defined. There may have been an old surveyed line from the colonial days, but of course nothing of it remained now. I was tempted to cut more to the west, to try to hit a creek where at least we could camp, but we were also near the Haieka - Kukui watershed, and I knew that in this no man's land, I would run the danger of getting sidetracked into the Kukui system. We had crossed a couple of fairly worn trails already but had not yet succumbed to the temptation to take the easy route they offered, for they would have led us inexorably out of our way, towards Kokadai or Kamarang. We had to keep going straight for another four kilometres at least, then maybe we could follow the country more and find the head of the Haieka.

Nic came back then with a three metre length of thick root vine, cut it into sections and handed them around, and we all drank our fill. We ate more bake and strips of dried steer, local pemmican.

I got stiffly to my feet. "About thirty more tallies north like this, Domingo, then we should be able to follow the country down. Let's go McDuff."

Thirty more tallies was easy to say. After only twenty, I for one would have been more than happy to give up. Domingo and his brother, however, being the indefatigable type, were in no mood to stop. The country now was heading steadily down, but was no longer the smooth surface of the laterite pediment. Small creeks crossed our path, mostly flowing northwest or west and as we walked on, they got progressively broader and wetter and then more deeply incised. We would slide down one bank, then have to search to find a place where we could scrabble our way up the other side, hands gripping on nothing more solid than crumbling shaly soil. I started to lose track of the distance we were covering and I gave up trying to keep any sense of direction, relying entirely on Domingo somewhere up there ahead. The physical, and mental, effort needed to cross each creek seemed like traversing a whole tally by itself. Midnight and his schoolmistress seemed to lag ever further behind me and I finally gave up trying to keep everybody in touch.

We found ourselves in one such creek again, but this time could not find an easy way to climb up the far bank. We waded, sometimes up to waist deep, and slipped on smooth green mossy boulders, searching the overhanging banks in vain for an old collapsed tree root system or something similar to give us a handhold. Downstream, however, the banks just overhung more and more, and crumbled more as the creek dug deeper into its bed. We were, in effect, trapped and were forced to follow the flow of the water. Go with the flow. So long as we kept north of west, I thought. I would hate to have to retrace our steps now.

Then, within the space of a few hundred metres, the country suddenly fell away in front of us. The creek was no longer incised and instead was flowing shallowly over a hard quartz-pebble conglomerate pavement. The forest opened up and we stood on the brink of a series of sandstone and conglomerate cliffs over which the creek fell in a single spectacular hundred and some metre drop. We could see for miles, right across to the Mazaruni itself, and there was not a single doubt now that we had hit the head of the Haieka spot on.

We regrouped. The Indians sat on the lip of the falls and smoked, in reverence. I thought of stopping there and then. What a view it would have been to wake up to, but it was still relatively early and the sight of the Mazaruni Basin in the hazy distance seemed to give me my second wind. Keep up the momentum, I thought. Everybody else seemed willing enough; sweet Josie looked a little on the pained side perhaps, and young Millie Macaw looked a little unsteady on her claws, but there was no outright dissension.

It took another hour, however, to find our way around the side of the falls and into the creek gorge below. We had to cut along the top of the cliff scarp for nearly a kilometre before finding a route down and even so, we needed to use bush rope to lower our loaded warishis down more than thirty metres of V. Diff. sheer rock face. The bloody noisy parrot got herself a free lift of course. Then, when we eventually did get to the creek again, the bottom of the gorge was choked with huge talus boulders which in many ways were more difficult to negotiate than the cliffs. We clambered over them on hastily constructed bush ladders and spindly hand-made bridges, squeezed past them, practically dug our way underneath them. We were all absolutely shaggy dog tired again but this time, there was no choice, there was simply nowhere that we could find to stop.

By late in the afternoon, we had managed perhaps another two kilometres down the gorge, then, as suddenly as they began, the rapids ended and the valley broadened out and we literally dropped at the first dry and level site we came to, and set up camp for the night.

The total distance we had covered for the day could have been no more than twelve kilometres.

With no Harald in camp, the cooking fell to me. Much as I admired everyone else in the party, culinary expertise did not feature conspicuously in their respective achievement lists. Don went fishing; Domingo and Nic went off in search of something, I was not sure what exactly; Midnight collected dry wood and got a blaze going, then the schoolmistress called him over, scratched his head, whispered what I presumed were sweet nothings in his ear, and sent him packing; as he passed by me he said, rather brusquely I thought, that he was going off to check on what it was the boys were up to.

As soon as Midnight had left, the schoolmistress eased off her boots and sat sideways in her hammock, scratching her bloody parrot behind its neck, then turned her attention to me.

"I saw your photograph in the paper from Manaus," she announced quietly. "I knew I had seen your face before, but I still cannot remember the connection. And your name, it is not familiar either." She rolled up the legs of her jeans exposing a pair of finely shaped calves, and very slowly pulled off her sodden socks.

"Well, perhaps it was my doppelganger, senhorita," I replied, "for I only have the one name and I don't believe I am quite that famous in Brazil!" I wanted to change the subject. For inspiration, I found myself staring open-mouthed at her legs. "Your feet! What's wrong with your feet? They look terrible."

Josephina's feet were red and swollen to double their normal size - so much for the fancy boots, I thought. I went over to her to examine them more closely and she pulled back in pain when I touched her heel; the skin was absolutely raw and weeping.

"We have to fix this, and quickly, before it gets infected. Why didn't you tell Maurice, or say anything?" I scolded her like a small child. Now that I had the initiative, I was not going to be cowed by this lady.

"There was nowhere to stop." Her eyes suddenly brimmed with tears. Her antagonism seemed to have melted clean away.

"Stubborn!" I scowled and tried to look hard. It was hard.

The macaw chattered to itself, "Ola Millie, ola," and swinging upside down from the scale lines, stretched out its head for another scratch, and the schoolmistress obliged.

I got busy. I boiled water, soaked towels and wrapped her feet and let the steam soothe them, then crouched down next to her and got to work on the boots. There was the sound of hacking and chopping in the distance, next the crash of a tree. The brothers Nic and Domingo were having fun. And Don had not caught the entrée yet. Dinner would have to wait for the time being. I soaked the back of her boots with coconut oil, rubbing it into the leather as hard and long as I could.

"I'm so sorry to give you this trouble, Thomas," she cooed, "I did not imagine it would be like this." She paused, waiting in vain for a response whilst my heart thumped, then continued more interrogatively, "How far must we travel tomorrow? I do not think Maurice will understand, do you?"

"I guess we are about half way, but..." I hesitated, "I don't think you'll be walking very far like this. Maurice will have to know."

I left the boots soaking up more of my precious supply of cooking oil and found the first aid kit. I lifted up her feet, very gently, and unwound the still warm towels. I would dearly have liked to hold on to those feet, explore a little perhaps, linger on a leg, consort with a calf, dally with a digit...but corny or not, she was my best friend's girl and I just could not do it. Instead I puffed sulphur powder liberally over those feet, holding them up by the toes, and dressed them, and told their owner to stay put.

Don came back right then with a brace of lukanani[19] and there was nothing more I could do than get the rice steaming! Josephina pulled those legs right back into her hammock and closed her eyes. Millie Macaw was balanced on the hammock scale lines, one foot retracted, feathers ruffled, one eye open, and as fast asleep as a bird could ever be, bloody freeloader!

The chopping sounds started up again, and as the dusk finally gathered in its skirts the local howler troop revved up in competition. I turned to Don who was up to his elbows in viscera lukananiensis.

"What are the others doing, Don? Do you know?" I asked.

"They went lookin' for woodskin. Creek's good an' clear below so it soun' like they have one."

---

[19] Lukanani are fruit-eating fish, very sweet, naturally.

"You mean they're making one... now?" It seemed incredible.

"Thas what it soun' like, Tom. I tell them earlier the schoolmistress foot hurtin' so I tink thas what they doin'. All that bangin' jus' then should be them wedgin' the skin off the tree. I tekin' a light to them jus' now."

It was amazing; I had not really noticed that she was hurting. It was now equally obvious that Midnight had not had a single clue either, but Don had seen her suffering. He had told the others, and there they were, building a woodskin canoe in the dead of night for this schoolmistress. At this rate, we might very well make it to the Chi Chi by tomorrow.

"Well you'd better take the lamp to them now, Don, before it gets too dark," I said, and Don left, and I fanned up the fire for some light, wrapped the fish in foil with a knob of butter, a shake of black pepper and the merest soupçon of turmeric, and threw it into a separate pile of hot coals...and started steaming the rice.

I stepped away from the fire and shivered in the evening air; it was starting to get distinctly chilly again. I went back to the schoolmistress, taking a blanket to cover her. She was lying still in the shadows of the flickering firelight, and I gently lifted her feet again, out over the edge of her hammock to stop the rawness from rubbing. She sat up abruptly and, focussing her beautiful bottomless cow-brown eyes on mine, planted a South American smackeroo on my cheek and practically pulled me into the hammock with her.

"I hope we can be friends, Thomas."

It sounded so trite, but then I put that down to the translation. If she had whispered into my ear in Portuguese, I think there would have been no stopping me. Instead, I shuddered and stuttered like a love-struck teenager. I put out my hands to stop myself from overbalancing and somehow, accidentally I am sure, collided with her upper torso fleshy bits. Oh bliss!

"Sure... I'm sorry... I..." I spluttered as I removed a last clinging hand.

She grabbed at my full-length, facial fur with both hands and planted a second and, did I imagine it, more enduring kiss right on the lips, then, school over, I found myself summarily dismissed back to cooking the tucker. Roast Jello should have been on the menu specials. I was on fire...

The lukanani was about midway between well done and charred beyond recognition by the time everybody came back to camp. The schoolmistress and I had eaten our fill already of course, while it was still succulent, and with lots of sauce. I saw the lamp light in the bush and hastily rearranged the sleeping schoolmistress' legs in her hammock, then retired to my own.

"So, howd' it go men?" I asked when all were assembled, putting on water for tea to wash down the food.

Midnight bent over sweet Josie and woke up the macaw which handed back a disgruntled chatter.

Don, as spokesman, updated me on the status of the impromptu construction. The skin was cut and had been successfully wedged off the tree, and the bush rope on the prow and aft was drawn and soaking and would tighten overnight. She was a fifteen footer, and with an efficient baler would carry two, possibly three, and a fair load. Nic picked his teeth with lukanani bones and Domingo smiled a satisfied, job-well-done sort of smile through teeth which would be difficult to pick with a whale bone. I asked Don if anybody had told Midnight about the schoolmistress' feet but nobody had done so and I decided to leave it till the morning, if at all. Midnight came back to join the rest of us by the fire and to pick at more fish bones and push rice around his plate. He had lost his appetite it seemed; he was quiet, subdued even.

The camp slept early but I was too tired to sleep, as well as more than a little confused. I felt lonely, in need of company. I sat on a bush chair by the lamp at the kitchen end of the tarp and leant back against a rough wooden kitchen bench. The camp 'furniture' consisted of rough hewn lengths of sapling strapped together with bush rope, and would be described in House and Garden as functional rather than excruciatingly comfy. Next, I found a tin mug and located my hip flask, and set about improving both the level of my physical comfort and my hyperactivated mental state by means of that age-old, tried and tested method known as alcohol-induced anaesthesia. You might have tried a good soporific book, by a well known author, a Stake mystery, or a Tasek horror... or a bland Keats anthology perhaps. I might have tried that last one myself, but I had not yet finished writing it.

I took a hefty slug from my mug, but somehow I was still

confused...but then at least I had lots of company. The night was dark, thick with clouds, and the solitary light in the tarp shone out to confound and confuse the very jungle itself. Every free surface within the radius of the light seemed coated with a resting layer of a particular species of large, pale fawn coloured beetle. Those individuals which could not find a place to rest flew, and buzzed and beetled annoyingly around my head and at random around the light, and some got swatted and stunned, and some got eaten. Three or four metres into the jungle, at the edge of the circle of light, lurked the voracious long-tongued hunter frogs... or toads, or whatever the hell they were...attracted not by the light but by this gourmet beetle supper feast which providence seemed to be handing to them on the finest china plate. The frogs... or toads... were green, brown, green and brown, shades of green, large and small, striped, spotted and streaked. They were of many different species I was sure (unlike the beetles who appeared all one happy family), but by the time I had finished with them they had two new things in common. Without exception, for I pride myself on being very fair when dividing out the goodies, they were fat and paralytic drunk.

You could say it was a waste of XM rum, but that night I treated it more as an important scientific experiment in live beetle pickling, and I am sure the frogs fully appreciated my generosity in tossing my experimental failures to them, lurking as they were at the edge of my light.

I slept with the croaking and clacking of crickets, cicadas, drunken tree frogs, survivor beetles, whatever they were, and woke with the screaming howlers again. It was barely light and the morning mist hung heavily over the still creek. A dozen different kinds of bird woke and sang a dozen songs, calling for a dozen different mates. The Amazon exults in its sheer diversity.

The schoolmistress was shaking me. "Wake up, Thomas." She was excited, intensely agitated.

I scrambled out of my bag, bleary-eyed and shivering in the cold morning air, and hastily dragged on a pair of trousers to preserve the general decorum, and only then did I start to focus in the half-light. She was barely dressed at all, in slinky and acutely revealing pyjamas, not at all the average sight to greet a bloke first thing in the morning in the middle of an Amazonian jungle adventure, but rather nice for all that. Everyone else was asleep, except Midnight...at least, everyone else was there and could be accounted for, except Midnight. His hammock hung still and thin and distinctly empty.

"Millie has gone, Thomas, wake up!" she continued.

"Midnight," I said, "where's Midnig... I mean Maurice?" 'What an anticlimax' is what I thought.

"Not Maurice, Thomas, I don't want Maurice! Millie's gone. I can't find her anywhere," repeated the schoolmistress. She was dancing about, wearing only thongs and, I suddenly realised, seemed to be totally oblivious to the state of her feet.

"Yes, I understand." It was my turn to repeat myself. "Where's Maurice? Is he looking for the parrot?"

"I don't know!" She sounded exasperated now. She stood very close to me and fixed me with those deep, brown, ruminating eyes of hers which could be so quick to fill with tears. She held on to my arm and squeezed, and her voice broke, "I don't care. He can look after himself. I just woke and Millie is not there! We have to find her. I don't know where she can go. I..." The eyes brimmed over.

I must have subconsciously held on to her. My mind had swung empathically back to her feet and I was on the point of making some deep and meaningful statement of commiseration like 'how are the feet this morning' when Midnight appeared with comic timing at the far end of the tarp. He was dressed only in his bucta[20], obviously fresh from a foray on nature. Judging by the far from comic expression on his face, however, I guessed he did not fully appreciate how his girlfriend and I came to be in such a compromising clinch.

Attack has always been one of the best means of defence, and came to me then like second nature. I snapped myself apart from the senhorita's grasp. "Where've you been?" I shouted accusingly. "We have an emergency here. Millie is missing. We have a case of a missing very large bloody papagaia," I said. "While you're out there having fun spraying ants and other ground dwelling life, we have a serious situation developing here."

The cold and misty dawn hour in the jungle, after a very trying and tiring day before, and with the looming prospect of an equally trying and tiring day ahead, is not the best of times for clear thinking or level headed response to an emergency situation such as we faced

---

[20] Bucta, spelling uncertain, is Guyanese for under shorts, swimming trunks, togs, dobies.

right then. My little histrionic outburst, however, had woken the entire camp and further explanations were not required; their schoolmistress was in distress and the whole contingent mobilised immediately, though in variously comic states of disarray.

The schoolmistress' hammock had been slung at the far end of the tarp behind a washing line of malodorous towels, placed for the sake of privacy. We now, all five as a man, pushed our disarrayed way through the limply hanging towels to gain access to the lady's boudoir in order to investigate the scene of the mysterious disappearence. Despite the time of day and the still poor light, all five of us agreed in short order that the lady had been quite accurate in her presentation of the facts; Millie Macaw was nowhere to be seen. Furthermore, it did not take more than a few milliseconds before our combined massive brain power and innate (did I hear inane?) ability at detection and observation provided us with the answer. Well, I must confess, the precedent had been set; the exact same thing had happened to me and my Amazonian parrot twenty years earlier.

When pet birds of the order Psittaciformes wake up in the morning, in a strange place with a rumbling tummy and 'spring is in the air', they have an almost overwhelming tendency to go climbing up towards the light. In the Amazonian jungle, the early morning light is about two hundred feet, or seventy metres, above the ground, that is, on top of the forest canopy which is where you would normally expect to find a wild Psittaciformes. Millie Macaw (the pet) had found a handy liana hanging next to the end of the tarp, and had used it that morning to gain access to the light and the great outside world, and was now somewhere rather high above our heads, no doubt feasting on an amazing variety of sweet things and seeds that she never before imagined, in her wildest of dreams, could have existed. One thing was sure and that was that she was most unlikely to come back voluntarily for her customary neck scratch and her dried-up, half-chewed, gourmet honey-seed tidbit treats packed in San Jose, Ca (i.e. the US of A), at least, not in a hurry.

We all shusshh-ed, and listened intently. There were sounds of birds all around us, the greenheart bird, the cow bird, the lesser maam and the greater maam, the little brown bird, the yellow bird up high in the banyan tree, but nothing that was distinctly Millie, nor anything that was even remotely parrot-like. She was obviously engrossed in breakfast and could not care less about the heartache and pain she was causing to some of us humans here down under.

There was very little that I could do. There was no sense in petitioning the schoolmistress, nor any of her devoted fans, it was obvious we were not going to leave camp without Millie, and at the time it seemed very unlikely we would ever leave there. Breakfast was consumed in silence and with eyes cast down to the ground but with minds intent on that other world of free air above the jungle roof.

"Nic, do you remember the time Waru[21] went missing out by Merume?" I asked. "We felled half the trees in the jungle that morning but we got him back."

Nic did remember..."Which tree to start on this time, Mister Tom?" he laughed, and went to fetch his machete and file...

Twenty years before, we had been traversing from Imbaimadai to Merume Mountain on the very edge of the Pakaraimas. I had been given an Amazon white-eye parrot chick the previous field season. He was bald when I got him, probably only three or four weeks old, taken from his nest and as ugly as sin. I had to hand feed him to keep him alive, wild berries and suchlike, but he must have suffered some deficiency for though he grew fat and healthy, he could never quite keep pace in the plumage department. He was never a handsome bird. After a few months, however, the then almost demi-feathered Waru and I were firmly bonded, true blue mates as an antipodean would describe it. We travelled literally everywhere together, he and I sharing one seat and one seat belt on the Caribou from Timehri to Kurupung and Imbaimadai. I carried him fly-camping. He would balance on a stick or on my shoulder for twenty or thirty kilometres a day. I had a pet kibahee[22] for a whole day and night till the jealous parrot chased it away. He shared my vodka and lime, and how much closer than that could two creatures get? So, when I woke one morning on Merume Mountain and Waru was gone, I was devastated. I searched, I called, but there was neither sight nor sound of him. The crew searched in vain also; he was, after all, one of the team.

There was no way I could delay my whole crew for the sake of a solitary parrot, but somehow breakfast was consumed very slowly, and striking the tarp met with all sorts of time-consuming and

[21] Waru is Wapishiana for parrot - I've always given original names to my pets.

[22] Kibahee is a small ring-tailed mammal, about the size of a huge squirrel or a possum, climbs around trees a bit like a monkey.

unexpected problems. By nine or ten o'clock as I remember, when we should have been two hours on the line already but in fact were just finishing with loading the warishis, Nic had recognised Waru's call from somewhere directly overhead in the canopy. The parrot was sighted, comfortably ensconced on a branch sixty or seventy metres up, looking down at us and calling. 'Look at me how clever I am!' It was patently clear that he was not going to descend voluntarily, at least not in the short term. The tree was unclimbable, except by a flaming parrot of course... okay, maybe by a British Columbia lumberjack... anyway, as far as we were concerned, the only remedy for the whole situation was to fell the tree. One small problem, however, stood in the way. Fell his tree, and it would tilt over maybe ten or fifteen degrees at the most, then hang up on another. Remedy, fell the other one first. Same problem, but with two trees down, his might topple thirty degrees.

You should have got the picture by now: eventually, in order to rescue one measly parrot, we, and I say 'we' with some reservation as I had neither the strength nor the skill to help, except in a consultative role, felled five trees in a row. I will never forget the sight of my Waru hanging on for grim death to that tree as the domino pack fell and his double six on the top came crashing seventy metres to the ground. He never let go, did not even attempt to fly, just screeched pitifully, and when it was all over sat and shook and chattered like a semi-bald nervous wreck. Incredibly, the trauma had no long term effects, neither detrimental nor particularly beneficial. His plumage growth neither slowed nor was it stimulated; his intake of vodka and lime neither increased nor moderated, he continued to drink all he was offered.

Imagine: five jungle queens exchanged for one semi-ugly, if personable, parrot. One hundred and fifty tonnes of prime wood pulping tabloid newsprint producing chlorine consuming timber and atmosphere rejuvenator in exchange for half a pound of scrawny bird flesh!

So it was that morning in the Haieka with Millie Macaw...except this time around only three trees were felled instead of the five at Merume in nineteen seventy-three. The reason for this had nothing to do with any recently developed environmental conscience, nothing so laudable, but rather because of our more favourable location next to a broad creek. Nicodemus had initiated the process by toppling a massive tree on the creek bank and Domingo was the first to see the flash of purple hyacinth that had been so rudely disturbed in her breakfast treats and had therefore come to investigate what was happening to her New World. There was another minor variation; where Waru had emitted a single tortured screech as he came crashing down, Millie let off a stream of highly colourful Portuguese invective that I am sure she could never have learned from the senhorita schoolteacher...more like your average Grade Ninerspeak I should have said.

So, Millie and her mistress were happily reunited. Heroes Nic and Domingo went off to put the finishing touches to the woodskin and to shape a couple of paddles and the rest of us struck camp. While Josephina clucked over her parrot, however, my friend Midnight brooded and, for the time being, I decided to refrain from disabusing him of his imagined accusations or, for that matter, myself of my own imagined pleasures that might have been. There remained a strained, Other World kind of silence between us.

After the excitement of the early morning, the remainder of our journey that day was something of an anticlimax, albeit still a strenuous one. The good ship Woodskin was launched and loaded with a minimum of pomp, and absolutely no champagne whatsoever, and the schoolmistress, her bird and upward of two hundred kilogrammes of high explosive and other gear. It sat low in the water, with at most two centimetres of freeboard. Josephina sat cross-legged and stock still, as she had been directed in the midships, with a large bailing pan poised and ready for action.

Domingo took up his paddle and pushed off. Josephina, forgetting her instructions, turned to smile and wave, just very slightly turned and...the boat listed and dipped and swamped briefly and... well, if it had been... any other captain in charge, would surely have sunk like a golden boulder to the bottom of the Haieka. Domingo, however, righted it in time, the schoolmistress learnt her lesson and set to bailing instead of waving, and the purple macaw flapped delightedly in the bath in the bottom of the boat.

The rest of us set off walking again. I for one, stiff-legged from the day before, keeping within shouting distance of the creek where possible, but occasionally cutting corners across the meandering river loops. The going was more or less flat, but the jungle was thick and tangled with undergrowth and ribbed with roots and we had to slash and cut and push and stumble our way through. Every few hundred metres there was another tributary creek to cross, or an abandoned loop of the main creek to negotiate, and as the morning passed the side creeks became progressively broader and deeper and, I convinced myself, they got wetter too. At first we could wade across but later were forced to swim. By midday we found we had to keep right on the levee bank of the Haieka itself as the surrounding country had turned into an endless and seemingly bottomless swamp, and that meant we had to walk out all of the river's loops and twists and turns which more than doubled the distance for the day.

Domingo and Nic took shift and shift - about in the woodskin. I am sure that was no less tiring because the river was mostly sluggish and tree-logged and had to be paddled all the way, but at least we were moving along. Without the woodskin to carry our gear and with the schoolmistress' delicate feet, we would not have got very far at all that day.

We reached the mouth of the Haieka on the Mazaruni at about four o'clock in the afternoon.

The woodskin had beaten the rest of us by a good half hour, and we met Josephina sitting on the bank beside a rough hewn landing, dangling her bare feet in the still water, to tempt any passing pirae I supposed. Domingo had stacked all the boxes and the tarp in the clearing and had gone on ahead down the river towards Chi Chi in search of a more robust river boat for the rest of our journey. Millie was sitting on top of one of the crates of tovex, unsupervised, chewing at the locking band.

Midnight, who had hardly spoken a civil word to me all day, sat with a protective arm around his girl.

Nic and Don threw up the tarp onto an old camp frame and I wandered off to get away from the jumping dog fleas and to be by myself. I had to renew my acquaintance with this great river that I had neither seen nor touched in so many years and with which I had once been so intimate. Despite an overwhelming physical tiredness... my legs felt like osmium, my back and shoulders ached... I wandered far in my solitude and eventually found myself at the end of a long broad stretch of gently swirling, sucking red water, and looking back some twenty kilometres away to the southeast, I met Mount Ayanganna standing green and alone and naked, for one fleeting moment bared of her skirts of mist and hanging clouds, but inviolate and timeless in all her glory. I sat there and breathed steadily and deeply, and chucked pebbles aimlessly into the water, and listened to the slap of the ripples, and reflected, and might have still been there now had it not been for a rumbling in the belly and the bloody evening mosquito shift.

Nic fished two pirae out of the mouth of the Haieka not far from the landing where the schoolmistress had bared her soles, and fried them up for tea. I drew the line at using my culinary skills on those pisciverous predators. They are bony beyond belief and taste, well, just too fishy for words. I ate rice with shreds of the dried and salted beef and slept early, listening to faint rhythmic river-slapping sounds drowning a whispered conversation from behind the line of towels.

CHAPTER TWENTY-FOUR

DEAD DOG FALLS

Domingo came back with King Harry soon after midnight. My dreams were interrupted by the high-pitched, prestissimo puttatata, puttatata of a twenty horse Evinrude, on the back of a twenty foot bateau. Torch lights competed with the gibbous moon and flashed briefly through the camp, and I turned my aching body over in my bag in my hammock and promptly fell back to my dreams till morning.

Tuesday morning, I woke feeling great; stiff and great. The sun was up but a cooling breeze blew down the Mazaruni like a giant evaporative air conditioner. For once I felt totally relaxed, mentally that is. There was no rush to strike camp, no rush to get anywhere in particular, no itinerary at all in fact. There were no jungle trees to destroy as Nic had thoughtfully cleared every liana for fifty metres around the campsite. Best of all everybody else seemed in a great mood too, not least Mr Midnight Tyler and the senhorita. The static was clearing between us.

King Harry was introduced to the team over breakfast. He was a round man, short but bulbously muscular from the neck down, with a weathered and shining round face and a bald head, like a shiny black cannon ball. He would have been about half-a-century old. He wore bucta and a vest of many holes... he could have chosen at least half a dozen ports through which to put his arms.

He was your standard grade A pork-knocker; he probably took up the bush life before he even turned twenty and had been working ever since towards the big shout[23]. He would have made a dozen or so shouts in his time, but none quite good enough yet to raise him out of his indebtedness to the shopkeeper or the dredge owner or the claim staker. If he made two thousand dollars[24] in a day, he was doing very well; one half he would spend on rice and the other half on a drink. If he made ten thousand dollars, which he could from time to time, he would buy some relaxation in one of the six Imbaimadai brothels.

---

[23] A find, the richer the find, the bigger the shout.

[24] One Guyana dollar is equivalent to about half a P, or just under one cent US.

When he made his fortune, only then would he get back to Georgetown to look after the children and the children's mother. But he had not been farther than Imbaimadai for as long as he cared to remember, and the only children he could remember fathering were right there on the landing.

He wore his wealth in his mouth, his teeth glittering with gold. His liquid assets, his sum total capital equipment consisted of a batel, a set of sieves, a spade and a plastic bailing bucket, and a half share in the Evinrude.

Music serenaded us from King Harry's canary yellow waterproof guaranteed to twenty metres ghetto blaster. It crossed my mind to wonder whether the music would not perhaps improve at twenty metres depth, but what the reception lacked in sound quality was more than compensated for by the programme. Breakfast Calypso Shots with the latest and greatest East Albuoystown band, General Ganja and the Evaders. Midnight was translating some of the finer verses for his school teacher, but he hesitated with:

lizard run up teacher leg.
and he dried up completely with:

Ding a ling a ling,
School call in,
Teacher panty tie wid a string,
String pop,
Panty drop,
Ding a ling a ling,
School over.

After our musical breakfast, I took King Harry over to one side.

"Well Harry, man, is everything we hear about this place as good as they say? We got all the gear we need." I was nodding over at the strapped crates. "We could take a look later eh?"

"Is a big shout, Sir," said Harry, "is a big big shout, Tom Sir, das for sure. We pull a tree carat las mont, crystal white gem, wort two hunned fifty thousand dollar, Sir."

"Not bad! How much you get for it though, Harry?" I asked.

"Pay off de bill is all," said Harry, "an' maybe sport up a lil... but nex time he gan all be differen'. Nex' time he gan mek pleenty money."

"So how much carat you pull out up to now? How many stones?"

"Thirty carat, maybe, gems, and fifty tousand dollar industrial. I keep back a some a dem gems fo show y'all."

King Harry fished inside his bucta, for a pocket, and brought out a tiny cloth wrap containing half a dozen stones which between them could not have weighed more than four or five carats. There were four whites, one pale green and one small, but exceptionally pretty flattened and curved deep bottle-green stone. There were no pink stones, but that did not surprise me. It was hardly what I would have described as a major major new diamond find! But it would do just fine for me.

"You'd best keep these to yourself for now, King Harry," I said. "We'll take all you've got but for now let's keep them separate, till we get in the caves. Don't show them around here even." I lowered my voice to a conspiratorial level. "Midnight's got himself a girlfriend, sister of a Brazilian police chief."

King Harry winked back and stuffed the diamonds back into his bucta, and we rejoined the others to help drop the tarp.

It took just about an hour to get down to the head of the Chi Chi rapids. The Mazaruni River through this section is nothing if not absolutely spectacular. It flows over conglomerates and smooth pavements of sandstone, diving inexorably down while the valley sides close in tighter and tighter. It is a little like riding down a funnel, the river captures you, swirls and churns and rushes you towards the falls, and suddenly it seems there is no way out, no turning back. The river banks are walls of solid rock. The thunder of the falls is constantly building and the red river ahead disappears into an orange foam below a mist of white spray, and beyond, all you can see are the dark deep green jungled walls of the gorge in the distance.

King Harry leaned over the motor and Nic in the bow leaned on his paddle and we came to a tiny landing on the south bank by the edge of a swirling whirlpool full of river flotsam. We had arrived at the Chi Chi.

King Harry's camp was right there at the top of the falls portage. That way, he said, he had fewer inquisitive visitors. Captain Beast ran a more than less irregular service on the river, from the bottom of the portage down to Imbaimadai, and would sometimes walk the three kilometres through the gorge to have a talk or pass on news. Captain Beast was about the only outside contact the Chi Chi pork-knockers had, except for the yellow ghetto blaster and the Guyana Broadcasting Service.

The camp was basic. There was no tarp, just a stick thatch type of roof on a lean-to frame, and some salvaged sheets of galvanised iron propped up as rain breaks and around a fireplace.

King Harry's partner was a redskin man, or dougla, of indeterminate and rapidly increasing age. His first, or it could have been his second, name was Clayton yet he was known throughout the region as the Grey Shadow, and the Shadow was to the King what the yin is to the yang, or the yang to the yin. He was tall and slender. His face was thin, his cheek bones prominent, his hair was thin and wiry and very grey, and his skin was blotched and flaky. His schoolfriends would have nicknamed him the matchstick or perhaps skeleton, but his adult peers were kinder. They named him primarily for his inner being.

There was a dog as well, a mangy cream-haired no-name hound. As we arrived, the dog had heard the motor and he and his Grey Shadow had come back from the diggings to greet us. The dog stood snarling and eyed the macaw with a mixture of outright suspicion and hunger lust, then, duty done, turned away to sit on its haunches and scratch fleas.

The Shadow came behind the dog and shook a round of hands and shouted hellos to all...

"Hello, Shadow."

"Pleased to meet you, Shadow."

"How are ya, Shadow."

... and then went to sit by the smoking fire and put on a pot of water for tea. Shadow was as deaf as a post.

Midnight and I went off with the King and the Grey Shadow, and the cream dog, to the diggings later that afternoon. The two men had been working in a dried-up creek channel which had cut through an earlier semi-indurated bed of river gravel, probably laid down by a former channel of the Mazaruni itself, I surmised. They had dug a metre or more underneath an overhanging cliff of loose soil and sand, about two metres high. There were no supporting timbers. They had diverted a second smaller creek and made themselves a small pond for washing the gravel, all by laborious spade, bucket and hand. The whole set up looked about as stable as quick-sand in an earthquake zone. Shadow jumped in the pool and started hacking away at the overhang with his spade, oblivious to the potential danger.

"Where are the caves?" whispered Midnight to me.

"Where are the caves, King Harry?" I asked.

"Ah, you wan' fo see de caves, Sir?" said King Harry. "We ain't worry wid dem fo some time now. Shadow, he nearly tek he life dere, Sir. Is a bad place dat. You all don want go dere, Sir. Dis place right dere here, Sir, dis de big shout now. "

"Is it this same creek," I persisted, "where the caves are?"

"Yas, up a ways on de lef bank."

"We could go see them now?"

"Yas, mebbe half a mile."

"Let's go then."

"Hmm, de water, she's mebbe a lil high right now."

"What water? The creek's dry."

"Not dere. She flowin' all right dere."

"Well let's go see."

"Is could be a lil danger dere, Sir."

"We just want to take a look, that's all. There's no danger in that is there?"

"Shadow, he near drown dere Sir, he don like to go back."

"Then Shadow need not come." I tried to control a growing exasperation. "You needn't come either if you don't want to, just tell us where to go."

King Harry stayed quiet for a while, then sighed theatrically and turned his back on us. I did not want to push him any further but he was becoming more than just a little frustrating. He gazed over at his mate, who had paused momentarily from his digging. It was as though he was telepathically communicating his thoughts. Perhaps he really was doing just that; the Shadow gave a grey shrug as if to say 'go ahead, tell them'.

"I tink you jus go up dis bank a ways, till you get to de cross," the King's tone was distinctly sorrowful now, "is where de other dog dead." He nodded back at Shadow. "Me an he an de dog, we gan stan back here an do some sievin' an wait for y'all."

I trudged along behind Midnight up the dry creek bed. It was the first time we had been alonc since the business with the schoolteacher and her dumb bird.

"Yesterday," I began, "me and Josephina, I hope you didn't misconstrue...

"Ah, forget it, Tom!" He interrupted my carefully thought out speech. "I did wonder at the time, knowing you and all, but Josie explained everything to me last night." He turned back and grinned innocently over his shoulder. "As if my old friend would ever cheat on me... perish the thought!"

"It was her feet, you see. You know me and feet!" I joked.

"Well yes, I suppose I do, you must be allowed one vice in this life, but next time maybe just stick to that one vice. It looked to me like you were moving in on the ankles at least."

"Oh, what a heel I must a bin, man. I should really resolve to control those disgusting fetishes of mine."

We reached a place where the creek bed had become ponded up against a bar of lateritised gravel and started to edge our way around the side of a deep black pool. The intriguing thing about it was that the water was not at all stagnant; it must have still been flowing but there was no obvious outflow.

I changed the subject. "Look at the water!" I said. "I wonder how it gets out of here, Midnight."

"Certainly not into the creek below," said Midnight.

The flow was sluggish. I threw a few leaves onto the surface of the pool and they seemed at first to just float around at random. I was on the point of putting it all down to the recent rains when we both noticed together that the leaves' motion was actually far from random. They had moved apparently upstream and were then circulating, barely but distinctly clockwise.

"There has to be a plug hole in here, Tom," said Midnight, taking the words right out of my own mouth.

"And where there's a plug hole, there's got to be a sewer." I spoke in my best metaphorical accent.

We each grabbed sticks and started poking around in the bottom of the pool like a pair of excited river urchins. This was great fun. Bubbles of foul smelling marsh gas rose from the rotting organic litter, then Midnight hit the jackpot and thrust his stick through the creek floor. The pool almost exploded sending a spray of stinking methane-loaded water over us both. The creek came alive and gurgled its way down the plug hole into the invisible cave system below.

In the next hour or so, the two of us systematically combed through the bush. We made a rough survey and a map of the dry creek and the local geology. We figured that we were on a former terrace of the Mazaruni river itself and that there must be an enormous system of caves and old gravel beds under our feet. Our two old pork-knockers had chanced on one small part of it, where their little side creek had happened to cut its way across, and the stones they were finding now had been reworked out of the old Mazaruni gravels.

This was one of those occasions when your mind starts to flip. This could truly be a major, major, major shout.

I came back to earth. We would need machinery, a D6 at least, dollars, more dollars, $$$, capital; it could be done, but we would also have to buy out the King and his Shadow and that might prove more difficult. For them, this place was a way of life. When the big big shout actually came, all their oft discussed plans to go back to the child's mother in Georgetown would evaporate. They could only ever be happy there in the bush. Perhaps all this should wait.

We came to the place where the 'other dog' was buried. It must have been quite a large dog, I thought, as I looked at the size of the mound under the cross. The diggings were similar in both size and design to those where the King and the Shadow were still working, a pond and a gravel bar overlain by sand and soil, except that these had all collapsed in on themselves. Maybe the dog had gone chasing a lizard or a snake when it had all caved in on him.

About one hundred metres beyond the dead dog diggings the creek was flowing again, over a series of falls down the rocky sides of a small gorge. There were some low roofed caves at the base of the falls formed where a bed of shale had been preferentially eroded out from beneath a thin dolerite sill, but the entrance to them was partly hidden and blocked by some massive sandstone boulders which had tumbled from higher up the gorge. This was not at all as I had imagined it would be. I could understand that King Harry might have had an access problem, but I really could not see that there would have been much of a future in looking for diamonds there. The creek was too small, there were no obvious trap sites and we were well away from any of the old reworked Mazaruni channels. Probably the pork-knockers had not even tried to work the caves for fear of some jungle spirit or bad obeah. For some reason the caves had become a side issue and why we had packed over fifty kilogrammes of explosives, fuse, detonators and cord and all that stupid paraphernalia all the way from Orinduik to here was all a bit of a mystery.

We returned to the King and his Shadow, and the cream dog. They had sieved a few more spadefuls of gravel, and sluiced a few more bucketfuls of water. The Shadow showed me a tail of gold in his batel worth three, four hundred dollars perhaps; the King, however, had not had such a successful day.

That night, over dinner, I asked King Harry what happened to the other dog.

"Ant bear tek she soul," Harry said. "is she soul bury by de cross dere."

CHAPTER TWENTY-FIVE

DEAD DOG FLATS

We sat up late listening to story after story of shout following shout and of the famous and the not so famous, of those drowned, of others murdered, of still others simply disappeared without a trace but surely had struck it rich before they did. Bush gaff. King Harry could barely write his name but he sure could tell a good tale. The cream dog and the deaf Grey Shadow, however, sat slightly apart from the rest of us, but then they had heard all the stories before.

Midnight started groaning around midnight, right on cue, and took himself off to bed holding his rumbling belly, degassing and blaming a tin of Shadow's piquant long life sardines in natural spring water. I was content that I had stuck with the beef strips. By two o'clock, Midnight's groaning had taken on a somewhat more sinister tone. The man was obviously in some considerable pain. By four, he had thrown up at least twice and had broken out into a fierce fever and was doubled up in agony, something of an over-reaction to what one would have normally expected from a tin of suspect fish.

Josephina was frightened and clucking like a broody galinha.

I woke. "Appendicitis, by the look of it," I diagnosed. "We'll have to get him down to Imbaimadai."

The whole camp was awake. The moon was close to setting but still bright enough, reflecting off the churning water, and Domingo and King Harry went off straightaway to the bottom of the Chi Chi Falls to look for transport. Hopefully they might find Captain Beast somewhere on the river, otherwise we would have no alternative but to drag the King's bateau the three kilometres across the portage.

About six o'clock, Domingo and King Harry came back. They had searched for some time but there was no sign of the Beast, they reported, and after further questioning it became clear to me that the King had not actually been expecting this Beast and his river boat for at least another three or four days anyway. What was even more frustrating, though, was that there was not even a woodskin we could take to go and fetch help.

In less than ten minutes, we were all ready to start the portage, even Josephina was coming along to lend a hand. I had been mentally calculating... an hour and a half, maybe two for the portage...another hour to bring the engine across and get Midnight himself stretchered on board... two hours for the twenty kilometres to Imbaimadai... midday then, perhaps, if we were really lucky... just time enough to get on the radio to Georgetown and call in a plane... and after all that the question and answer session would be bound to come...

Who were we?

Where had we come from?

Where were we going?

When had we come from?

Why had we come?

To Chi Chi!

Who was the lady? What about her feet? Brazilian?

... and the Englishman? Visas?

Explosives?

... Ohh shit!!...As if by magic, right at that moment Midnight remobilised. He came shambling out from under the tarp and, suddenly accelerating, disappeared, crashing through the undergrowth... silence... a haunting silence. We stood quietly and waited. I grasped Josephina's arm to stop her from running after him. There came a resounding fart which even the deaf Grey Shadow appeared to register on his personal Richter scale, followed by a long drawn-out sigh, and a few minutes later an ashen-faced,but smiling and obviously very relieved Midnight reappeared. His fever had broken, and his peristaltic tubing was evacuated...so much for the doctor's expert diagnosis. There would not now be any idle pleasure seeking side trips for him to Imbaimadai, no sir, instead he would have to spend the rest of that day and most of the next recovering in bed, in camp with the nurse - or would that be in camp, in bed with the nurse?

The King and his Shadow would have nothing more to do with the caves, but gave us permission to blow them and anything else in the forest to hell and fury if that was what we truly desired. Midnight was in no shape to do anything other than lounge in his hammock, and the schoolmistress stayed back to minister to his needs.

The pork-knockers went off to their dangerous little puddle, and

Nic, Domingo, Don and I set off to wreak havoc and destruction on Mother Nature. I calculated that half the tovex we had brought would be more than ample to waste on the famous caves and what was left over, I could blow on that first pool which Midnight had unplugged the day before. There, there might indeed be a good chance of finding some nice stones.

I wrapped det cord around a couple of giant trees whose presence was particularly annoying to me, crimped on a length of fuse and blasted them to hell and fury, as per our earlier permission. Shards and hard-wood spears flew through the air with the destructive force of some new antipersonnel terrorist weapon, murdering and maiming goodness knows how many as yet uncatalogued life-forms. I think Domingo may have sensed I was losing my tree.

To properly dispose of the sandstone boulders blocking the cave entrance, I would have had to core drill them first and pack the blast holes with the explosive. We simply did not have the right equipment. Instead we dug around the boulders and unceremoniously shoved the tovex underneath and packed it with mud and unclassified jungle shit as best we could. The shot exploded most inefficiently. Most of the blast was directed externally and just lifted soil and water and air. It made a cracking good show and let off a bang to rival Midnight's fart but did little to anything of substance except to nudge one of the largest rocks over to one side. Not exactly an open sesame but it was enough, and after the mud settled, Don and I squeezed past the rock and behind the shower of the falls.

Inside, the cave was dry but still full of the echoing sounds of water. I waved my torch around and its light penetrated no more than about five metres before crashing against the black back wall. There, on a low shadowy ledge, crouching or perhaps cowering, was a pile of none too ancient bones and the remains of what must have been fur. Whatever it was or used to be, it stank abominably, vomitous and soulless in the stale cave air. It heaved with microlife in the torch light. I decided against investigating too closely and somehow, I could not think why, my mind flashed back to the large mound under the cross. "Ant bear tek she soul," I remembered.

We scraped out a few buckets of gravel from the front of the cave where the air was fresher, and washed them and got a small tail of gold but no stones. Like I said, I was not really expecting anything different.

I was a good deal more careful setting the charges at the pool. I figured that the bar that dammed the creek originally would have been on one margin of the palaeochannel, but I could only guess at how extensive the cave system was beneath the dry creek bed. By way of investigation, we drove a series of pick holes as deeply as possible, and to my surprise, broke through the crust to the underground drainage system in two out of every three holes that we drilled. I imagined an old river bed, full of interconnected pot holes, churning with gravel and boulders in the rapids, ideal trap sites for glittering stones and precious metals. My plans changed with each new exploratory hole, and in the end I decided on a charge array which would blow out a single trench at right angles to the direction in which I calculated the former river system would have flowed. That way, we could take samples right across its width. It was a far from perfect method, I knew, but it would give me a fair idea of the area's potential, and certainly more than enough information to sell on to some unsuspecting stock exchange. I tried to conjure up a good name for the new find; Dead Dog Flats stuck in my head, but somehow I did not think it would sell too well.

We cleared a few trees by hand, but on a dozen or so of the largest, I wasted more det cord. There was some guilt I guess, but it was like a drop in the ocean. I figured Counsel for the Defence could argue that if anybody else had found the place, they would have clear felled for hectares around. The way it panned out, the trench ended up a little over twenty metres long, two metres wide and two to three metres deep, and one to two metres full of assorted inorganic and organic Amazonian shit. It was not the tidiest of shot firing jobs I had witnessed, but being not vastly experienced in that type of work, a specialised sort of business after all, I actually felt quite chuffed with my handiwork. It had been a little like using a sledgehammer to crack a peanut perhaps, but then at least the tovex was a tightly focussed explosive and had made a reasonably straight sided and rectangular trench. ANFO, on the other hand, would have left nothing more artistic than a shapeless Picasso-form crater.

A back hoe might have come in very useful for the clean up, but since the closest suitable machine was somewhere in south-eastern Trinidad, that did not seem too practical a solution at the time. We therefore took hand channel samples in the trench every metre. Nic and Domingo shovelled and bucketed the samples to Don and me at the upper pool where we sieved and sluiced. And after the first pass, we all four of us dug and shovelled again and speared another half metre deep into the rubble in the bottom of the trench and repeated the sampling process all over. By the end of the day we were all, to put not too fine a point on it, positively knackered, not least since we had all been on the go since the early early morning having our beauty sleep disturbed by the chunderous Midnight. It was already dusk, in fact, before I even remembered that we had missed luncheon!

The rewards of our labour, however, were there for all to see and much much more than I could ever have hoped for. I estimated that between noon and dusk, we washed out between a tonne and a tonne and a half of gravel. We had recovered over five ounces Troy of gold and, wait for it, about seventy carats of diamond... of which a good fifteen carats were gem. No pink fancies, but gem for all that! And we had hardly scratched at the surface. This was going to be **the** big big shout.

The next day, Thursday, Midnight was mostly recovered but still very weak. He was, in fact, far too weak to do anything more than sit around in his hammock having Josephina rub his poorly head, poor lad.

I had already accomplished what I had come to Chi Chi for and was in many ways itching to be off again. Every time I looked at the cream dog, in fact, it responded perversely and delightedly, scratching off yet another hundred thousand jigger fleas, fresh bred to leap onto me, to torment me, to dig under my toes and fingers and breed anew in me. Itching to get back to Orinduik, get on with phase two of the great caper.

My thoughts swung back and forth like a pendulum. On the one hand, only a few hundred metres away, there was the age old lure of precious stone and metal, diamond and gold just waiting there for the taking, gravel just sitting there asking to be sampled. And then if I did too much work, got too excited, up would leap King Harry's price, faster and higher than any bloody jigger flea. I had the demand and he controlled the supply, and this was a classic supply market... but then again, if I did too little work, had too little to show, my prey at the stock exchange might not be sufficiently impressed to part with their pension funds.

One simple fact remained, however, which was that Midnight was essential to the plan and could not be left behind. Therefore, I too had to stay back another day at the Chi Chi. I had never had the patience to spend a whole day fishing, and was especially disenchanted with the idea since the only fish to bite in the Upper Mazaruni River were bony pirae. I had nobody to rub my head. I could have happily spent time with a good cook or even a good cook book in my hammock, but I was certainly not going to hang around that flea pit of a campsite. I could do no other, therefore, than gratify this inner all-consuming greed and go wash me some more diamondiferous gravel.

Don, Domingo, Nic and I duly returned to Dead Dog Flats to blow up a second line of trees and blast out a second trench a hundred metres from the first, and to repeat the whole sampling process of the previous day. And for our efforts that Thursday, I am happy to report that we were rewarded with equally spectacular results.

Again we made no secret of anything since there would have been little point in trying. Josephina, I know, abandoned her sick charge and stood and watched us playing with our explosive charges for much of the afternoon, though she did not approach us openly. King Harry and his Shadow kept their distance, well beyond the obeah, though I am quite sure the cream dog paid us one haunting, fleeting visit.

I paid King Harry with the gold, ten or eleven ounces in all which would give them close to half-a-million in the local, chronically, devalued currency, and I divvied up the diamond as he and I had earlier agreed. I persuaded him to promise me faithfully that they would hold off from going down to Imbaimadai, at least for a few days.

Back in camp, I made up some small separate packets of diamond, one for Midnight, another for Don.

CHAPTER TWENTY-SIX

LAST OF THE SARDINES

Friday morning, early, we were packed and on our way, back up the Mazaruni in King Harry's bateau. I reasoned that one of the best ways to keep Harry and his Shadow from sporting up in Imbaimadai, and therefore from spilling the beans too prematurely, was to take them and their boat with us as far as we could. The bean spilling, I knew, was as inevitable as an empty bottle of rum, but I needed just a few days to clear the country.

With the bateau, we headed straight back into the Haieka. It was as though we had all been given a new lease of life; we hauled that boat up through white water rapids and over tacoubas as if it were made of nothing more substantial than balsa wood. By mid morning, we were already back at the place where we had camped the previous Sunday night, and we tied the boat up to Millie's erstwhile freedom tree, now reduced to just another languishing tacouba. Millie, for one, paid it no heed.

We said our farewells; the cream dog looked the saddest of the bunch as it watched those tins of long life sardines and strips of beef disappearing into our packs. We left the yellow ghetto blaster crying out its message of civilisation to the empty jungle.

Sun is shining,
The weather is sweet, yeh,
Make you wanna move
Your dancin' feet now
To the rescue,
Here I am,
Want you to know Jah,
Can you understand?

The deaf Grey Shadow waved, and for once smiled a cavernous black smile, and the King rubbed his shining black pate and flashed his teeth of gold.

"We'll be in touch, Harry," I said, "soon as we can."

Domingo was already on his way, and the rest of us quickly filed along behind. He cut directly away from the creek to avoid the gorge and its cathedral boulders. Mind you, we still had to scale the cliff walls but it was all so easy now without any loads to speak of. Even the schoolteacher and her Askew-softened boots seemed to be enjoying themselves this time around. Sheer faces, overhangs, soggy lianas, everything was a piece of cake. In less than an hour, we had reached the top of the gorge and the Haieka Head Falls and invested a little of our precious time resting and gazing a final awestruck gaze over the Upper Mazaruni Basin. It was laid out below us like a plush green carpet, wall to wall, no rucks, pristine. The midday sun directly overhead beat down on the open face of the falls and when you squinted at just the right angle, played the most magnificent rainbow across the gorge below. I heard an echo playing:

...Want you to know Jah,
Can you understand?
When the morning
Jah the the rainbow, yeh, yeh,
Want you to know
I'm a rainbow too.

To the rescue
Here I am,
Want you to know Jah,
Can you understand?

Sun is shining,
The weather is sweet, now,
Make you wanna move
Your dancin' feet, yeh, yeh,
Want you to know just if you can,
Here I stand...

The afternoon was tiring. The afternoon was the grudge that followed the excitement and elation of the morning. We retraced our path back up to the watershed, trudging the tallies again, limbs protesting again, and stopped at last at the last small creek which only Domingo could remember crossing. It was not much more than a sluggish puddle and it was full of mosquito larvae, but it would do for one night.

We were back in the clouds and a chilly clinging mist. We had been carrying a minimum of rations and that night finished up most of what we had left over, irresponsibly mixing the little red tins of long-life sardines in tomato sauce with the green-tinned long-life sardines in fresh spring water. The flour was done, the XM rum was long since gone.

We parted company in the morning.

Midnight, Josephine and Millie set off to follow the rest of our outward route back to the VW cabriolet. Don would go with them as far as he was needed, but not too far. I hoped the trail would be clear enough for Midnight to follow and I was half convinced there would be some sort of reception committee waiting at the track. Don's brief, therefore, was to improvise and stay away from anything remotely authoritarian. Midnight was the sacrificial-lamb-with-friends-in-high-places, hence the small packet of sacrificial diamond he was carrying.

Domingo, Nic and I found and followed an old trail east across the watershed towards the head of the Ireng. It was one of half a dozen Indian hunting and trading trails leading from the Kukui Basin to the Kopinang Mission area, not often used but nevertheless kept open. These were the trails which we had studiously avoided on our journey to Chi Chi, but now, going this way I had no hesitation at all in making full use of one. It might not have been part of the original plan, but was a pretty obvious piece of improvisation.

We skirted right around the western head of the Ireng, keeping to the Guyanese side of the border and keeping to clear open bush, then crossed the Sukabi river and several other creeks fed by Mount Ayanganna. For much of the way I could feel and even smell the presence of Ayanganna on my left shoulder and at my back, though I never got to see it again. Eventually the trail followed the country and the laterite pediment down more to the south east, and that way didn't become entangled in the Ireng River itself. We walked about forty kilometres that day, twelve hours straight and lean and hungry, in the end our branch of the trail dropping back down to the fast fading sunshine in the Ireng at Saveretik village.

Saveretik consisted of one long house and two out houses, two dozen people at most and nearly as many dogs. We were welcomed by half a dozen small children when we were still a couple of kilometres away, and escorted in style. We drank pawacarrie[25] and munched on discs of sun-dried cassava bread dusted liberally with dog hair. We told the villagers that we had been off prospecting and exploring west of Ayanganna, that we had had some luck and wished to steer clear of the authorities. The villagers of Saveretik have little truck with outside authority, having been born to the land they occupy, and accepted us for precisely what we told them, no more and no less. That is the ingenuous way of the uncorrupted South American Indian and similar endangered species. And besides all that, we were more or less expected; there was a message waiting for us from the Asio-Celtic engineer and the Buxton tallboy.

---

[25] Cassava liquor fermented with enzyme of spittle, usually brewed by the half boat load.

PART FOUR

CHAPTER TWENTY-SEVEN

INDIAN DIGGINGS

While we had been slogging over to Chi Chi and back, Harald and Tall Boy Osborne had been enjoying their own adventures. They had followed the track west for the best part of fifty kilometres to the Rio Cotingo. The country they found was inhospitable, some had been half-heartedly cleared but just in isolated patches and for some reason no settlers had stayed. What remained of the cleared land had degenerated into a tangle of bright and bloated secondary undergrowth. What remained of the primary jungle was alternately barren and sandy or swamp.

It had taken them most of two full days to clear the track and drive to the Cotingo. There they found the vestige of a track leading south along the east bank of the river. There was certainly no way to go any further to the west as the Roraima scarps rose precipitously from the west bank and continued uninterrupted to the clouds on the Venezuelan border.

The next day, our friends had tried the southern trail. It rapidly degenerated, however, into little more than a hand cut survey line and they and the Tojo were eventually forced to a complete halt after only ten kilometres or so.

They had kicked around for a while, debated their chronology and decided that if they had the inclination, they had the time also, and then set off for a little afternoon prospecting in the river. Harald told me later that he had a weird sort of feeling about the place, he felt somehow detached, a premonition he said. They were wandering down the river and came across some recent and quite extensive diggings, very recent diggings by the look of them but quite high up on the bank, well above the flood line. They had washed out a couple of batels of gravel, and had got hardly a tail of gold in them. So why should anyone be working out here they wondered. What was more, there was no sign of any campsite, no frames, no recent clearing, not even a dead fire. They searched around some more but all they found were a few piles of horse shit, recent also, half washed away by the river, and a mass of hoof prints leading away to the south. So they assumed the garimpeiro camp must be away down the river somewhere.

Our friends were about to leave and head back up to the track, back to the truck. Harald said the hairs on his neck bristled; I was surprised for I never knew he had any. In fact they had already turned to go, together, when they found themselves, all of a sudden facing a small group of Indians in full war paint and armed to the back teeth with the slings and arrows of misfortune. Head hunters hunting Harald in the headwaters of the rio Cotingo, was how Harald described them to me.

The Indians were not overfriendly at first. For some reason, they did not fully appreciate the way Harald and Tall Boy had been investigating the diggings, uninvited. Their diggings they indicated. On second thoughts, thought Harald, these diggings were less like miners' excavations and more like bloody great burial mounds. Fortunately for this tale, however, the awkward confrontation was short lived for as soon as our Guyanese friends opened their calypsonian mouths all their social digressions were quickly forgiven.

Portuguese being neither party's strong point, the Indians used a combination of sign language and drawings in the sand to tell Harald and Tall Boy that, yes, there were garimpeiros further down the river, and warned them against travelling that route. Garimpeiro justice, they explained, in the upper Cotingo was run by a kangaroo court - they may not have used that exact antipodean metaphor, but you get the gist - and meted out by the lynch mob. Foreign prospectors were very definitely persona non grata. Then, even if the Englishmen managed to sneak past the garimpeiros, they would only run into the vaqueros and yet even lower forms of life.

There was also mention of a crack Manaus police squad in the area, in league with the vaqueros. There was talk that rewards had been posted for a group of Englishmen.

There were rumours that an Indian village had been burned, and there was news that Brazilians had been killed in revenge.

Harald and Tall Boy had driven back the way they had come, very circumspectly. They came to the turn in the track where we had camped and found the VW still there, untouched, and no other recent tracks, and had therefore continued south. The new tyre tracks, a hell of a lot of them in fact, had started up no more than two kilometres from the collapsed bridge and therefore realising that repairs must have been made, they abandoned the Tojo and hid it off the side of the road and hoofed it across country, eventually coming down the creek which emptied into the Ireng right opposite Saveretik village. That had been on the previous Thursday. They had left a message feeling that we might also come that way, then thumbed a lift in a canoe down to Orinduik the next day. The canoe had returned Friday with yet another message for us: There was a reception committee waiting at Orinduik as well! No charges were being laid as yet, but the Corporal had been asking some awkward questions about explosives.

CHAPTER TWENTY-EIGHT

WAR GAMES

Sunday, the day we had set off walking to Chi Chi from the end of the north fork track, comissario Color and his boys, if you remember, were driving out of Enamuna to save Brazil from the ravages of creeping democracy. You will also recall that the meteorological conditions pertaining during the previous night were such that this particular morning after was far from conducive to driving a short wheel base Tojo, notwithstanding its Gleaming Glacier White paintjob, loaded with crates of munitions and a mountain of supplies (including an inordinate number of cigarette cartons) on a foundationless and snail-infested mud track. Your real expert might have done alright; Pedro, however, had not yet advanced to that level. Our heroes made barely a couple of hundred metres from the safe and dry stucco street and then stuck fast.

Riaz was unshackled, then reshackled and put to push. Being a weasel as well as work shy, however, he proved to be not a lot of help. Perez pushed, also inconsequentially. Pedro spun the wheels, something at which he was becoming quite adept. Comissario Color peeled open his first carton of cigarettes and set about organising his team.

The church bells pealed, calling the faithful to morning mass. No villagers came running to help our stranded heroes though.

Color soon hit on the smart idea of using the winch (he had acquired a new battery) and picked out the very shack to which his men should attach the grapple, a good strong looking structure. The grapple and cable, of course, proved infinitely stronger than any Enamuna shack could ever be and pulled out an entire wall, just like that. Then the villagers, motivated by nothing more than their acute sense of self preservation, came to help. The bells for mass continued to ring unheeded.

Juarez and his men looked on through field glasses from their bunker at the southern end of the stucco street, smirking, tragically misjudging the terrible situation which would ensue.

The assembled villagers crowded around the little truck and pushed en masse and ran the MUTS unceremoniously out of the shanty town, out past their boundary and out onto a low ridge of drier ground. There the Tojo wheels gripped at last. Pedro gunned the motor and took them slewing down the track out of sight of the village and its miserable inhabitants for whom the bells tolled. Riaz was the only one to look back.

Somehow Pedro kept the truck moving round the corner by the north fork turn-off and pointed it due west. Color sat clean and erect in the front passenger seat, smoking from a slim ebony and ivory cigarette holder, directing the momentum, his close-spaced black eyes piercing the very air in front of him. He might have been a tank commander in some revolting jungle campaign. In his mind he uncrated bazookas and fired salvos at his imagined foe who hid behind every tree.

Pedro positively flew along the track as it kept to the higher ground. Quartz gravel shot out from behind the wheels and drummed on the subframes and the sump guard and transmission cases.

Color, the very epitome of sartorial elegance, white gloved on the trigger, let off burst after burst of rapid small arms fire. Pedro skimmed the Tojo over laterite corrugations.

Color brrrrrdd and dadadadaaddd his heavy machine gun, playing from side to side, into the hostiles. His monocle flashed silver in front of one black eye in the alternating stripes of deep shade and bright sunlight on the jungle track. His medals flashed in unison. His face beamed with pent-up energy and excitement.

The quartz ridge came to an unexpected end, rolling away to the north. In front of them, the ground dipped, dove under the water table, and suddenly the game had ended with a wall of red mud spray which plastered itself onto the windshield. Pedro, to all intents and purposes blinded, desperately pushed on the Toyota high-tech washer controls, and flicked at wiper switches, but to no avail. He had neglected to fill the washer tank, for all the good that might have done him. His foot hit the brakes for the first time since leaving Enamuna and they promptly locked up. The Tojo went into an uncontrolled blind spin and finally came to a halt, amazingly still upright though totally disoriented, sideways off the track and planted somehow in the middle of a small but highly noxious itchy bush.

Color, spinning, knew immediately, instinctively, that they had either hit a mine, or had been caught by rocket fire, but he held on through it all, a leader of men, returning his own fire, spraying venom blindly into the enemy that surrounded him.

The Manaus Treason Squad set up a temporary camp in the middle of the enemy territory, set up its perimeter defences, one man at each door of the truck, to wait for the rain puddle it had encountered to evaporate, and to dry out the motor. Pedro was put in charge of locating the spark plugs! Riaz was set to defoliating the itchy bush.

"There is a ranch house not far from here," volunteered Riaz in mid scratch. "I came this far yesterday. There are people there for sure."

But comissario Alfredo Color was not about to lose face twice in one day. He had the enemy on the run and he would make sure he arrived in befitting style.

The tropical sun was already hard at work, sucking moisture from the earth, baking the slick mud into hexagonally cracked clay. The Manaus Treason squad dried out the motor (Pedro never did find the plugs, surprise, surprise) forded the rapidly receding puddle and was back on the road before it could scratch itself where it itched most.

Comissario Color had come to deliver his message of national doom and to recruit the vaqueros' sons for his posse. Senhor Moreira had been one of those persuaded by Toni Juarez only two days earlier to keep the peace, but now, faced with this comissario from Manaus in the flesh, and bewizarded by his silver tongue and the promise of unimaginable rewards, that resolve quickly vanished.

They came behind in proper style on horseback, the two youngest sons from the Moreira Ranch, and Color went on ahead, steadily westwards into the setting sun, collecting more young cannon fodder and cavalry, Pereda, Vale, Guilherme De Freitas, Adalberto Fernandez and young Eduardo Teregha.

The posse camped behind the Teregha Ranch on the banks of the Cotingo. The evening air was still and thick with a smoke haze in the north. The sunset was magnificent.

The vaqueros' sons played music, and drank cachaça and ate rare steaks and raw alligator eggs and swapped exaggerated stories of the conquests of women.

Color and his elder hosts discussed manoeuvres well into the night.

No Englishmen had been seen on the road, definitely no vehicles had passed that way, and that could only mean, to these wizards of tactician's logic, that they must have abandoned and hidden their vehicle and headed up the Cotingo by foot. There was a particular Macushi village, not more than ten kilometres away, which was known for being a hotbed of insurgency. These people had tried to block senhor Teregha himself from clearing the land for his beef. Troublemakers they were, without a doubt, and well worth a visit in the morning. More cachaça was poured and the nation toasted. The munitions crates were unlocked and their contents distributed.

I think I need not elaborate here on what happened the following day. Suffice it to say, the naive and gutless but well-armed and impeccably dressed idiot Color, still firmly anchored in the self vindication of his one man putsch, besaddled, led his posse of still drunk and armed to the teeth pig-ignorant, red-necked, too young companions up the river to pay the Macushi village a lesson in what they considered to be civilisation; a lesson that they would not forget in a hurry. It was a classic case of chronic Cowboys & Indians.

They rode in proper posse style, single file, up the broad rio Cotingo. They found the renegade village and surrounded it and burned it to the ground, ostensibly to make way for another half-dozen head of prime beef. They forgot all about the Englishmen. They would have raped those old women who could not run into the bush, five star fuel for the next generation of tall stories of cross gender conquest, and they would have slit the throats of the youngest children just for the sheer hell of it, save for the fact that the villagers had felt their coming from a long way off and were equally long since gone. Instead they aimlessly razed all they could find, wrung the necks of the free-range chickens and slit the throats of two old porkers, then roamed the neat small fields trampling the cassava bushes and shooting machine gun rounds into the fruit laden pawpaw trees, just like that.

Romero and De Silva, to their everlasting redemption, took no part in the aforementioned proceedings. They had not taken kindly to life in the saddle and, falling back by degrees, had eventually turned tail and sneaked back to the Teregha Ranch, to the still shackled Riaz and the safety of their faithful Cool White Tojo.

Having tasted the sweet delights of victory, of having indefensibly destroyed the undefended trappings of an alternative culture, the stark raving mad Color and his power-drunk posse set out in search of even greater accomplishments, driven by a terrible and terrifying inertia. They headed on up the valley of the Cotingo, now mindlessly crashing through the garimpeiros' camp, kicking over the lean-to structures, again burning whatever they could find, and on up to the workings, shooting up the sluices and scattering everybody and anybody foolish enough to get in the way.

They drank the garimpeiros' cachaça in the midday heat. They took their gold. They would have taken their women if they had been capable of it. And then the garimpeiros gave way declaring the Macushi had passed by that very morning, not more than two hours earlier.

On they rode, up the valley of the Cotingo, still not having quite satiated their lust for wanton destruction. They rode up to where the valley walls were closing in, beyond the cleared land and the open trails, barren jungle country. They found Indian spoor on the gravel banks of the rio Cotingo. They drunkenly led their horses on, the very latest and bestest of weaponry strapped to their strong and tolerant backs, and they met their ignominious and humiliating fate from the curare-poisoned tips of neolithic arrowheads, paralysed, on a secluded sun-drenched stretch of peaceful sand and gravel bank, quite high above the gently swirling water.

Death comes suddenly to this tale, but how else should it be? In death, one minute you're there, and the next you're not. Exit, finally, character comissario Alfredo Color; fade to the next scene. Meanwhile, his world and his legacies live on.

Two cowboys survived, or rather were allowed to survive to tell the tale. They carried the news to our two stout cabos at the Teregha Ranch. They were the two youngest sons of the most fortunate senhor Moreira.

CHAPTER TWENTY-NINE

LOOSE ENDS

It took a day for the two survivors to make their way back down the river and past the garimpeiro camp. It took quite some further while before cabos Romero and De Silva could fully digest the unpalatable news brought to them by the youngest of the Moreira brothers. They were at once disgusted yet fascinated, sickened yet elated, and above all else very afraid. They had their rule books but this was not covered and there was no one to whom they could pass the baton. Certainly they could not take off to investigate because they had their prisoner Riaz to consider.

Old senhor Teregha, when he was told, did not wait to clarify the official rules of engagement. He was all for raising the whole neighbourhood and striking an immediate and bloody retaliatory blow, and our two cabos could not find the internal fortitude to even try to dissuade him. The remaining Teregha sons were duly dispatched along with the serendipitous Moreira brothers to carry the news back to the Fernandez, the De Freitas, Vale and Pereda ranches. Romero and De Silva found themselves involuntarily drawn to follow on behind.

The tale which the boys recounted grew ever taller with each telling, graduating from mysterious slings and arrows to ambush, and then to torture and degradation. Cachaça bravado became hardly worth a mention. The sacking of the Macushi village faded into an insignificant blur in the background, The garimpeiros became the allies of the bastard Indians, had offered them protection and sustenance. For senhor Teregha, the Fernandez, De Freitas, Vale and Pereda families, comissario Juarez' erstwhile threats petered out to contemptible triviality in the light of their combined tragedy.

The vaqueros had gathered and headed back west for sweet revenge. What they thought they might accomplish is anyone's guess. What or who they would find I doubt they could have thought through to any logical degree. The Macushi were wrapped in their native land and now not only had their bows and arrows and blow pipes and Amazonian alkaloids and natural strychnine derivatives, but most of the contents of the late comissario Color's twentieth century munitions crates as well! We will leave these characters now, riding once again into their self made sunset, back to augment the still billowing black clouds of wanton destruction, back to back on the irresistible march of progress.

De Silva and Romero arrived back in Enamuna late on the Wednesday night. Toni Juarez took what they told him straight on the front of his unshaven chin, without flinching, expressionless. Riaz was unceremoniously thrown back into the holding cell and the comissario got on the radio to Boa Vista. Flares were blazing on the tiny Enamuna airstrip within less than an hour, and in the early hours of the morning, a convoy of trucks rumbled into the village and into the empty army barracks. The war was on.

At first light, Juarez left to make peace between the vaqueros and the Indios, and the garimpeiros if they would listen, accompanied by a company of light artillery. Apparently the colonel still owed this comissario a favour.

His offsider Santos stayed back in Enamuna to coordinate whatever would need to be coordinated, and the ever faithful Rodriguez was sent off with a platoon of engineers to rebuild the collapsed bridge on the north fork track, and be ready to receive any stray Englishmen who happened to come passing that way. Just one Englishman would suffice for Juarez, to be used as a sacrificial lamb.

We could also leave Juarez and the Brazilian army out of the story at this juncture. It is mere detail. Just to say the vaqueros and the garimpeiros were hard at it when the army arrived, and the Macushi had taken to the hills and vanished across the international borders within their own ancestral lands. Armed with only machetes and the odd rusting antique Colt 44, yet faced with the odd well-greased and polished cannon, the garimpeiros winged a great deal but gained no recompense from the mediators. The vaqueros were rounded up into stockyards like the cattle they herded.

Juarez could see, however, that there would be no lasting peace, at least not in his time and under his influence. Any true peace would be generations away, between the survivors. He left the army to tie up loose ends as best it could, search out bodies if there were any left, at least to make a show of tracking the Macushi to the borders.

Juarez had a report to write. He could make no links between

Riaz, the Englishmen and the explosives and what had happened in the Cotingo, but still would have liked a more substantial scapegoat than the weasel Riaz to take the heat off his own misjudgement. Rodriguez would have to catch him an Englishman. On what charge was largely immaterial; if gun running or receiving would not stick, then diamond smuggling, anything, dangerous driving or speeding for Christ's sake would have to suffice. He knew comandante Malcenski would not be too impressed with his handling of the situation, however much the tragedy had been of Alfredo Color's own construction.

That night, Juarez flew directly to Boa Vista from the Teregha Ranch; senhor Riaz joined him there next morning.

CHAPTER THIRTY

RUNNING AWAY

The messages from Harald and Tall Boy were a bit of a concern. First, there was a moderately long tome detailing their trip out to the Cotingo and their suspicions regarding the rather large mounds by the river side. I can only guess to this day whether there were bodies or Color's munitions buried beneath those gravel banks. The note contained news of rewards for Englishmen and on the same line, killings of Brazilians, and whether linked or not, I had no desire to test my legal prowess in that regard in any Brazilian kangaroo court.

As far as I knew, I was not known to the Brazilians, at least not as Tom Askew, and I could easily avoid Enamuna, in fact I had not the slightest desire to renew my acquaintance with the place. That was one thing I had going in my favour. More worrying, perhaps, was the second message from Orinduik and explosive questions from the Guyanese side! There, I was known as Tom Askew and it would be tricky to bypass the place, and downright difficult to find answers to those questions.

When Don turned up at the village, however, alarm bells really started to ring. Midnight had been arrested at the bridge and carried off in cuffs for goodness sake! Whatever had transpired over in the Cotingo, the Brazilians were taking it pretty seriously. Not even Midnight's privileged position as a potential brother-in-law to the Boa Vista chief of police was enough, so it seemed, to afford him protection.

"What the hell happened, Don?" I asked.

"Jus' that, Tom! Midnight, he get tek at the bridge, get tek sweet!" answered Don.

"What about senhorita Josephina?"

"Not a ting, Tom, the schoolmistress, she jus' drive off back towards Enamuna..."

"... and the police, they're still there?"

"Police, and the army, they all tek off far as I could see. But I ain't staying about too long, y'unerstan'..."

"...and the truck, did you see it? Did they find it, the Brazilians?" I continued my interrogation.

Don took a deep breath as if to indicate this was to be his final speech. "We see the tracks when we comin' up to the bridge, a lil' way before. Midnight say it best if I walk on from there, in case they got people at the bridge. I see the truck hide off the road in the bush, but I don' tink Midnight an' the schoolmistress seen it..."

"... but surely the girl must have told them you were there. Why didn't they come after you as well?"

"Maybe she didn' say nothing." Don smiled and held his hands up in the air, "Maybe she like me."

There was no answer to that.

I was tempted to go back and take the truck, maybe sneak through Enamuna, but the risk was just too great. The Tojo looked like being an expensive tax write-off! And if the Brazilians found it, and traced tracks back to the Cotingo, well, Midnight's position in Brazilian law might become positively untenable, long term,one could say.

All I faced now was a couple of days and a hundred and fifty kilometres of savannah trail through Paramakatoi to Lethem, assuming I could get past Orinduik in the first place.

We jumped on the first available woodskin the next morning, very very early, before dawn and whilst misty vapours were still languidly swirling across the river. It cost us next to nothing, a few left over rations and a couple of dollars. We navigated by torchlight. The river sucked and slurped and red caiman eyes bobbed and danced in the beams of light, caught and entranced, disturbed from their nefarious purposes, or perhaps just primitively curious. Other than those eyes, however, I observed little; my mind was elsewhere.

It was barely light as we pulled in to a secluded landing on the north side of Orinduik village. Nic and Don crept off towards our old hut to find Harald; Domingo stayed back with me to wait at the edge of the jungle. We looked out in the gathering light at the savannah hills which smoked with wisps and trails of cloud, snaking down tree-lined gullies, and listened to the village roosters call. I hoped Petal would remember Don more favourably this time around. I started to say my goodbyes.

The symbiotic seven were breaking up, but fast. Midnight was incarcerated in some hot Brazilian jail house, quite possibly for the foreseeable future, and certainly beyond any help from me. Harald and Tall Boy would try to act cool and collected, ship out the jasper, go home to Golden Grove and Buxton with just a few foreign dollars for their rewards. The brothers Nicodemus and Domingo eventually would make their way back to Sand Creek and Wapishiana normality, and would reflect on these past two weeks as just another anomaly in their aboriginal dreamtime.

Don and I were still hanging in together, saddled up on a pair of the gaudiest and roughest running Trail Suzuki 250s you could have found in the whole Rupununi. Modern vaquero gear in its impurest form. From Orinduik, we crossed the Tumong river to Kurukubaru, then on to Kato and Paramakatoi. We reined in and sat by the side of the trail, bum-sore and hot and half deaf and nauseated from breathing the dust and each other's exhaust, each wrapped in our own memories, tucking in to fresh bake with roasted powis and lashings of pepper sauce. Don fingered a fresh scar on his right cheek and bit voraciously into a drumstick. Then south to Monkey Mountain and the Echilebar river.

Thus far along the trail, I could remember in almost frightening detail, every hill and every creek, each turn and lonely shade-giving tree. The path was ageless, an ever so slightly glorified walking trail of polished sun-baked red clay, but we had not had the luxury of bikes then. With every turn on the track, with every skidding and spinning wheel, my mind spun back to nineteen seventy-two. Then it had taken a week or more to walk, necks straining at the warishi straps, footsore, fly-blown, sun burning, taking it hill by hill, turn by turn of the path permanently engraved by the flashing neurons.

At every village we passed, I got a growing impression that our passage had been expected. I wondered whether it was the Indian telegraph or a more sophisticated communication system.

Don James left me at Monkey Mountain. The trail south now would be unfamiliar to me, but should be straightforward enough as it led to Karasabai, and would eventually turn into a fully fledged two-wheel-mud-rut track at Velami Outstation. Don turned north up the Echilebar; he was chasing his own dreams and memories of a two carat stone washed out on some former expedition, but was also on a last errand for me.

I was on my own now.

Just north of Karasabai, I knew it was not just the Indian telegraph, superbly efficient though that system was. A small GAC plane sat on the strip. I had seen it from some distance glinting in the sunshine, and now waited and watched, very patiently for once. Shortly before sunset, two uniformed policemen walked out from a shadowy hut and hopped on board. They had had their fill of watching over an empty savannah for one day and now were eager to be off back to their feathered beds for the night.

Much later, in the dead of night, I pushed the bike around the village. The dogs smelled me for sure, for they howled; I guess the villagers knew I was there as well, but I doubt they would have said a thing. I slept the rest of the night and most of the next day some distance south of the village, whilst the plane sat on the strip again, then travelled on through the second night... Bell Avista, Macaiba, Sunnyside, Pirara, Manari Ranch...

... Lethem. The bridge and the border post beckoned; it would have been so easy, well the bridge would have. I skirted round the small town and dumped the marvel of modern Japanese technology that had brought me from Orinduik on less than a tank of gas, and swam over the Takutu, back once more into Brazil and into my alter ego.

EPILOGUE

CHAPTER THIRTY-ONE

DOCTOR SIMON TWEAK

The name on the hotel booking is Doctor Simon Tweak. it matches the name on the passport, and the credit cards. Just arrived from Paramaribo, capital of Surinam, by KLM.

Georgetown, Timehri airport; WELCOME TO TIMEHRI INTERNATIONAL AIRPORT in unlit neon tubes; a pair of white and green DC3s parked angularly, nose up, ready for a one of these good days soon flight to one of those places no 'international' could hope to go; red, black, yellow and white arrows on green flags...

The face in the passport photo is clean shaven, green eyes peeping through unseen contact lenses. A middle-aged man of business with a seven day visitor's visa and an onward ticket.

... the compressor in an Ice-Cold Coke machine in the corner shudders into action, successfully competing with the familiar snippets of language.

On holiday, just taking a short break, you know, winding down. Oh yes, passed through before but that was many years ago. Prefer to get off the beaten track, you know.

The piece of pale red meat sizzles in the roasting pan and combines its fishy juices with shallot and peppers. Water dragon tale. Water dragon tail. Harald is peeling eddo and sweet potato. The two Indian lads prop themselves up in the corner, now smiling wildly, smoking sweet leaves. The camp oven belches water dragon smoke.

I stood by my bags and allowed myself to be taken over by the taxi touts. I rode with the flow like any other white middle-aged business man, cum-tourist My bags moved and I followed, by chance by taxi-bus into town, cheap and incognito if not exactly road-safe. 'Main Street, please, the Park Hotel.'

We pull up outside the Park Hotel, a three storey colonial style wooden building on stilts; the impressive polished hardwood staircase leads impressively up past peeling paint to the foyer on the first floor; everywhere is polished wood and peeling paint; it's all very confusing; large fans turn lazily in the ceiling.

"Welcome to the Park Hotel, Doctor Tweak. Did you have a pleasant journey?" I was greeted by the desk clerk, a Grecian Two Thousand version of a former Bikram.

"Thank you, Bi...yes I did." I nearly called him Bikram then. "Are there any messages for me by the way?"

"Just the one, Sir, from Mr Van... I forget, Sir, a Dutch name." My Bikram handed me a small sealed envelope. "Will you be taking dinner, Doctor Tweak?"

"Ah, no thank you, I think I'll just go to my room and have a rest. I'm a little tired," I said. "Good evening to you, ah...?"

"Bikram," said Bikram.

"Good evening, Bikram," I said.

My room on the upper floor is so huge that it looks quite bare; there is the polished wood floor, and, centrepiece, an antique heavy wooden bed with an enormous circular contraption in the ceiling from which to hang a mosquito net; dark, smooth-black wood, and hospital-crisp worn thin white linen and sheets; a small small fan in one corner turns but has hardly any effect; my window looks hotel-inwards, overlooking a kitchen roof with appetisingly steamy vapours extracting beneath my nose.

I did not want to eat. I was tired, that much was true, but I felt hot and I could not have slept anyway with that lousy next to useless fan and the kitchen cabbage smells. After a few weeks in the bush, I could not bear to be so enclosed. I went out to explore the rest of the hotel, to see how it had survived its aging alongside myself. Which of us was made of the stouter stuff? Who had the better paint job? Inevitably, of course, I ended up in the lounge, feet stretched decadently out on top of the veranda railings, gazing out over Main Street. I ordered a rum punch and set to watching the front doors of the Cambridge opposite, peering with green eyes over the bougainvillea in the central reservation.

The Cambridge Hotel was even more seedy-looking than I had remembered. The large double green door was still there, and so was the doorman...

... through which and past whom I can catch very occasional glimpses of a dimly lit interior; a faded sign outside advertises 'ch...ke.-i.-a-bas ...t'; music blares out over more human sounds - 'Don't chain my heart', an open invitation to see in the New Year at the Cambridge Hotel.

I looked over the note from Van Bemmelen again, and then at my watch. He had suggested nine o'clock at the Cambridge. Fair enough, I was getting a little peckish now, but the chicken-in-a-basket sign was so faded, I wasn't sure that that was still on the menu. The hollow stomach feeling was less hunger than sheer unadulterated fright.

I was half-way through another rum punch of still unimaginably unbeatable quality when a son-of-Bikram informed me that there was somebody waiting at the front door to see me.

"Show him up then," I said, but the East Indian waiter 'would prefer not to, Sir. The person is an Amerindian.' This, evidently, was another man's country. I glanced around the lounge at the sea of pasty pale foreign faces, at those who would surely be affronted to have an Amerindian walk into their lives.

Don did not seem to mind though. He greeted me from the bottom of the impressive staircase.

"What happen to de face Tom?"

"Simon, Don, Simon Tweak," I said under my breath as we grabbed hands. "Who did you ask the doorman for?"

Don laughed, "It's okay, Tom, I jus' say the Englishman who

come in today. But I tink I say he had a beard."

Don handed me the small packet of incredibly valuable diamonds that I had entrusted to him. It contained over thirty carats of unblemished Argyle pink fancies and had travelled with me more than halfway across the world, through any number of customs checks, thrown into the bottom of however many bags, rubbing shoulders, so to speak, with all forms of dirty laundry. I had never had a moment's doubt that I could trust Don James with it for the final leg of its journey from Monkey Mountain.

"Don, there's a Mr Van Bemmelen going to be in the Cambridge tonight, at nine. He is expecting me, but I think I would prefer if we did our business here, among the giant cockroaches and with old Bikram on guard. Could you do me this last favour? Tell him I'm waiting for him in the lounge."

I handed over a wad of American dollars, enough to set my old friend up with his own dredge if he wanted.

I've also got this letter for you, it's a finder's reward for the Chi Chi claim. See if you can get it to the King and his Shadow. Let them sign it and it'll make you rich for sure. Don't come back."

A final goodbye and I made my way back up those impressive stairs wiping real tears from my eyes, for it was I who would never be able to come back after this.

Van Bemmelen, a Dutchman from Antwerp with connections in Paramaribo, had heard on the grapevine that there had been a major new diamond discovery in the Upper Mazaruni Basin. The news had filtered out by a couple of different routes. It was currently all the rage at a pork-knocker landing known as Imbaimadai and he also had it on good authority that the Brazilians had jailed one man trying to smuggle stones down the Ireng. He might not have believed the pork-knocker stories alone, as exaggeration was a way of life amongst those people, but the Brazilian arrest seemed to confirm that this was no run-of-the-mill find.

He lowered his voice to the level of international conspiracy. He had also heard that amongst the stones recovered were some pink fancies, of a quality hitherto only known from the AKI pipe in Western Australia. These so-called Chi Chi pinks must be considered unique, beyond any shadow of a doubt, and would naturally command a very significant premium for any seller. The cartel itself would no doubt show a great deal of interest. If I could guarantee...

We were interrupted by the discrete ahem of another son-of-a-Bikram, "Doctor Tweak, there is a telephone call for you, international, Sir."

I excused myself and went over to the desk to take the call. It was Josephina, back in Paramaribo, just checking on progress. She'd booked next day's KLM flight and we'd go on to Trinidad together, and then, well who cared! Napoleon would be baby sitting Millie.

"... yes, as I was saying, if you could guarantee, Doctor Tweak, that there would be no more stones like these found..."

A large black shining cockroach scuttled across the floor towards us and met Van Bemmelen's leather sole with a sickening crunch. I closed my eyes in recognition and yet could see Big Patsy in the dark adjoining corridor, not a day older, still no signs of grey, wielding her broom, overwhelmingly saddened by Gregor's sudden and very final demise.

"Thank you, yes, a bank cheque drawn from Antwerp will do just fine."